THEN SHE RAN

RAN

An absolutely gripping crime thriller with a massive twist

CHARLIE
GALLAGHER

JOFFE
BOOKS

Published 2018 by Joffe Books, London.

www.joffebooks.com

ISBN-13: 978-1-78931-011-5

For Harris. We miss you man.

Author's Note

I am inspired by what I do and see in my day job as a front-line police detective, though my books are entirely fictional. I am aware that the police officers in my novels are not always shown positively. They are human and they make mistakes. This is sometimes the case in real life too, but the vast majority of officers are honest and do a good job in trying circumstances. From what I see on a daily basis, the men and women who wear the uniform are among the very finest, and I am proud to be part of one of the best police forces in the world.

Charlie Gallagher

Chapter 1

'Jenny, honey, we've got to go! We've got to go now!'

Jenny's eyes opened and she tried to move her arms, but they were weighed down; their four-month-old daughter, Isobel, lay across them. Beyond her tiny, sleeping form was a digital clock with red numbers. They looked angry, as if they'd been scorched into the black face. The numbers advanced one digit, to 10:01 a.m. — Sunday morning. Once, this would have been her favourite day of the week: lazy and carefree, a cooked breakfast and a stroll — no work until tomorrow. But recently, days of the week had come to mean nothing. Time meant nothing. Sleep meant nothing.

'What are you talking about? I only just got her off.' It had been a terrible night. Isobel's teeth seemed to be coming all at once. There was no doubt the poor thing was in a lot of pain, inconsolable for much of the time. But Jenny's patience was frayed — damned near severed. Neither of them was coping with sleep deprivation very well.

'We need to go. We need to go — now!' Joseph said again.

Jenny was now wide awake. As gently as she could, she pulled her arm out from under Isobel's neck. Isobel stirred enough to sigh but stayed asleep on the big bed. Joseph's eyes were wide and filled with fear. He was serious — she'd never seen him like this before. 'What's happened, Joseph? What are you talking about? Leaving?'

'I've put some bits in the bag, stuff for Issy. We have to go now, Jenny.'

'Don't be ridiculous. We're not going anywhere.'

'We need to go NOW!' Joseph's raised voice got a reaction from Isobel. She scrunched up her face in a scowl, made tiny fists with her hands. Jenny knew the signs, knew what was coming next. Sure enough, Isobel's cry was instant and powerful.

'What the hell, Joseph?' Jenny moved to the end of the bed. The curtains were drawn; Joseph walked over to them and tore them apart. Isobel's crying got louder. Jenny could see their suitcase laid out on the floor. It was stuffed with Isobel's clothes, her nappies and wipes. He pushed it shut and zipped it up. Jenny still sat on the bed. Joseph was like a man possessed. He picked the case up and stood it on his wheels. The handle clicked out. He had laid out a few bits and pieces on the unit at the end of the bed: his wallet, his phone and the papers they had been given when they had hired the car. The hotel room key was there too. He scooped up everything but the key.

'Are you not taking the key?'

'We can't come back, Jenny.'

'What the hell is going on? Like hell am I just going to take Isobel out like this — with no explanation!'

'There's no time. You have to trust me. We have to go now!'

Jenny couldn't help but absorb some of his panic; Joseph didn't scare easy after all. She found her feet. She picked up Isobel and tried to shush her. She pulled her in tight to her chest and she calmed down a little. Joseph strode into the bathroom. When he came back out, the keys to the car rattled in his hand.

'Now!' Joseph walked to the door and stepped out. Jenny saw him look both ways before disappearing a few paces down the corridor. She scooped up the keys to the room and stuffed them in her jeans pocket. She had dressed for the day hours ago and only needed to slip her feet into loose trainers. Joseph strode back into the room and took hold of the suitcase. Jenny looked around the room. She had clothes strewn over the chair, her toiletries and hair straighteners in the bathroom. She had other belongings on her bedside table and across other surfaces.

'I can't just leave all this. Can we not just take a few more minutes to pack all the stuff? I need to change Issy.'

'We can get more stuff. There's no time. We have to go now.' Joseph walked back into the corridor and held the door to stop it swinging back closed. His eyes fell on Jenny, still full of panic, still desperate. He was pale and the hand that reached for hers was cold and clammy. He moved them towards the stairs. Isobel had calmed down enough so that her sounds were just unsettled moans. The crying had stopped at least. Joseph strode past the lift to the top of the stairs. Jenny stopped at the lift and pressed the call button.

'We take the stairs,' Joseph said.

Jenny followed him through a door to the stairwell but he was already out of sight, moving down the stairs two at a time with the suitcase held over his head, his footfalls echoing off the bare walls.

'What is going on?' Jenny called after him. Joseph ignored her; it sounded as if he was already on the landing below and moving to the next flight.

They'd been on the third floor of the Dovorian Hotel. Jenny had thought it to be a strange choice from the start. It was a budget hotel; there were no real facilities for families, certainly nothing for a four-month-old baby. Joseph had said it suited their needs; it was close to the centre of Dover. Jenny didn't understand why this was important; there was nothing in the town for them, nothing in the county. But Joseph had just told her to *trust him*. He'd been saying that a lot recently.

She made it to the ground floor. They had to pass the reception desk. It was vacant. She had needed to summon someone from the back office when they were checking in; she was glad there was nobody there now. Joseph was moving away from it at speed.

He was already halfway along the ground-floor corridor, which ran the length of the building to a side exit. The door was swinging open when Jenny got to it. She was going as fast as she could manage but she was some way behind Joseph, who was once more out of her sight. She stood still for a second. She could feel her heart beating in her chest and she was breathing heavily. Isobel wriggled and she tried to hold her firm against her chest. She knew it was the best chance she had of keeping her quiet. She heard an engine revving hard and their hire car pulled up in front, Joseph at the wheel. He was already out of the driver's door by the time she got to the rear. He pulled the door open and unclipped the baby seat. Jenny hated it. It was rear facing and she would rather be able to see Isobel when they were moving, but the internet had told her how much safer it was.

Jenny tried to make Isobel cosy, wrapping a blanket around her as tightly as she could and tucking it under her tiny body. Isobel liked to be wrapped up tight and warm.

'We have to go!' Joseph bent over her, she had put the baby seat on the pavement. It was sloped, the hill was steep and it wasn't easy.

'We have to make sure she's wrapped up and safe first, Joseph. What the hell has gotten into you?'

Jenny lifted the seat. It clicked into place on the second attempt. She kissed her fingers and rested them against Isobel's cheek. Joseph was already revving the car.

Jenny moved to the front passenger seat. The car was already moving as she pulled her door shut.

Jenny snatched at her seatbelt. In her haste it stopped short. She tutted and pulled it again. 'What the hell is going *on*, Joseph? You have to tell me. Are we in some sort of trouble?'

She gave up on her seatbelt. They made it to a junction at the bottom of the steep hill. Jenny saw a sign that said Folkestone Road. The flow of cross traffic was relentless. Joseph had turned away from her, looking at the stream of cars coming from their right. The car was rolling further into it; there were no gaps and Joseph was starting to make noises that could almost be described as whimpers. Still holding her seatbelt, Jenny looked back to check on Isobel. She noticed a figure running towards them along the pavement on the opposite side. He wore a long, black coat and his right arm was tucked underneath it. The car bounced forward a metre as Joseph tried to bully his way onto the main road. Jenny's head rocked and she lost sight of the man.

That was when Joseph's window blew in.

It sounded to Jenny like an explosion. She had wrapped her arm around the driver's seat for leverage, so she could lift herself enough to see into Isobel's seat. She dropped back into the seat as her right forearm flashed with a stinging pain. Joseph cried out, the car lurched forward and Jenny was pushed against the headrest. She could hear car horns blaring and Joseph shouting at her to get down. The car was rammed from the rear, just enough for her to feel it. She heard more car horns and then the revving of the engine.

'ISSY! Jesus, Joe! Issy!' She pulled herself onto her knees, clinging to her seat back and facing the back seat. The car swerved suddenly and Joseph overtook something. She tried to lean into the seat back. She could see just enough of Isobel. Her tiny arms and legs wriggled and contorted in the air, as they did when she was confused and trying to understand her surroundings.

The back window popped inwards. In the same instant she could hear the air move, something fizzed past her ear and thudded into the roof lining. Instinctively she ducked back into her seat.

'They're shooting at us! Why are they shooting at us?'

Joseph's cheek was rippled where he was biting down hard. The car swerved again, this time hard left at a roundabout — more angry car horns. Isobel was crying — at least Jenny knew she was breathing. Jenny spun in her seat to face forwards.

'Joseph, talk to me! You need to pull over, we need to get Issy out of this car!' Jenny was screaming. Joseph was still peering forward.

'Joseph!' She hit him on the arm. He had to brake hard and she was pushed forward in her seat. Issy screamed louder in the back. The car moved off at crawling pace; they were in two lanes of one-way traffic.

Joseph turned to face her. 'We can't stop.' The right side of his face was slick with blood.

'Joseph, you're hurt!'

'I'm fine. It's a nick from the glass.'

'A nick! You're covered in blood.' She reached out to gesture at his face with her right arm and saw that her sleeve was also soaked in blood. She tried to pull it up to inspect her arm; it felt boiling hot. She clenched her fist — it was still working at least. She would have to inspect it later.

'What do these people want, Joseph? Jesus, what have you done?' Joseph was peering forward. The car jerked and shuffled as he tried to move. Jenny could see both lanes of traffic were now at a standstill. They were in the right lane and there was a row of parked cars to their right and shop fronts the other side of them. People walked along, seemingly oblivious to the gunshots that had taken out

Joseph's window completely and left glass scattered over the parcel shelf.

When the left lane started moving, Joseph cut across immediately. Once more the horns blared but the lane was clearer and the car set off as if it had been stung. She could see green traffic lights ahead and a parked van that had been blocking the right lane. The left lane was clear and Joseph kept his foot planted.

Ahead, a car pulled out from a side street. Joseph was going too fast to brake in time so he wrenched the wheel right and changed lanes again. Jenny was thrown against the window. Isobel was now inconsolable in the back.

'You're going to kill us, Joseph!' Jenny spun again in her seat, trying to get into a position where she could talk to their daughter. The car lurched forward and she was pressed back into her seat. She could see a black SUV behind, matching them for speed. It was in the other lane and now it seemed to be gaining on them.

'They're still chasing us, Joseph! What do they want?'

There was a jarring thud into the side of the car — then two more in quick succession. She felt the car lurch, as if the last blow had been a sucker punch. It skewed sideways as Joseph yelled out. Jenny was thrown to the front of the car and she struck something hard with her right side, and then came a savage blow to the side of her head. Suddenly, all she could hear was a whistling.

She faced out of the side window. She couldn't move. The black SUV seemed to drift past in slow motion, part of a stream of traffic. She could only watch as a muzzle flared from the back window. She was aware of more thuds, the tinkle of glass, another shout from Joseph maybe. She watched the vehicle pass — and then its brake lights flashed red. More car horns, the black SUV stopped completely, a rear door pushed open. Jenny was transfixed.

'Jenny!' Her hearing returned all at once and the confusion came with it. Joseph was shouting in her ear, she snatched her head towards him. Isobel was crying at the top of her lungs from the back, it pierced her mind directly.

'Joseph . . .' It was all she could manage.

'You have to go. You have to get Isobel out.'

'What?'

'Get out. You have to go. With Issy! GO!'

'Aren't you coming?' Jenny felt dream-like still. Her voice was soft, she was confused by the pain in her side. Blood trickled into her mouth and she licked her lips.

'They're not here for you. Take her and go. Please! You have to run, Jenny!'

Jenny turned to her door. She pushed it open. Her hip shot with pain as she stepped out of the car, and there were pins and needles in her thigh. From the corner of her eye she saw someone walk towards her, he stepped off the pavement — a middle-aged man. She smiled at him as if it was all a dream.

'You okay, love? Everyone okay?' He looked into the back of the car. He must have been able to hear Isobel crying.

'I have to go,' she said.

She walked around to the pavement and pulled open the driver's side rear door. She lifted Isobel to her chest and pulled her in tight, just how she liked it. She was still crying. Joseph looked out and he still looked panic stricken. His whole right side was a mass of blood, his hair was matted and what had once been a light blue, long-sleeved jumper was shredded against his arm and neck. The car had a scorched look, too: the whole door was a rash of black bits and dents. Movement caught her eye from the other side of the car, a man was walking directly towards them, towards the passenger seat she had just vacated. She looked back to Joseph.

'Are you not coming?' she said. Isobel was calming down a little. Joseph glanced over his left shoulder and then snatched his head back to her.

'Run, Jenny!'

Jenny could feel his panic. The man was almost to the car when he extended an arm. There was a sound like a firecracker. Joseph flinched. He was looking away from her. Another firecracker — he flinched again.

'What the hell?' The middle-aged man shouted in her ear. He must have followed her and he now ducked in front of her. Suddenly Jenny's mind un-fogged and everything was clear. She ran round the middle-aged man as she heard another *bang*! The middle-aged man cried out and she heard screams. She had Isobel clutched to her chest and she was crying. She blundered into the crowd, everyone was still; they were all either ducking or stooping but she could hear at least one set of footfalls behind her. And they were running too.

Jenny made it to the end of a row of shops. There was a gap for a narrow lane, then a chemist on the other side. She spun right into the lane. It was tight, and didn't look wide enough for a car — or so she thought. A second later she knew she was wrong; a car engine revved behind her, then a noise like a tyre struggling to gain a grip. The pavements were suddenly gone and she had an eight-foot wall on her left and the brick side of a building on her right. There was nowhere to go but straight on. This road ahead was empty, there was no one else on foot and the only sounds, amplified by the high walls, were her footfalls and a revving engine.

She ran harder, her right arm so tight around Isobel that she was scared she might hurt her. In front, she could see the dull grey of a multi-storey car park. She sprang through the entrance, running around the barrier. She heard the screech of a car stopping, then the sound of its doors opening and closing. She ran through the car park until she burst out on the other side. In front of her was a small grass bank, well worn by foot traffic taking the same route. It led into a small retail park that contained a couple of supermarkets and a shop selling beds, clustered around yet another car park. Though the area was thronged with cars and people, she remembered the busy scene she had run from: the presence of other people hadn't mattered then.

Jenny slowed to a walk and stooped, trying to lose herself among the parked cars. She made it to the car park entrance where a line of slow moving cars meandered slowly in a one-way system looking for parking places. She approached the first car she came to, walking in front of it and holding out her arm. The car stopped, but the couple inside locked their doors and shooed her away. She moved to the next car that rolled in behind it. The same reaction, only this time the driver tooted his horn. Quickly she ducked lower and moved away towards the supermarket. She caught her reflection in the windows of parked cars: her eyes were wild, her hair slick with sweat and her right arm was still a mass of blood. She was still clutching Isobel to her chest but her white blanket was stained a deep red and her hair was the only part of her that was visible. 'Please let it be my blood!' she whimpered.

Jenny realised how she must look, she realised that no one was going to help. She turned back towards where she had entered the car park and dared to stand taller. She could see a dark figure moving among the cars. He wasn't far away and was scanning for something. He was looking for her. She was running out of options.

Three rows closer to the supermarket she saw a police car parked up next to a vacant parking space. She ran to it. It was empty. She peered desperately towards the supermarket entrance, praying for the officers who owned the car to emerge, to be armed, to shout for her to stand behind them.

They didn't come.

She looked over to where she had seen the man walking among the cars. He was closer still, facing the other way but still moving. He hadn't seen her yet. She pushed herself up against the police car, peering at him through the windows. He turned towards her, his arm held

10

out like before. She could see he was holding something and people around him were starting to react. Someone screamed. Jenny couldn't stay where she was. He was going to kill her — and Isobel — and he didn't care who saw.

Jenny looked frantically around. The outside perimeter of the car park was fifty metres away where there was a short slope to a pavement. Hiding wasn't going to work. She had to get away. Quickly she checked Isobel over. Her eyes were wide and she was running through some fretful expressions but she was fine. The blood on the blanket was all on the outside; it was all Jenny's. Jenny dared to look over to where the man had come closer. He was still searching. She slammed her eyes shut and begged for this to work. She stood up, facing away from the man with the gun. She fixed on the pavement and ran as hard as she could.

Chapter 2

PC Ryan McGuiness stepped through the supermarket doors. His colleague PC Natalie Sawyers was close behind him.

'Maybe we've got it wrong, you know,' Natalie said.

Ryan slowed so Natalie could catch him up. He saw a playful twinkle in her eye. 'Got what wrong?'

'Well, life in general. We're in there taking our report and tutting at the man who walked in and stole three bottles of gin at seven in the morning, but I mean, who's right? I love gin.'

'I know what you mean. We won't be able to have a gin until at least our lunch break.'

'We should just quit? Maybe nick a bottle of gin on the way home — job done. I wouldn't have to worry about my sergeant's exams. Well, I wouldn't have to worry about anything.'

'Except prison.'

'Oh, come on! How much gin would you have to nick to go to prison? Much more than I'd ever need! And that's only if you get caught. What description did we get today?

A tall bloke in a white crash helmet, with a limp. It's not a great deal to go on, is it?'

'Do I detect you are feeling a little less motivated today, Nat?' They stopped outside of the shop. Ryan joined the queue for the cash machine. He was struggling to open a packet of sandwiches. He'd been running too late for breakfast before his shift.

'I wouldn't say less motivated, Ryan. I'm just tired, I guess. And maybe looking for alternatives to spending my nights studying and my days waiting for you.'

Ryan looked up from his sandwich wrestling. 'Jesus, Nat! I'll be two minutes! You got somewhere you need to be?'

'*Zulu One from Control.*' Ryan's radio came through loud from its position strapped to his chest. It caused two people ahead of them in the queue to spin and face him. He smiled and quickly turned it down.

'Maybe!' Natalie called over, she gestured at her own radio. She dipped her head to reply, 'Zulu One. Go ahead, Control.'

'*Zulu One, you are tracking close to a shots fired call in London Road, Dover. We have multiple informants. Received so far?*'

'So far,' Natalie replied. Ryan pushed his wallet back into his pocket. They both started towards their parked car.

'*At this time we do not have anything confirmed and it varies from shots fired, erratic driving and the last call is regards an RTC. We're pretty sure they're all the same incident, Zulu One. We just need someone on the ground to take a look.*'

'Received that, Control. Show us en route. What's the exact location?'

'*The RTC is described as being outside of the old indoor market, if that means anything to you. So you are aware, this is being assessed by the firearms commander and an armed patrol is making its way. We just require you to make an initial assessment.*'

You are to remember the stay-safe principles. Do you need reminding of these principles, Zulu One?

'No. Thank you, Control.'

Ryan looked over at Natalie and rolled his eyes. 'By stay-safe principles they mean don't get hit by a bullet, right? I mean, it's good advice but I'm not sure anyone really needs reminding of that.' Ryan made it back to their car first. He slid into the driver's seat and threw his sandwiches onto the bench seat behind him. He fired the engine and snatched at first gear for a quick getaway. He knew the location: it was a quick trip round the one-way system. He was suddenly aware that his colleague hadn't joined him, she still stood at the passenger door, apparently unmoving — he could just see her hip. Ryan cursed and slid her window down.

'Nat, we gotta go!' She stepped further away, towards the front of the car. She moved far enough for Ryan to see her face. Her eyes were wide in panic, her hands covered her mouth and she was staring back towards him. He saw what she was looking at, what he had missed in his urgency. A white blanket, bunched up and lying on the bonnet was pressed lightly against the windscreen. It was stained red — blood red. It was so fresh that there was a spot on the screen.

'Jesus, Nat! What is it?'

'Ryan,' Nat managed. 'It's a baby.'

'A what?' Ryan got out of the car. His attention was dragged away to the unmistakeable sound of a gunshot. Members of the public were running towards him. He turned back to his colleague who was still staring at the bundle on the bonnet as if it was too hot to touch. 'What the hell is going on?'

Chapter 3

'So how have you been?' The words drifted out of Sarah
Elms' lips like small talk. Like the exchange of pleasantries
at a workplace water cooler. George Elms took a moment
to look around, to quell the immediate response that he
wanted to give his wife.

Outside the large window, Langthorne's Old High
Street bustled under light rain, a shiny strip of cobbled
nostalgia. Unchanged since the turn of the previous
century and once the hub of the town, it was now mostly
art galleries, bars and coffee shops, like the one in which
George and his wife were now sitting. It was his favourite
in the town. The coffee-tinged air that helped set off the
atmosphere was complemented by a bookshop theme. Just
about every inch of wall was covered with books, old
novels with aging brown jackets and yellowing pages. He
had chosen it as a venue for their meeting on purpose. It
was a public place, so it came with the natural pressures of
social etiquette, where his wife could feel comfortable.
And it was somewhere he knew and liked so he could feel
comfortable too. But his wife had just asked him casually
how he had been, after she had disappeared with their

daughter for the best part of twelve months. The comfortable surroundings suddenly mattered very little — he wanted to bang hard on the table, maybe get to his feet and tip it right over, throwing their carefully presented lattes all over the floor. He wanted to shout, to swear, to demand to see his little girl.

'I've been okay,' he said, instead.

'Quite a pause there, George! Is that what you really wanted to say?' Sarah's chuckle had a nervous ring to it and she seemed to be studying him closely for his reaction.

'Well, I mean obviously it's been hard. I've missed my family every day. I missed you, both of you.' Their daughter Charley especially, if he was honest. She would be nine years old in two days' time — nine years old! How had that happened? Sometimes he thought about it, about how much time was passing since he had last seen her and it just about brought on a full panic attack. He would have sharpness of breath, even palpitations. You get one shot at being a dad to your kid and they don't stay kids for long.

'I can imagine.' Sarah said.

George bit down hard on his tongue. There was no way she could have a clue. 'So are you back down this way for good?'

'Probably — I mean that's the plan. We're in with my mum at the moment until we can get a place sorted. But it will be in the area.'

'Okay.' George tried to quell another feeling that came on quickly: excitement. His wife and child were going to be a twenty-minute drive away. The last year had been nothing but sporadic phone conversations and messaging — and now this! And from nowhere.

'So we won't be far. We can sort out some regular arrangement for you and Charley. At least once a week or something, but starting with her birthday. She's missed you.' Sarah smiled. She was so beautiful, the more so when she was happy.

'Oh God, I've missed her too!' George took a rushed intake of air as his emotions threatened to get the better of him. 'I've got Tuesday booked off. Her birthday. Just let me know times.'

'We'll sort something. You can have her all afternoon. I didn't want to bring her today, but does the afternoon suit?'

'That's fine. Are you not going to be with us?'

'Well, I thought I would give you some time on your own, just the two of you. We can have dinner in the evening maybe? After you've done the cinema or whatever you want.'

'Is that what she wants to do? There's something on at Leeds Castle, I was thinking of taking her there.'

'She'd like that. She can't wait to see you — I don't think she'd mind if it was a few hours on a park bench to be honest! She wanted to come today, but I wanted to speak to you first. I didn't want her here, in case . . . you understand, right?'

'Sure, I understand about today.' George leant back in his seat. He had been disappointed about today but there was no need to share it. Not now. He was about to get Charley for the best part of a whole day. And on her birthday! He knew he had a stupid smile on his face; there was nothing he could do about that.

'So, an inspector now!' Sarah was back to watching for his reaction. She peered out over her raised coffee cup.

'Yeah, it's all pretty new. Just a couple of weeks really.'

'How did that happen? Detective Inspector George Elms! No offence, George, but I had you as the last person they would promote.'

'I know! None taken. I don't think anyone saw it coming — me included. I suddenly got a nudge in that direction and I sort of went with it. I never expected to actually get the promotion. I just wanted to see look on the faces of certain people when I turned up for my interview. As it turned out I had some really good evidence in my portfolio, I passed the exam and then the interview. Then I was endorsed by someone in senior management and they had no choice but to make me up.'

'Senior management? Who stuck their neck out for you?'

'John Whittaker.'

'Whittaker?' Sarah seemed to be mulling the name over. 'Ex-army, right? Older fella. Always stands to attention. We met him at some award ceremony.'

'Well remembered.'

'He's not the sort of man you forget. We liked him, right?'

'We did yes. We certainly do now. He's one of the good guys.'

'Few and far between at that place.'

George couldn't disagree, not with Sarah. No one had been affected by bad apples in his police force more than her. No one except him, maybe. 'So here we are.' George tried to move away from his work. 'I feel like I've missed out on so much. Thanks for all the photos by the way, but I still feel like I've missed it all.' The photos — Sarah had sent through photos of their daughter at significant events. Dressed up for a Harry Potter party, a witch at Halloween, surrounded by presents at Christmas and on a sun-drenched beach during a summer break on a Spanish island. In every one their daughter was beaming with delight, in every one she was getting older, and every one had the ability to stop George in his tracks and bring him to his knees.

'I know. You shouldn't miss any more George. You understand that I needed to take her away. We both needed space — and time.'

George did understand. He didn't like it, but he did understand. His job had brought evil right to their doorstep, to his family home, and George had made the mistake of thinking he could control it. But he hadn't been able to. Now the threat was gone but the scars and the fear . . . they would take longer.

'You're back now.'

'I am. I needed to talk about me, too, not just Charley.'

George was suddenly aware that she had tensed up again, where she seemed to have been starting to relax.

'Okay.'

'There's no easy way, George, you know, I tried to work out how to say it—'

'Just say it then.'

'I'm going to need a divorce.'

George had picked up his coffee cup. He bumped it back down on the table. Hot coffee slopped over both sides. 'You didn't have to break it to me like that!' He smiled, but he kept his eyes downwards on his drink.

'I did say there was no easy way.'

'I guess not.'

'Are you surprised?'

'Well, yes. I mean I didn't think we were there yet. Obviously I was way off.'

'We've been apart for what, two years? More than that, really. Can you really say it hasn't even crossed your mind?'

'Divorce? Never.'

'That I might ask?'

'No, never.' George was aware that his voice carried an edge. He supped back at his coffee to try and calm his mind.

'Well, then, I'm even more sorry if this is a bit of a shock. I didn't think it would be *totally* out of the blue. We don't need to talk about it now, I'll give you a little bit of time to get used to the idea and we can talk again.'

'Get used to the idea?'

'You know what I mean, George.'

'I don't think I do. This isn't changing the wallpaper in the living room, Sarah. This is everything to me. I know

19

we have been spending time apart and I know the reasons for that, but they were all about you feeling safe, you and Charley.'

'I know.'

'So who is he then?'

'Who is who?'

'Don't play games. You said you *needed* a divorce. The only reason you would need a divorce is if you wanted to get married. So who is he?'

Sarah sighed. She looked flustered all of a sudden. 'George Elms, detective. It has been two years in total.'

'I know that.'

'Well, what did you expect?'

'It's probably best I don't answer that.'

'You've got no right to be angry with me, George.'

'That another one of your rules?'

'What do you mean?'

'You take yourself off, tell me I'm not allowed to make contact, not allowed to come and find you, that you would call me. Now twelve months down the line you're back to tell me how I'm allowed to feel about it all.'

'Because when you *did* contact me, when you *did* find us, our daughter was taken. *I* was taken. Who knows what could have happened. I still can't even think about it, George, after all this time. We were at the mercy of a madman and there was nothing you could do about it.'

'I did do something about it. We survived that. As a family. We came through it. It was a tough period, but that's all done with now. I can understand you needed a little time away, I know why. But it's done. He's gone.'

'Yes, George, that madman has gone, but he brought something out in you. Suddenly my husband was an utter stranger. And can you promise there won't be another madman further down the line? A queue of them, maybe? Look at what you've gone through in the last few years, even if we weren't directly involved. You couldn't just come home from that and play happy families. You can't just be a normal dad getting off early for sports days or being there for Christmas. How damaging do you think it is for Charley when her dad comes home with black eyes, or blown up, or shot at? Or what if you don't come home one day? Lord knows that would be hard enough right now, but if we're back as a family unit, if we let you back in? There would be no coming back from that. She would be destroyed. And so would I, George, so would I.'

'I always said that I would quit the job if you said I should. If that's what it takes, I'll put my notice in the second I walk back through that door. My family is all that matters to me. There's nothing else. Just say the word and I'll do it.'

'Really? You got promoted, George! The last time we saw each other you were waiting it out for the right offer. Then you got it. They said you could walk — full pension, all that you could want. And here we are. What happened?'

'You happened! You left — remember? I had some time off on my own before and I did nothing but self-destruct. I'm terrified, Sarah, that I'll go back to who I was then if I don't have anything to get up for in the morning. That's the only reason I stayed. We go back to being a family and I know I'd be fine. I'd have everything I want. I'll quit, I'll go in now and I'll quit.'

'It's not that simple. There's too much. There's *been* too much.'

'This other fella?'

'It's not just that.'

'He exists then. Who is he?'

'Does it matter?'

'What does he do? Sits around at home wrapped in cotton wool, I hope.'

'Don't start being funny, George. He's an architect. He's unlikely to get me kidnapped.'

'Well, he's off to a good start then.'

'He's good with Charley too.'

George bit down hard. The image of Charley sitting on another man's shoulders, giggling at him with the delightful belly laugh she had when she was tickled, tugging on his hand at the zoo. It made him feel physically ill. He was aware that he was starting to lose control. He needed to get away. 'I need some time. The irony, eh?' He was aware his voice broke a little. He stood up. Sarah fixed her gaze on him, those big, brown eyes suddenly full of sympathy. It made George angrier.

'Okay. We'll be around. I was serious about sorting something for you and Charley for her birthday.'

'Yeah, I'll be in touch.' George pulled a crumpled note from his pocket and dropped it on the table. He heard Sarah say something but he was already making for the door and he didn't hear it. He had to get away before he broke down completely.

George made it back out onto the street. The front of the café was made entirely of glass and they had been sitting by the window. In his periphery, he could see the figure of his wife where he had left her. He pushed his hands into his pockets and dipped his head against the rain. He walked up the steep hill, back towards the town centre. His phone was ringing in his pocket. He ignored it — let it ring out. Almost immediately after, it vibrated again. He peered at the screen; he had missed a call from Emily Ryker.

George was new in post as the detective inspector for Major Crime covering the east of the county. Emily Ryker was his intelligence officer. They had always gotten on well — too well at one point. But that was ancient history. Soon after, he had met Sarah and settled down. Since that moment he'd never considered anyone else. Never considered that there even could be.

The second vibration had been a text message. It said simply, *urgent*. He and Ryker had an understanding: they could ignore each other's calls, but if it was important they would send a message straight after. George knew he was expected to call her right back, but he couldn't muster the energy to speak. He wanted somewhere dark and quiet that served something stronger than coffee, where no one could find him. He had taken a Sunday off to meet his wife, hoping that it might turn into an all-day affair with his daughter involved. Sundays used to be his favourite family day. He couldn't have been more wrong. He switched his phone off. Whatever it was Ryker needed to talk to him about, he was in no fit state to be of any use.

Chapter 4

Jenny made it to the grassy verge that ran along the edge of the car park. She half-turned to get a last glimpse of Isobel and the raised lip at the edge of the verge caught her out; she was sent sprawling onto the pavement, her knees and elbows scraping against the tarmac and the air forced from her body as she grunted. She heard another *crack*! And then a thud that sent a clump of grass and mud flailing towards her. For a second she was frozen to the spot, looking back towards the source of the sound. A man dressed in black had climbed into the back of a large truck. He was facing her. He still had his weapon levelled in her direction. She scrambled to her feet and sprinted down the pavement. It was sloped, down towards where the River Dour rushed against its concrete sides, the natural riverbanks having given way to the straight walls. The path dropped quickly below the level of the car park she had left. It would provide her cover at least.

She heard another gunshot. This one sounded further away. In the distance she could hear sirens. The pavement sloped back up and the river slipped underground, but Jenny was facing a road. Traffic moved along it but she ran blindly out. She heard the urgent squeals of car tyres and blaring horns but she ignored them and made it to the other side. The sirens had been louder too but she didn't consider stopping, not even for a second. She needed to get away from there; she couldn't afford to stop.

The river reappeared on her right. It flowed a little quicker and was shallower, enough that she could hear its gurgling. She was still running, but the adrenalin that had fired into her body and enabled her escape was all but consumed. She was running on empty. She was exhausted. She braved a glance behind her and saw a long, empty pavement. No one was behind her. She heard more sirens. Surely anyone seen brandishing a gun would now be focussed on evading the police? She slowed to a walk and concentrated on filling her lungs with deep breaths, trying to recover. Her leg was painful all of a sudden. On inspection she had ripped her jeans at the right knee and it was bleeding quite freely — her elbow too, and she dusted some grit from her forearm.

'Isobel . . .' she muttered. She turned back to face the sirens. Maybe the police already had Isobel — maybe she was safe? She'd had to leave Isobel on that police car. The shots were meant for her. Her last glimpse of the gunman had been of him walking away from where she had left Isobel. She was so much faster without her. It had been the right decision; it was the *only* decision. She considered walking back to the car park, which would probably be swamped with police cars now. Then she thought of Joseph, of how he had been sat in his car in broad daylight, of how that animal had fired through the window. She rubbed at her face — she had to get the images out of her mind for now — at least until she was safe.

'You okay?'

Jenny spun back round. She hadn't been aware of anyone approaching. A man smiled at her, he was mid-thirties, overweight and wearing a *Goonies* T-shirt. He had a tattoo of faded red lips on his neck.

'Not really,' she said.

'The sirens, they for you?'

'Sort of,' Jenny's voice was croaky. She was still trying to get her breath back under control.

'You in trouble?'

'No. I mean, yeah, but I was running away from whoever the police want. I'm not that person.'

'I know the police. I know all of them. They joke. They say, "Stephen, you know us just by our boots!" I got a window, see. I live in the basement flat, and when they come see me they have to walk past my window. I always know who it is by their boots!'

Jenny patted her pockets. They were empty. She must have left her phone in the hotel room. She last remembered plugging it in and sliding it under the bed.

'Do you need some help? You're bleeding. I did some first-aid classes. I can put a sling on if you needed that. Or I can do the recovery position.'

Jenny looked him up and down. He was wearing loose-fitting tracksuit bottoms that were pulled high and stained and gripped tightly at his ankles. He had cheap-looking formal shoes with no socks. He was a little simple, she thought, but she did need some help.

'Do you have a phone?'

He patted his own pockets. 'In the flat!' he said. He seemed delighted. 'You can use it. I rushed out, I heard the police, see. I must have forgotten to pick up my phone!'

'Is it near?' Jenny looked around. They were still on the river path. It seemed to cut between rows of housing.

'Just over there.' He wafted a finger in the general direction in which she had been running. 'You wanna come?'

'I need to use the phone.' Jenny said. She tried to smile in a way that was reassuring.

Stephen led the way. It was less than a two-minute walk. Jenny found that, having stopped, she was now limping from her hip a little as she followed on behind.

She could still hear sirens but they were more distant. Stephen's front door was down a set of tight, stone steps and was unlocked. He had to push it hard to open it enough for them to get through. Jenny stepped in after him. There were reams of unopened post lying behind the door, getting jammed underneath. She pushed it firmly shut and the post immediately slid back. She had to apply her weight to get the door to click shut. The flat was starved of natural light, cluttered and smelled musty. It wasn't dirty as such, but on every inch of surface stood an action figure — mostly *Star Wars*. Jenny recognised some of them but there were a lot she didn't.

'Do you like *Star Wars*?' Stephen said excitedly.

'I guess. I've seen the films. Look, my baby is back there. I need to call the police and make sure she's okay. Did you find your phone?'

'You need to call them here? I can do that! They know me, they come here all the time.'

'No, it's okay. I need to talk to them. I need to tell them what happened. It's very urgent!'

Stephen beamed wildly. He plucked a phone from under a toy spaceship on a low table and held it close to his face. The keys looked oversized, the whole thing looked like a toy phone. 'I'll call!' he said again.

Jenny's attention was dragged suddenly to a movement at the front room window. The stairs down to the front door were visible, just like Stephen had described, they were like a diagonal stripe from the top left to the bottom right. She could see legs moving quickly down the steps. She stepped forward, her pulse racing. Stephen pushed past her. Jenny could see more of them now: two men, both wearing black shoes and black trousers. They had black vests on too — with *Police* written across their back. Police officers! Thank God.

'They're here! Stephen, they're here, I don't need the phone! I'm safe.' She moved across the floor towards the front door.

'Wait!'

She stopped. Stephen looked stern, his brow contorted in confusion. 'Them's not police boots. Not even police shoes. Where's their belt, their handcuffs?' He was leaning into the window now, trying to get a view to the right where they would be stood at the front door. Jenny heard a knock. She could see the front door from where she stood. It was a half-length frosted pane and the men appeared as two dark distortions. She saw them turn to face each other and heard a murmur between them, though not well enough to pick out the words. A face pushed against the glass. They tried the door again, this time it was thumped with the underside of a clenched fist by the man on the right.

'POLICE!' One of them shouted. They thumped again. Jenny didn't know what to do; it was as if she was cemented to the ground. She turned to Stephen, who was walking towards her. He was still scowling.

'We'll see about that, won't we?' He brushed past. The hallway was so tight Jenny felt his stomach push into her. The two distortions were still at the door. They would have seen Stephen coming. Suddenly there was a tremendous bang. Stephen stumbled backwards immediately. There was another tremendous bang, then a thud against the door. Stephen was on the floor, almost at Jenny's feet. He had a hole in his chest, it was bright red but Jenny could also see bits of white. His eyes stared up at her, his mouth gaped open and shut.

Jenny turned away and she ran. The back of the house was just as cluttered. She was in the kitchen, crowded with plates and cups now, rather than figures. There was a long window high above the sink. She stopped, desperate for a way out. There was a back door, partly concealed behind a full-length curtain. She snatched it out of the way and it came away in her hand, the curtain pole clattered to the ground making her jump. She heard another thud and the tinkling of glass. She could hear the pushing of a mountain of paper . . . they were coming in.

The handle to the back door rattled but it wouldn't open. There was a metal knob under the handle and she spun it right around and tugged at the door. It still wouldn't move. She spun it again, the door moved slightly, it opened inwards but it was blocked by a cat box and some litter in a tray. The scent was suddenly pungent. There was no time to move it. She yanked it as hard as she could. The cat box tipped out, the door opened enough to get her leg through. She wriggled in the door and was half through, her shoulders caught; she could feel them scraping on the metal frame, peeling her skin. She heard heavy footfalls coming through the house. Suddenly the door let her go and she stumbled out into a tiny courtyard. There was an eight-foot wall all around her; she could barely see the sky. She heard another noise behind her that came from the kitchen. She pushed off the door and ran as fast as she could at the wall. She threw herself at it. She lifted her right foot to meet it flat and reached up with her hands. Her fingers caught the top of the wall. She heaved herself up, the toes of her shoes scrabbling against the concrete. The door blew out behind her. It made her flinch, so much so that she nearly lost her tenuous grip. She managed to get one of her elbows over the top. She could see a garden spread out in front of her. The grass was overgrown, a wall had collapsed and had been left where it had fallen. She managed to hook her left leg over, her nostrils filled with the scent of dog mess. She heard a shout.

'JENNY! WHERE YOU GOING, GIRL?'

She rolled into the grass — far enough from the edge that she couldn't be seen from below. She heard a scrabbling sound, someone was trying to climb out the way she had. She peered down the garden. She could run, which would put her back out on the streets of Dover, or she could turn and follow the river back to the police but she couldn't be sure she would make it. There were now fingers on the top of the wall, they were blanched white and they fidgeted as someone hung from them. She picked up the biggest chunk of collapsed wall she could find — three house bricks seized together in a roughly triangular lump. A man's head appeared — slick black hair and a sweaty brow — concentrating on the climb. His eyes met hers. Jenny stood over him, the piece of wall over her head. She brought it down as hard as she could on the top of his head. He fell away out of sight, she heard him hit the floor, the bricks too. She heard someone else shout something — she didn't know what. She was already running.

Chapter 5

The Major Crime floor of Langthorne House Police Station was usually a quiet, calm place at just before eight on a Monday morning. But as soon as George stepped out of the lift he could tell there was a bit of a buzz about the place. The buzz got louder as he pushed through the double doors into the department where his team of detectives and support staff lived. The department was a spacious area, open plan save for a large meeting room and two offices right next to it, one of which now belonged to George. The recent cuts to policing meant that Major Crime was now a far more transient occupation. Often George would walk through the department to acknowledge just a smattering of DCs, spread out among the banks of desks. The bulk of the team were used to moving all over the county to wherever they were needed. No one knew what would happen if there was a serious incident in more than one district.

Today the banks of desks were still unoccupied by people, but they were occupied by things. Bags and coats, steaming mugs, lunchboxes and paperwork were strewn across just about all of them and every monitor was alight and alive. Something was going on.

George had to walk past the meeting room to get to his office. Sure enough, it was teeming with movement and noise. George could see through the glass panels that ran the length of the room. He saw DS Jason Carter standing with a marker pen in his right hand and gesturing for calm with his left. The whiteboard had what looked like the start of a timeline drawn roughly through its centre. George continued his walk to his office. He pushed the door shut behind him. It barely had chance to settle in its frame before it was pushed back open again. Emily Ryker stepped through.

'We don't knock anymore then, Ryker?' George flopped in his seat as he spoke. He was still carrying a travel mug with coffee in it. He rarely drank coffee, especially black. Today it was black and it was strong.

'What are you doing in here, George?' Emily demanded.

'I work here, Ryker. The more pertinent question would be what are *you* doing in here?'

'I came to get you. We were all summoned for a meeting. 7 a.m. start. Where have you been?'

'At home. I didn't know there was a meeting.'

'I called you. What happened to our system?'

George looked puzzled. He took a sip of his coffee.

'You know . . . where we're allowed to hang up on each other if we don't want to talk, but if we get a message that it's urgent we call straight back. I sent the message, George. It was urgent.'

'What's up?'

'That's what I get? What's up?'

'*Is* there something up?'

'I was calling you about this job. The reason most of the county's detectives are in the room next door.'

'What job?'

32

'Jesus, George. I know you weren't answering your phone but it's all over the news. You couldn't avoid it if you wanted to. The shooting. In Dover. People dead, others missing. Broad daylight. Is any of this ringing any bells?'

'Blimey!' George took another sip of his coffee. 'Sounds like I chose the right day to have off.'

'Are you coming next door or not? Whittaker has already asked where you are.'

Chief Inspector John Whittaker was the reason for George's promotion, his only ally it seemed — among anyone of rank, at least. Normally George would be excited to come in and hear about shootings and missing people. Today he could really do without it. He had planned on hiding in his office and drinking strong coffee.

When George walked into the meeting room, he realised very quickly that there was nowhere to hide. There was almost nowhere to sit. He was still swigging at his coffee. There were a lot of voices all talking at once and it took the entrance of John Whittaker to silence the excited detectives. Whittaker stood at the end of the table, talking into his mobile phone. He soon pushed it back into his pocket and looked straight at George.

'Can I have a word?' Whittaker said, before addressing the room as a whole. 'People, I asked for the timeline. I'll be five minutes with Inspector Elms and then I'll be back. I need to have this timeline up and visible to everyone, okay? Let's get it done, please.' He led the way out of the door and towards his office. George followed.

'What the hell happened to you, old boy?' Whittaker called everyone *old boy*. He had risen to the rank of Major in the British Army before moving to the police. He still spoke like he was on the parade ground.

George did his best to look indignant. 'What do you mean?'

'You look like rat shit, man. I've seen men come back from a tour of Afghanistan looking more up for it than you. What's gone on? Emily said she couldn't get you by phone.'

'I was on a day off. I booked it—'

'I know what you were, George. Major Crime, however, can't always recognise a *day off*. Seems some selfish bastards are still content to shoot at one another on down days. You need to be contactable by phone at least.'

'I'm sorry, boss, I know. I had a shit day and I turned my phone off. It won't happen again.'

'You must be sorry, calling me *boss*.'

'Major, then. Sorry.' George called him Major when they were in the right surroundings. He found it funny; Whittaker didn't seem to.

'What's the matter with you? You were seeing the wife, right? She's out of hiding. Did she not turn up?'

'She turned up, sir.'

'I might have known. I'm always pretty distraught when my wife turns up too. Every time she pops out to go shopping I live in hope.'

George managed a weak smile. 'She wants a divorce.'

'And I suppose *lucky bastard* is not the response you are looking for?'

'Not really.'

'Fine. Well, look, George, I know this is big for you but I don't have time for one of my legendary pep talks where I tell you to dust yourself off and get back to work, okay? So I'll just say that you need to dust yourself off and get back to work. Can you do that?'

'I'm fine.'

'Well, you look like shit and you smell worse. Did you drink it or bathe in it?'

'I don't remember.'

'Of course you don't. Jesus, George, of all the days.'

'I know, I'm sorry. It was a blowout, I needed it, but I'm fine now.'

'Well, let's hope so. I just got off the phone with a patrol sergeant. Totally separate to this whole mess. He's at an address on the outskirts of Canterbury. He has a body up there, sus circs. I'm going to need you to go up there and fly the flag for Major Crime. Everyone else is tucked up with this other job from yesterday. Murder victims, they're like London buses.'

'You don't want me involved in that? In the shooting?'

'Well, yes, I did, but that was yesterday. It's actually worked out with this other thing coming in. It means I have a volunteer to send.'

'Well, I guess I can't argue with that.'

'It won't do you any good. I have CSI on the way. Uniform will hold the scene. I'll call the sergeant back and let him know to expect you around ten.'

George glanced at his watch. 'The outskirts of Canterbury, you said? I'm only twenty minutes away.'

'That's right. So that gives you time to go via your home. Get a shower, George. Comb your damned hair and maybe find a shirt you've actually ironed. I need you switched on up there. I can't spare the usual team. You're it — for now at least.'

'What do we know? Is it a good job? What makes it suspicious?'

'The job number is fifty-two of today if you want a look at the log. I have a printed copy somewhere. It has what we know up to this point — which isn't much. The suspicious element is a shotgun wound to our dead woman's gut. Suspected robbery, elderly couple, that's a brief summary.'

George stiffened up a little. 'A proper job then.'

'Sounds that way. Now get yourself presentable. I feel bad that we can't send the full team to these poor saps. I think I should at least send someone who is sober.'

Chapter 6

George hadn't seen the point in Whittaker sending him home to freshen up. Now he was glad he had. He felt much better — almost normal.

He was back to work and moving through the village of Elham. It was a beautiful smudge of green and brown set mostly in an area of outstanding natural beauty. Its closest civilisation was the equally beautiful city of Canterbury. It had extended patches of wild fern meadows and trees on either side of the road shedding their leaves as if George was part of some ticker-tape procession. He had found a detective who hadn't been sucked into the Dover investigation to keep him company, an old friend — Paul Bearn. He was a good detective, once part of George's team before George seriously injured him in a moment of noise and confusion. Paul was damaged forever, but it had done nothing, it seemed, to damage the strength of their friendship. Paul was in the passenger seat and he was reading out loud from the printed 999 call.

'So, 4 a.m. this morning, or just before, we get the call from a panicked male saying his wife has been shot. There's lines of input here where they're trying to get some sense out of him and then just a summary from the uniform patrols when they turn up. Looks like a group have turned up and tried to rob them and it's gotten out of hand. Looks like the murder weapon might have belonged to the couple.'

George scowled. 'This is gonna need some piecing together.'

'Lucky you brought me, then.'

George grinned. 'I heard something about your latest light duties being as some sort of analyst, right? I thought you might appreciate a day out.'

'Yeah see, that's a common error. Most people don't realise the importance of analysing crime trends in urban areas. But what would you say if I told you that I can now show, statistically, that more crimes occur in areas that are the most densely populated? What would you say to that?'

'That I could have told you that before you started the study.'

'Exactly what I told them. Honestly, they're running out of things to ask me to do. I'm terrified to finish one job because I know the next will be worse!'

'Well, today at least you can do some real police work. You're wasted in there, Paul. I meant what I said about you coming into Major Crime.'

'Thanks, mate. If you can square it then I told you, I will.'

'Excellent. The department really needs a good tea maker.'

'Wanker!'

Both men laughed. George suddenly slowed the car, his eyes right. He read the house name out loud: 'Kismet.' It was etched in a solid slab of oak that was nailed to a thick tree trunk. A farm-style gate next to it was jammed open. George could only see a drive stretching away from them, he couldn't see any part of a house. He swung into the drive.

'*Kismet*. Means fate, right?' Paul said.

'It certainly did for these people.' They drove in silence, the atmosphere instantly less jovial. George took the time to contemplate what had happened here just a few hours earlier. He couldn't imagine the fear and the panic that the couple must have been through.

Apple trees lined the drive and were dotted across the wide lawns. A low, double-wire perimeter fence wrapped around the estate. There was woodland on the other side, thick rows of mature trees reaching over and beckoning in the breeze. The drive turned gently to the right then straightened up. A large and very traditional-looking farmhouse stood in front of them. It was immediately imposing in a way that only buildings that had stood for hundreds of years could be. There were three marked police cars and a marked police van that had *Forensic Investigation* emblazoned down its side. They were all parked in the gritted expanse at the front of the property. To the right of the house was a substantial double garage. One of the doors was lifted and George could see the rear of a smart-looking Range Rover. Someone stepped out through the big front door that was dead centre on the ground floor of the main house. They were dressed in a white paper suit, blue boot covers and a blue mask covering their mouth. She pulled her mask off and the hood on her suit down as George's car approached. She flicked a long, dark ponytail free from a hair net and beamed a smile. Allesandra. George was always glad when he turned up at something serious and she was the one in the suit. She had an excellent eye for detail and more importantly she was always cheery.

'Hey!' George stepped out. Allesandra was beaming.

'Long time no see.'

'This is true. It's been a little quiet recently. Someone must have said that out loud a couple of days ago, I reckon.' George referenced the age-old superstition among police officers that saying the word *quiet* would swiftly invoke the opposite. To police officers, 'not busy' was always referred to as just 'Q.'

'I know, it's gone crazy all of a sudden. I checked on my phone earlier, it's not even a full moon.' George smiled broadly.

'What?' she said.

'That's where we are these days, isn't it? We want to know if the moon is out so we consult our smart phones!'

'You know what I mean.'

'I do. Paul Bearn you know and love, of course.'

Paul walked round to join them. Allesandra pecked him on the cheek. Her eyes fell to his left arm, it was tied off in a sling. The nerves had long since shrivelled and died in it and he no longer had any movement in it at all.

'Hey, Ali.'

'How come he gets a peck on the cheek?' George complained.

'Because he's special.'

'I see. What do we have here, then?'

'We have a murder, George. I don't think we can be any more certain about that. Single gunshot wound to the abdomen. Looks close range but far enough away not to be self-inflicted. Ian Banks is the patrol sergeant. He's assigned the front here as the common approach path. Seems a van of some sort has driven to the rear of the house in the early hours of the morning. We've got tracks I can recover at the back. There's another drive that leads to another gate back out onto a side road. It's normally padlocked but it's been snipped. The lock was tossed but I've recovered that already. I've only just moved inside. The husband is still in there. I managed to get him out of the main rooms at least, but he won't leave the house. Not until his wife does. She's still in situ.'

'Sounds grim. How's he doing?'

'Not good — as you can imagine.'

'What are your first thoughts around him?'

'You mean, did he shoot his wife in the belly with his shotgun? That's a brave call, George. Luckily it isn't mine.'

'He might have done then?'

'I don't think so. Not for a minute. I don't think I've ever seen anyone more devastated. It didn't stop me seizing his clothes and swabbing him for gunshot residue. Be gentle with him.'

'So you stripped him and swabbed him, and now you're telling me to be gentle with him?'

'Yes. The difference being that I have a way with people. I don't just look at them and they think I'm accusing them of something. We actually talked a little. He wasn't massively engaging, but he told me enough for me to know that I was wasting my time.'

'Wasting your time how?'

'He will be covered in residue. He was firing his guns just a few hours before. He's fairly regular with them, even at his age. I think he does it for a bit of sport now. Whatever the reason, evidentially any residue found on him will be easily explained.'

'That already gets me suspicious.'

'Because you're a police officer. You people see the guilt and then work backwards. Like I said, be gentle with him, he's had quite a night.'

'That I cannot argue with. Is there somewhere we can speak to him where we don't have to suit up? It's not ideal trying to build up a rapport when the subject gets the impression he's ET.'

'You want to speak to him first or do you want to see the scene?'

'I'll talk to him first. The scene isn't going anywhere.'

'Okay. Well, yeah, there is then. They have a living room at the front here. The door was shut throughout with no suggestion anyone's entered there. I've processed it already. It's where he's sat. If you go through the living room and turn hard right you'll see him in there with Sergeant Banks.'

'Perfect, thanks.'

'And don't go in any other rooms. Not *any*!'

'Yes, ma'am!'

George recognised the sergeant who stepped towards him as he entered the living room. He was a big man, tall and imposing, even more so in his size twelve boots, body armour and vest with his cuffs and spray attached. The radio lit up suddenly on his chest then faded back to black. George didn't know him well; he had seen him at a few incidents before, maybe. Certainly he had seen him around the police station.

'Sergeant Banks.' George extended his hand. The sergeant took it up but not with any vigour.

'Sir,' he said. Even in a whisper George could sense the acid in his tone. George was maybe a little sensitive to it now. He knew his past meant that he wouldn't always be a popular figure with some colleagues. He had become more in tune with it since his promotion. He still didn't really give a shit.

'How is he?' George nodded towards the elderly man sat on a large sofa. He was leaning forward, looking down at the floor, his elbows resting on top of his thighs, hugging himself almost, like it might be providing a crumb of comfort. He had to be the husband.

'You can see for yourself. The poor fella's had a rough time. We all have actually — *sir*. We were night turn. Due off three hours ago. Any chance you can stand me and my people down? Early turn have the scene. It's just us left in here. They are sending someone over to sit with him, but really we should only be waiting for Major Crime to arrive.'

'Yeah, of course. There's no need for you to stick around. We'll be here a while I reckon anyway.'

'Thanks. Early turn have the scene log. CSI are happy for you to stay in here but I don't think anywhere else is open yet.'

'No, we spoke to CSI on the way in. I understand you set the common approach path as the front, right?'

'Yeah. We've taken initial accounts. It's been hard. Stanley there isn't really talking too much. He's not being obstructive — I just don't think he can speak at the moment. I've never seen anyone so bad. But all the action was at the back of the house. Mrs Wingmore is still lying in the rear porch.'

'Rear porch?'

'Yeah, it's like a boot room, I suppose. It leads into the kitchen. I think they use it as the main door.'

'Okay. We'll need a copy of your pocket books before you go off-duty. Can you throw them at someone in the office in Major Crime? Then get yourself off to sleep, yeah?'

'Will do.' The sergeant nodded at his two colleagues, they moved silently out of the room.

'Paul, can you get on the phone, make sure we've got a FLO assigned for this. They need to be here sooner rather than later.'

'Will do, boss.' Paul Bearn turned away, already clutching for his phone. A FLO, or Force Liaison Officer, was someone assigned to work with most victims of major incidents, and always where murder was suspected. They were sold as support for the victims of crime — or their surviving relatives at least. They did fulfil this function, but really they were a key part of gathering intelligence around the family when trying to identify suspects. They could still be with family members after some time had passed and when guards might have dropped.

George approached Stanley Wingmore. He hadn't moved — not even turned his head to see who the new people were in his front room. George thought maybe it didn't matter to him now. Nobody here was going to be able to change what had happened. There was a sofa directly opposite him.

'Mr Wingmore, I'm Detective Inspector George Elms. Do you mind if I sit for a moment, sir?'

The man raised watery eyes. George guessed that he was in his seventies. He looked in good shape, not an ounce of fat on him — that was certain. Maybe a little too thin. He wore a green suit with sewn patches on the arms, a chequered shirt underneath with a thick tie pulled tight against his scrawny neck. George had seen on the call log that CSI had already seized his clothing from him, a set of blue and white pyjamas. They had been described as *stained red*. Despite everything that had gone on, the man had still made the effort of changing into a day suit. He looked every bit the gentrified farmer that his surroundings suggested.

'Please, Inspector.' He gestured with a wrinkled hand. George took the invitation, but perched on the edge.

'Call me George. There's nothing formal about today, Mr Wingmore. And I have come to really hate the *sir* thing.'

'Stan.'

George smiled warmly. 'Stan. Thanks. I know you probably don't want to be talking to the likes of me, Stan. I know I wouldn't. But I need to talk to you about what happened last night. About all of this. I'm so sorry you got caught up in it. I'm so sorry for what's happened. I've been a cop a long time and every time something like this happens I know deep down that we've failed. I'm sorry we couldn't have been here.'

'There was nothing you could have done. Nothing I could have done either. I'm too old and too feeble to even protect my own wife. Have you any idea how that feels? They laughed at me, George. That's evil. How could they do this . . .?' He petered out, his voice quieter, but there was no sign it was breaking. George had seen it before — his expression, his demeanour, his body language. He was empty, devoid of any emotion. A combination of shock, denial and not being able to even contemplate what had happened. This was all going to get a lot worse before it got any better.

'Old and feeble, young and athletic, ain't neither of them that's bulletproof, Stan. Don't you start beating yourself up now. Your night's been bad enough.'

'It would have been different when I was younger. You have to trust me on that.'

George smiled again. 'Quite the formidable one, I bet.'

'A farmer. Man and boy. I used to be able to look after myself. And my family.'

'Stan, I want to find the bastards that did this and now I need your help and all of that fighting spirit you've got. I know you've spoken to my uniform colleagues already, but I want to go through it again with you, because I'm the one who's going to find them. I'll ask you for every detail, Stan. It won't be easy, but I know you're strong enough. Does that sound like something you can do?'

Stan had been back peering at the floor. He lifted his head again and looked right at George but it was like he was looking into him. 'Nothing matters anymore, Inspector, none of this. What is there left for me to talk about?'

'The men that did this . . . let's make them our focus, you and me. There's nothing else worth talking about Stan, not right now. But those men, they're out there somewhere and between us we can find them and we can lose them their freedom.'

George heard movement behind him. He had been leaning in, the intensity between him and Stan bringing them closer. The noise broke it like a spell. George turned to where Paul Bearn was standing at the door.

'You okay, Paul?'

'Yeah. I need a word is all. Nothing urgent.'

George looked back toward Stan. His head had sagged again. George reached out and took hold of his hand. Stan reacted to the touch.

'Stan, I'm gonna pop out to my car and get something to write on, okay? I want to take that detail from you. It gives me a place to start at least. I want you to know, Stan, I'm a fucking good detective.' George jerked a thumb at Paul. 'Me and him . . . we're good at what we do. And what we are doing from this moment until it is done is finding the bastards that came to your home early this morning. We need your help, Stan, okay? You up for that?'

Stan nodded. His jaw creased, just for an instant, but he held his head up this time. George stood and let go of the old man, about to move away. But he stopped as Stan started talking.

'You see that.' Stan gestured towards the fireplace. It was huge, the entire bottom half of one wall cut out. A double-doored, cast iron wood burner stood in its centre. The top of the brickwork ran with a knotted beam of beautiful oak that had bronzed horseshoes dotted along its length. It was in keeping with the room as a whole. Above it, the white ceiling ran with dark wood beams. George's eye fell on a picture rail hung with memories — all of them smiling. To George, the house smacked of a family home that had been built around its occupants, and had grown as they had. Now it was just the pictures that were left. And Stan.

'It's beautiful, Stan. You don't see fireplaces like that anymore, most new-builds these days don't even have—'

'Not the fireplace, the floor. The mark.'

George looked down at the floor. The fireplace had a brick hearth that finished against a wooden floor. They looked to George like original floorboards, polished and worn by centuries of use. 'What mark, Stan?'

'In front of the fire. Me and Janice. We met at a barn dance, George. Back then, it really was a dance in a barn. Her dad's barn. The one right outside our back door. We didn't really have the opportunities to go out on the town that young people have now. That was how you met the women when you were a farmhand. I danced with Janice that night. It was the first thing we did. She could see I was shy, I was sat on a hay bale with my brother and I was watching her but I couldn't move towards her. I just couldn't think of anything to say. And you know, it was like my legs wouldn't work. She was so beautiful, everything about her. Then she walked over to me and she took my hand and we walked out into the middle of the barn and we just started dancing. We didn't speak, not for a minute or more. And do you know what I realised, George, in that first minute before we had spoken to each other?'

'What's that, Stan?'

'I realised that this was the woman that I was going to be dancing with for the rest of my life. And suddenly I didn't feel shy at all, suddenly I felt like I was dancing with my oldest friend. And of course I was.'

George beamed. 'I love that story, Stan. Beautiful.'

'Janice thought it was too. And we kept it up. We've been married sixty-two years, George. Not a cross word. And every Sunday evening, no matter what, we would come in here and we would dance in front of that fire. Those marks on the floor are where we've damned near worn the boards through. I used to rush the Sunday jobs to get back. Janice talked about fixing it once. I couldn't think of anything worse. Sixty-two years, Inspector. Now those marks are all I have left.'

George looked closer. He knew what he was looking for now. The marks were clear — tiny scuff marks, but it was more than that, the boards were worn down, there was an almost circular dip in the floor, the wood slightly lighter. 'I can see it. I can see exactly where it is!'

Stan was looking over at it too. His head dropped again. 'Sixty-two years married. She was everything, George. What do I do now? What do I do now?'

George exhaled in a loud sigh. 'What can I say to that, Stan? Me and Paul here . . . we can't possibly understand what you are going through. We can't know how you're feeling. All I want to do, Stan, is to appeal to that angry, stubborn, tough old bastard that lives inside of you. I want

46

that man to shake this morning off for just an hour or so and to tell me exactly what happened. And I want to see you angry when you do it and sad by the end. I just want to know that you are still feeling *something,* Stan, because right now I've never seen a man more empty. Life will go on, you know — even after what's happened. I know you can't see that right now and I don't know how long it takes to get there, but life goes on. The little bit I do know about you mentions that you have children, right? Have you called them?'

'One daughter. Just one. My Louise. I haven't even thought about what I might say. She lives in Europe. She has her own life now, George.'

'We can help. Let me take the strain with that a bit. I'll take some details from you in a minute and, with your permission, I can make those calls. Or I can get someone round to speak to her in person — whatever you think is best.'

'I don't know. I just don't know.'

'Okay, Stan. We've made a start though. There are things that need to be done and we'll take you through them. We'll get your girl here and we'll start to piece together what we can. What you're feeling right now, it is going to get better. I know it's easy for me to say that, but trust me. And helping us . . . that's a big part of *how* it gets better. Do you think you can summon that tough old bastard for me? I just need him for an hour.'

Stan might have smiled. It was weak and his eyes lit for just a second. 'Yeah, I know he's in there somewhere.'

'You can't keep that man down, Stan. Let me go and get my paperwork, okay?'

George left the room; Paul had pushed out ahead of him. They stepped down onto the gravel drive. Allesandra was leaning into the side door of her van and back in full forensic garb. She pulled her mask away to speak to them.

'How's it going? With Mr Wingmore, I mean?'

'Okay. As well as can be expected at least. The poor fella's a bit of a shell in there. It's going to take a bit of time to build him back up before we can even start to find out what went on.'

'I spoke briefly with the uniform skipper,' Ali said. 'They have really scant details. He said that three blokes turned up in a van and demanded money. Stan in there tells them he doesn't have any. They get a bit more insistent and he loses his temper, gets his gun out of his cabinet and they get it off him. The rest is laid out for us in the kitchen.'

'Horrible, isn't it? I'm conscious I've left him in there on his own, Ali. I'm only getting some paperwork and then I'll be back in to make sure he doesn't move around the house.'

Ali smiled. 'You're alright. I'll keep my eye on him. I had a chat with him earlier. I reckon the last place in the world he wants to be right now is in that kitchen.' She pulled her mask back over her face. 'It's not high on my list either to be honest!' She stepped back towards the house.

'Paul, where are we with the FLO?' George asked.

'A couple of minutes and I'll have a name for certain. I've been waiting for the coordinator to call me back. It looks like Tim Betts is next in line. They're just checking he's able.'

'Okay, that would be good. Tim's one of the better ones.'

'Yeah, I agree. He would be perfect for this one too, he's good with people like our Stan.' Paul gestured at his vibrating phone. 'Ah, that'll be him.'

George opened the boot of the car, pulled out the black folder with his blank statement forms and walked back into the house. He stopped to wipe his feet on the mat — habit when entering someone else's home. He could hear some soft music and the sound of movement. It was coming from the living room where he had left

Stan. Silently he peered round the door. Stan was still in there. He was at the fireplace, gliding in a rough circle over his worn mark, his arms outstretched as though they were still wrapped around his wife of sixty-two years. His eyes were shut tightly, accentuating his wrinkles, as if he had aged a decade since George had left. But his lips were pursed tightly together in a kind of smile. It was growing, spreading over his face as the music quickened. His slippers scuffed against the floor as his strides got longer.

George slipped back into the hallway. He could see the big kitchen, through internal doors with glass inserts. He could see Ali in her full, white forensic suit. She was dusting surfaces, trying to piece together who had come here in the middle of the night for the sake of their savings and then gone, taking everything but fading memories.

George stepped back out onto the gravel. Paul was just coming in.

'Is he not doing the statement?'

'He will,' George said. 'Let's just give him a minute.'

Chapter 7

Jenny stood at the window where she had been for most of the night. She had kept the light off in her hotel room and peeked around the thick curtain, or pulled it back and stood behind the net curtains when the night had been at its blackest and she had been at her most confident. Now, the sun was back up and she was hidden again, just one eye checking for movement on the street below. There was a lot more of it now, mostly cars queuing in two solid rows for the port of Dover that was just off to her left. There was some movement from people out on foot, but their heads were bent into the driving rain, their hoods pulled up and their chins dug into scarves or collars. No one seemed to be taking any notice of the hotel. *Hotel* didn't really describe it. It was a drab B&B. The night before it had displayed *No Vacancies* in a stern black font in the window. But Jenny had run as far as she could away from the town. She was by the sea and more and more desperate. She didn't know where else to go. Yesterday afternoon the weather had been better. A group of tanned foreign-looking people had been out on the forecourt when she'd approached, gathered around an old black car with the bonnet up. They'd all stopped to look at her as she walked to the door. More than once she nearly turned and ran away again. But it was practically the last building before the port. She was out of options.

An elderly woman eventually came out of the ground floor flat. She'd looked Jenny up and down and then said in the slowest English she could muster that they were full. Her body language relaxed a little when Jenny spoke back in English. She told her she was in trouble, that she just needed somewhere to stay. The old woman admitted that she did have a spare room, but said she wasn't allowed to put guests in it anymore. It was a converted loft and new fire regs meant that it was no longer deemed safe enough. She could lose her licence. Jenny practically begged her. The woman folded, she said she could put her in there for cash, but if anyone asked, she was staying there as a non-paying guest. This had suited Jenny more than she would admit. The woman hadn't even taken her name.

It was the very top floor. She could see that it had once been a fully functioning suite, but it smelled as if it had been closed up for a while. The woman had warned her that it was used for storage. There were stacks of old towels and linen, and piles of plates and cutlery. The stuff had been in the middle of the room when Jenny went in and she'd spent the first twenty minutes pushing it all over to the side. The bathroom was the worst for the closed-up smell; it didn't have a window. The bath was covered in a layer of dust. The bath water popped and burped when she'd first turned it on, but eventually it did run and it got warm. She crushed up a bar of soap that had hardened edges but was good enough to produce a thin lather. A bath was the first thing she'd thought of once she'd felt safe enough. The room felt like a million miles from civilisation. Surely no one could find her here.

Her paranoia came back, though. It snuck in with the shadows that replaced the daylight. The other residents were noisy too, most of the time it sounded like they were angry, like they were shouting at one another. At one point she considered the fact that she might have to leave to get something to eat. The thought of going outside was terrifying, but her hunger pains were getting stronger. Among the piles of linen and cutlery, she found a wicker basket full of individually packed biscuits, the sort you would find resting against your coffee. She devoured eight or nine. She would offer payment for them when she saw the proprietor in the morning.

Much of her evening was spent cleaning and dressing her arm. She'd soaked it in the bath and picked out the tiny little bits of black metal that had penetrated the skin. It was slow going and painful. She'd had to keep stopping, she couldn't see to work through her tears. When the pain got so bad, she would curse Joseph, a man she hadn't known much more than eighteen months and who had always had an air of mystery about him. That was a big part of what she had found so damned irresistible. But she cursed him still, for whatever he had done to bring this on her and for staying in that car while she had run away with their daughter.

And what of Isobel? The room had an old portable-sized tube television with a stiff piece of wire looping from the top for an aerial. She had manipulated it to get BBC 1, the national news. The shooting in Dover was the headline piece. The report had confirmed two men dead but said they believed there to be more. They hadn't named anyone yet. Jenny accepted that Joseph was one of them. She was surprisingly numb about that. There had been no mention of Isobel in the early reports. The ten o'clock headlines, however, were shown live and displayed a sombre row of police officers. The one in the middle introduced himself as a chief inspector. He was appealing for the mother of a young baby left at the scene to get in touch.

We want you to know that your baby is safe and well and being looked after by appropriately trained officers and staff. There is round-the-clock protection. I can't imagine the stress you were under, the pressure, when you decided to leave your child in the care of our officers and to flee the scene, but we know you did that for your child. Now we want you to get in touch. Just to tell us that you are safe. And from there we can work with you to make sure you stay safe. Please, there is a number on your screen . . . Please, just give us a call or come into any police station and make yourself known. I will personally guarantee your safety. Just a phone call.'

It took Jenny a little while to recover from knowing that Isobel was safe. The relief ebbed out of her and with it all of her energy. She had fallen to her knees in front of the television and sobbed Isobel's name. She managed to note down the number on a napkin taken from a pile. It was only three numbers in truth: 1-0-1. When she was calmer, she considered the inspector's offer — just a phone call. That could wait for the morning. The last time she had thought the police were there to help her hadn't worked out so well. And she was so exhausted. But she could not sleep a wink.

The morning light and the driving rain seemed to come together and she was awake to see them both. She had no idea how long she had stood at the window; she wasn't wearing a watch, and though the time was shown on the rolling news channel it was too small to make out from where she stood. The television was on very low as she still didn't want to draw any attention to her room. Then, suddenly there was a knock at the door. She froze and let the curtain fall back shut. She moved over to the television and flicked it off. The room was suddenly as dark as it had been. She moved to the door and stumbled on some boxes.

'You in there, love?'

Muffled as it was through the door, Jenny still recognised the voice as belonging to the proprietor, the elderly lady who had given her the room. Jenny rested her right hand on the handle. 'Yeah, I'm in here.'

'I do breakfast, love. At least I used to. You can come down to my flat and have some if you want. There's no one about.'

Jenny still held the door handle. Her hunger pains were far worse than last night and she couldn't face another biscuit meal.

'It's included, see. You pay for the room, you get your breakfast. I was going to do some bacon for me anyway.'

Jenny pulled the door open, just enough to be able to see out. The woman's features were softer than Jenny remembered. She smiled, her hair was long and dyed dark, the roots were grey. She had pulled it back into a tight bun. She wore a fleece top over leggings and rubber Croc shoes with socks. Jenny smiled back. 'Sounds lovely, thank you.'

Jenny had to walk from top to bottom, past every door of every room to get to the woman's flat and she heard nothing, not a peep.

'Is everyone out?' she asked.

'Yeah, the place always empties early in the morning. It's one of the best things about this business. They all get picked up early to go to work.'

'They live here?'

'Yeah, for now at least. Most of 'em are asylum seekers, a mixed bag, all at different stages of trying to stay here. Some have already been rejected, some are going through appeals, some arrived on the back of a lorry last week.'

'Some have been rejected? How come they're still here?'

'They won't be for long. And I don't mean they will be sent home. As it gets nearer to immigration turning up on the door to deport them, they will disappear. Most go to the big cities, easy to get lost up there.'

'And they work all day?'

'Not legally. You can't work if you're waiting for a decision on your asylum status. That's why they stick them in places like this. They have to give them somewhere to live, but the system's a bit of a joke. They all work cash in hand somewhere, the takeaways, carwashes, deliveries — anywhere that will take the risk on a bit of cheap labour. There doesn't seem to be a shortage of that either. I think the authorities are well aware, but they don't cause any problems and it helps keep the wheel spinning on the economy. I don't ask any questions and I certainly don't tell no tales. This setup works nicely for me too.'

Jenny followed her into her flat. It had a corridor that ran the length of its left side and a neat little living room was the first room off to the right. They passed beyond it and moved through to the kitchen at the back. Again it was tidy. The cooker and the fridge were oversized, almost industrial, but it was the only sign of it being the hub of a B&B.

'So I suppose you don't need to make them all breakfast in the mornings. How many evening meals do you have to do?'

'Oh, I don't cook for them, love. I mean I get paid to and it's part of the contract but I don't. I tried to at the start, but they want halal meat and they can't eat for Ramadan or whatnot. I'm much more of a Sunday roast, and fish and chip suppers kinda girl. I tell them that and they soon find other arrangements. They eat a lot of takeaways, the ones who work in the chicken shops or the kebab houses. They tend to bring home enough for everyone. I still take the extra cash from the government for feeding them, why wouldn't I? The way I look at it, I offered and they refused.'

'Well, I won't.'

'You what, love?'

'Refuse. I won't refuse bacon. And don't worry about it not being halal. I haven't eaten for a couple of days.'

The woman chuckled. 'Fine then. I've missed it if I'm honest. I used to like the banter, cooking for people in the morning, setting them up for their day.'

'You'll certainly be doing that.'

'Well, then, now you know my secrets, I take government cash and spend it on my own bacon and exotic holidays rather than feeding my tenants, so now it's your turn — your secrets.' She was still smiling. She poured out two cups of strong-looking tea from a pot that had been hidden under a tea cosy.

'My secrets?'

'A girl turns up at a place like this with a bloody arm, begging for a place to stay and she hasn't eaten for a couple of days. That sounds like a girl with secrets to me.' She pushed one of the teas at Jenny. A bowl of sugar lumps followed. Jenny took the tea in both hands and slurped at it immediately.

'I don't even know your name,' Jenny said, grinning nervously.

'Anne,' the woman said, 'and I've seen something like your arm before. My husband got himself in an argument with a farmer. This fella had a shotgun for chasing away the vermin on his farm, only he'd sawed the end off so he wouldn't miss. Close up it'll rip you apart, but a bit further away and you get a nasty rash like on your arm.'

'A shotgun, eh? Would you believe me if I said I didn't know what it was.'

'I would. Hurts like hell too, I would say.'

'It's better now. The bath helped.'

'The girl on the news, the one they're saying ran away from all the chaos down in the town. They reckon she was attacked by a man with a shotgun. A lot of people got a look at him. Not many got a look at the girl, though.'

Jenny sipped at her tea. She was looking away, knowing that if she made eye contact she would give herself away. 'Really?'

'That's what they said. I guess when there's a man running around with a gun, he gets all the attention. The only description of the girl is that she's got dark hair, quite long, and she was wearing a white top and blue jeans. And she left her baby at the scene. They say she did that to keep the little dot safe. They don't think that little girl is more than six months old.'

Jenny did now look Anne in the eye. Anne hadn't made any start on breakfast yet. Jenny knew she was being studied for a reaction, but Anne's expression was soft and sympathetic.

'You learn a lot, running a place like this. Just that all the guests have their own back stories, their own reasons for hiding in the attic. All I'm saying is that if that girl came here, if she needed help, then she would get it without any questions asked.'

Jenny finished her tea. The second she put it back down on the side Anne filled it up again with a tip of the pot. Jenny added the milk. 'I'm sure that would be appreciated. Sounds like she would have had a hell of a day.'

Anne's face broke into a full smile. She lit up some pans and pulled the fridge open. Soon the air was filled with the delicious smell of sizzling bacon.

'So your husband . . .' Jenny said, '. . . you said he got shot at. I take it he got himself a rash and nothing more?' She was peering around for signs of co-habitation.

Anne cracked some eggs. 'A nasty one. All down his right side. I was picking shots out of him for a good couple of hours. Healed up fine though. And after that he never again picked on a man with a shotgun under his arm.'

'Sounds sensible. Does he work here with you?'

Anne pursed her lips. 'I'm afraid not. He was a good man, he was good to me his whole life and then he was good enough to die first! The insurance bought this place outright. I don't know whether that makes me lucky or not.'

Jenny broke into a smile for the first time since the previous morning. She covered it over swiftly, realising that perhaps it wasn't appropriate.

'Don't worry,' Anne said. 'It was a long time ago. I've had plenty of time to get used to it. He was good man. One thing we always had was the jokes. I know I can say things like that, I know he'll be up there now laughing hard. Now, love, please find yourself a seat at the table, it won't be long now.'

Anne turned back to her stove. Jenny moved a short distance to the table, the chair caught on the wooden floor and squeaked. Anne had turned the radio on; it must have been on the hour because the news headlines kicked in. The shooting dominated the report, then they went live to a press conference. Jenny looked over to Anne, she was still facing away but she had half-turned back to Jenny, no doubt waiting to see if there was any reaction. Jenny didn't give her any, she just swigged at her tea, but she was listening. It was the same voice as last time: the chief inspector, though she couldn't remember his name. He said that they were still looking for the female who had fled the scene. He confirmed that at least two men had died as part of the incident, and then he made another appeal to the missing woman. Only this time it was different:

Jenny, we can't imagine the stress you are under right now but I want you to know that you will be safe with us. Please make contact with us, even if you just let us know that you are safe. We want you to know that your daughter is safe, we want you to know that she slept well last night, despite all of the excitement. She's been checked over by medical staff, Jenny. She's perfectly fine. Call us, Jenny. You can call 101 or 999 — it doesn't matter. We will come straight out to you. Thank you and I'm sorry but I can't take any questions as this time.'

The reporter cut back in. He talked immediately about the fact that the female had now been named, or at least her first name revealed. He then appealed for witnesses and quoted a number to call. Jenny's head had fallen forward into her hands. She snapped upright as a plate was placed in front of her.

'I'll drive you down there, Jenny,' Anne said. 'Whatever you're running from, it doesn't matter anymore. The police have your baby and she's safe. Just go and see her. But we'll eat our breakfast first, okay? I can't be having a bad review on TripAdvisor now, can I?'

Jenny wiped at her face, she jerked a nod and took an intake of breath. She managed a smile too. She didn't want to be running anymore. Whatever Joseph was into, it was nothing to do with her. They would see that. There was nothing for her to worry about.

Hungrily, she bit into her sandwich.

Chapter 8

John Whittaker moved into the foyer at the Force Headquarters and pushed his way through the second wave of reporters, those who hadn't made it into the main briefing room. He had been involved in some high profile jobs in his past, but he had always been a bit part, able to sit back and watch the more senior members of staff provide the lip service, while he actually got some work done. There was very little getting done right now — by him at least. Even as he was led out of the front of the building and ushered into a car that had pulled up directly outside he could see his phone was going off. Another *unknown number* call. He knew what that meant. Some chancer from the associated press had gotten hold of his number and was trying to penetrate the interior of his getaway car with one last question. He pressed to reject the call and threw the phone onto the front seat. Detective Sergeant Melanie Richards was in the back seat next to him.

'I do hope this is the right play.' Whittaker voiced his doubts. It was rhetorical, really. There was no answer to it.

'Why wouldn't it be?' Melanie asked. Another sergeant, Jason Carter was driving. Whittaker saw him flick his eyes to the rear-view mirror. The car was moving towards the exit gate. Jason was under strict instructions to get him back to Langthorne House as soon as possible after the press conference.

'I don't know. Maybe I shouldn't be using a six-month-old child as a way of stoking up a response from dangerous criminals, no matter what the circumstances.'

'I thought we were just after a response from the mother?'

'For all we know she *is* the dangerous criminal. Naming her made sense to me at the time, but the second I said it . . . I don't know . . . it just didn't feel right. I was a mean poker player in the forces, Mel, because I never revealed the cards I had.'

'I'm not sure there's a right answer in this situation, sir. This could end up being exactly the right play. Now we just need to wait and see.'

'I've never been a fan of *wait and see*. I can live with not finding the right answer — I just can't live with getting it wrong. Wrong in this case means another body on my patch. And an orphan not nearly old enough to know what that means.'

'This woman's been pretty good at keeping herself out of harm's way so far. Anyway, sir, we're pretty certain that whoever attacked that car knew the occupants, right? I'm sure we're not telling them anything they don't already know, which means we're not putting her in any more danger.'

'Let's just hope she is still out of harm's way. Has Inspector Elms been in touch yet?' Jason had been tasked with getting an update from their second murder scene of the day.

'No, sir. I tried him maybe ten times. His phone went straight to voicemail every time. I left a message on the last go asking him to call as soon as he gets it.'

'Voicemail, you say? George Elms can be trusted. There'll be a damned good reason for him not getting back to us. Get me back to the ranch and I'll try him myself. Anywhere in fact that isn't this wretched place.' Whittaker sat back in the leather of the big BMW saloon that was his allocated car for the operation. He was happy to see the exit gates sliding open and for the car to drift through and pick up speed. There were two things that he hated more than anything else — the associated press and Lennockshire Police's senior management team. And right now they were all gathered at the same place.

* * *

George Elms fiddled with his facemask, despite knowing that you weren't supposed to handle it once it was in place. It was so damned uncomfortable. The science around DNA was moving far faster than the competence of a thirty-something police detective and George was tired of hearing about it. It was just a few weeks since he had attended a conference on this very subject, where he had been cheerfully informed that advances in DNA detection were very quickly approaching the point where DNA would no longer be a viable form of evidence. Any defence solicitor worth his salt would soon be able to argue that the discovery of DNA at a scene could be the result of transference, had any persons who had attended that scene *ever* been in the same room as the accused. And not necessarily at the same time. *Try and prove they haven't*, the speaker had said, a smug look spreading over his face while he enjoyed the stunned silence of his audience. The news very quickly got worse and most of George's attention was lost while he had carried on with tales of DNA *blowing in the wind*. George and his colleagues would soon be back to the methods used before DNA and forensics — *pissing in the wind* as George referred to it. It had prompted laughter in the bar after. George wasn't laughing now.

The Wingmores' kitchen was very much in keeping with what George had seen so far. No country farmhouse was complete without the country kitchen. It had a grey, flagstone floor with a huge Aga range cooker that radiated heat and set the atmosphere just right. The room was all chunky wood, earthy colours and ornate ducks — all very tasteful — only now with a splatter of red. Janice Wingmore was on her back. Her legs lay over a stone doorstep leading into the boot room that Sergeant Banks had described. The victim was in a navy blue robe that was obviously too large for her. She had long socks on, pulled up almost to her knees. The robe was lying open to display square knickers and a light pink vest-top. Her hair was messy and spread out on the floor, as were her intestines. The gunshot wound was a mess of black and different tones of red. Ali had assured him before he had gone in that the shot had gone right through. The hole was the size of a side plate and the size was how the CSI officer had been able to tell him that it was not a self-inflicted wound. Nothing made sense about that anyway, she looked every bit the woman who had been shot in the midriff when repelling someone from entering her home. And now George had a little more of an understanding as to why it was her lying there and not Stan.

Stanley had given a good account. It had taken nearly two hours, but George was skilled at getting to the finer details and Stan was sharp — too sharp almost. He could remember times, places and descriptions, but he also remembered sounds, smells and cries of pain. George didn't know the way back for Stan, not from this. When the life had left the frail body of the woman lying on the floor in front of him it had left Stan as well. While taking his statement, George was always aware that he was talking to a shell of a man.

Stan told how, at 4 a.m., the couple had been roused by strong lights — possibly headlamps — then a banging on the door and calls for help. He specifically remembered checking the time. He had leant out of an upstairs window to ask what the hell was going on. His wife Janice put the lights on at first but Stan had scolded her — he couldn't see with them on. When she turned the lights off she couldn't find her robe and so must have grabbed Stan's from where it was hanging on the back of their bedroom door.

Downstairs, Stan could see just one man. He was agitated. He said that his daughter had gone out with a boy from the village the previous night for a drive. He hadn't heard from them since. He said that one of the boy's friends had told him that they would sometimes park up on a track that he thought was on the land of this farm, only he didn't know where they might mean. Stan felt bad. He wanted to help and promised he would. When he ducked back in to close the window, Janice was holding her phone; she said she was calling the police. Stan told her not to, that the man had already done that, that they were already out looking for the girl.

Stan walked to the back door. He turned the lights on in the kitchen, his guard was down and he wasn't concerned about being able to see out. Had he been able to, he would have noticed that one man had become four men. They were all dressed in dark clothing. The three he didn't see until they were pushing their way through his back door were wearing balaclavas and holding blunt weapons. They demanded money instantly. He was pushed back into the kitchen and someone ran past Stan and grabbed hold of Janice, who had followed him down the stairs. He threatened her with what Stan thought might have been a cosh, something short and solid looking. There was a scuffle. Stan remembered someone gripping his arm so tight that it was really painful. He showed George a bruise. They kept screaming at him for the money, he told them he didn't have any money. He fell to his knees, the pain from his arm was excruciating. He heard Janice scream and he said okay, he would get the money. He said it was in a locked cabinet under the stairs. It was a stupid move, Stan reflected. It wasn't money in the cabinet; it was his shotguns. He had three. He thought he could get hold of one, he didn't think they would follow him so close behind. He never stood a chance, the guns weren't loaded — not until the men took the shotguns and tipped out the boxes of ammunition. They led both Stan and Janice back into the kitchen. Stan argued some more — he was so angry that people would come to his home and threaten his wife. A gun went off. Suddenly they just left. Stan ran out after them, but they were fast. The headlights were bright again, he remembered they drove at him and he had to run back to the kitchen. He watched them leave. He could hear his heart thumping in his ears, he could smell the shot, it hung in the air but it was mingled with something else, something metallic. It was blood. Janice was on the floor. He didn't move her. He fumbled with his phone to call an ambulance. He still had a vision in his mind of how he'd bent down to pick up his wife. He cradled her head, lifting her towards him and he spoke to her. He asked if she was all right, if she could hear him. She didn't speak. She would never speak again. That last image was all he could think about. He couldn't shake it.

George took his time getting the account. But he rushed over the end. He had the detail he needed; he didn't want to interrupt in case there was something significant, but there was no need to labour the painful bits. George was well aware that he'd have to sit Stan down to go through it all again on video. For now, at least, he had been tortured enough.

When Stan was finished, George left him in the living room. Paul was still with him. George felt bad about that. He could only imagine the atmosphere in there.

Now he walked back past the lounge. Ali led him out through the front door and into the fresh air. To see the scene from outside meant walking the long way round.

The back door was completely off-limits. Ali pulled her mask away. George did the same. They walked up the side of the house, stopping just a few metres away from where they had started. Ali's attention was fixed on the rutted ground.

'So those are the tracks I mentioned. I got a good lift from those. They will go off for analysis, but I can tell you from experience that they are from something four-by-foury. The tyres in general are wider than a normal car and the treads are too far apart. They're from a 4x4, but something with proper off-road tyres on.'

George was careful to step where Ali had. He could see clear tracks, a tread mark with tyre knuckles pressed into the mud. He could also see where the tracks slipped, as if a car had skidded close to the kitchen door. It fitted exactly with Stan's account.

'So not your Chelsea Tractor type.'

'Exactly. Maybe even a farm vehicle, like a proper Landy. That sort of thing.'

George nodded. Land Rovers were the vehicle of choice for a lot of farmers. 'And the analysis, will that be more exact?' he said.

'Well . . . yes and no. It will usually give you the make of the tyre, sometimes we can do wear analysis too. Of the tyre, that is. That can be useful if you have something to compare it to. It's like a footprint for tyres — each one has a unique wear pattern.'

'But we need something to compare it to.'

'Exactly. And the sooner the better. As for our victim, the wound and the positioning of Mrs Wingmore is consistent with a single gunshot wound to the stomach. The size of the wound puts the weapon at around five metres away from the victim — possibly a little closer. Judging by the splatter and her position, it would put our shooter outside of the house when the trigger was pulled. We'll be able to do a little bit more on the slab with the wound. With gunshots we can often tell about angles and trajectory, but shotgun wounds are harder. Her wound is basically a clump of mess. A more clinical weapon would have a far more obvious entry and exit route. I've measured the wound front and back, and it's level enough for me to suggest that the attacker fired from the hip. But that's not going to appear written up formally in any report. And it won't appear in any court papers. They may have just aimed blindly at the doorway, but that's for the investigation to decide.'

'The levels?'

'Yeah, put very simple, if the wound is higher at the front than the back the round would have been fired downwards. That's consistent with a rifle held into the shoulder and aimed — looking down a sight. If it's lower at the front than the back then it's fired from the floor and if it's level — as in this case — then it's likely to have been from the hip.'

'Sounds logical.'

'It is. Whether that's helpful or not is another question. I've seen it become significant in self-defence cases. One offender I remember claiming he fired blindly from the floor because he was getting a kicking. I showed very easily that that was utterly impossible. I could show he had aimed with a high velocity rifle butted up against his shoulder. It was fifty-fifty to that point — but he got twenty-five years.'

'That sort of result would do me here,' George said. 'This scene may not be in our favour though. To prove murder, we'd have to prove intent. I'd rather you said our killer was aiming.'

'Shooting at a doorway where you know people are stood . . . that's not enough these days.' And a shotgun spreads out. It covers a big area. From this range you can't miss and any centre-mass wounds will always be fatal.'

'It's enough for me, Ali. A jury is an unpredictable animal, though. You get our shooter in his best suit saying he was chased and he panicked and fired a warning shot from the hip? I've seen it work.'

'UK justice at its finest.'

'We need to prove what we know is all — and beyond reasonable doubt. Anything else you can tell me?'

'The scene will take a couple of days, George. It's just me for now and I don't see me getting any help soon. It'll take hours just to pick up all the shot and wadding. I will give you the full report as soon as I can. Janice may give us some more when she is laid out in the morgue, but I'm not sure what else she knows. I think she was stood at her kitchen door when a shotgun round was fired into the home, through her. If that's consistent with what our friend in the living room has said then I can say I know *how* she died. His account also gives us the *why* and the *when*.'

'So we're just missing out on the *who*.'

'Indeed. The best bit. I'll do what I can with that. The log said there were four offenders and we know they entered the home. There aren't any foot impressions that I can see — I've had the UV out, and there were no obvious prints. But I'll do a proper dust and sweep again. I'll get a search team through for a fingertip search too. If a hair, a flake of skin or so much as a bogey has fallen off one of them I want it found. We need to get lucky. But, then, don't we always need a bit of luck?'

'We do. And if karma's a thing then lady luck will be with us on this one. These were decent people woken up from their beds.'

'Seems that way, George. You need anything more from me?'

'Don't think so. I have every faith. I'm genuinely surprised you're bothering with the search team — like you would miss anything!'

'I know, right! It's protocol. I had this tutor at uni — a forensic scientist and a right perv, he was. I always turned the UV on his crotch by *accident* — that sort, you know? Anyway he always advocated as many initial searches as possible when everyone else was saying to be aware of keeping your scene as sterile as possible. He had this saying: *every torch casts a different shadow.* I thought *yeah, whatever,* but he's right you know. I'll never forget that.'

'He definitely stole that from somewhere!'

'You're probably right. I still like it though. We all see the world ever so slightly differently, George. That includes a crime scene.'

'This just got a little deep for me. I'd better let you get back to casting your shadows.'

'I'll call you with anything really important.'

'I know you will. In the meantime, I will lean on the boss and see if I can't get you some help up here. This is a big job on your own.'

Ali smiled. Her mouth was covered again by a new mask ripped from its packaging, but George could see the twinkle in her brown eyes. 'Keeps me busy up here, George. Sometimes it's nice to just be left alone, you know.'

George suddenly felt his phone buzzing but knew there was no way he would reach it in time through a layer of clothing and a forensic suit. 'I certainly do,' he said. He walked round to the front of the house where Paul stepped out to meet him.

'Sorry about that, Paul. I didn't want to leave you alone with Stan but until Tim gets here one of us will need to stay with him.'

'I spoke to Tim on the phone. He can't do it, George. He's got leave booked and he's going away in a few days. He said he could do the next couple of days but I told him not to worry. I didn't think you would want him to come in only to be swapped out.'

'Shit!' George said. Paul was right, the whole idea of having a FLO was to build a relationship with the witness, to get right under his skin, to become trusted. That needed someone who could be there for as long as it took — no interruptions. 'You're right, Paul. We need someone who can be in right from the start and keep it up. Someone Stan will trust.'

Paul bit down on his bottom lip. 'I don't really know who's on the list anymore. It's a shame, George — Tim would have been perfect.'

'He would. I need someone just like him, someone who is good at listening, who comes across as supportive and trustworthy, but who also understands investigations. Now . . . where could I find someone like that?' George lingered on Paul.

It took Paul a couple of seconds to cotton on. 'Oh no! No way, George!'

'Mate, I can't think of anyone better. I don't know why I didn't think of it before. I honestly wouldn't have even bothered Tim — you're perfect!'

'No, George. I can't do it. You have to do the course and get signed off — it's a big job, you can't just play at it.'

'You'll do it right, Paul, I know you will! And don't you worry about courses and all the rest. You have every attribute in spades. And, right now, Whittaker would be more than happy for us to take the initiative. I reckon he's about to have a shortage, don't you?'

'George, come on! I don't know what I'm doing. Really.'

'None of us do! Look after Stan. Be here with him at some point every day, help him get over this shit state of affairs and find out anything you can from him that might help. You've worked with enough FLOs. You know what they can do.'

'Yeah, but Stan! George, he's been smashed to pieces. He's like Humpty Dumpty in there.'

'And you are all the king's men, Paul. I can think of no one better.'

George could feel his phone start vibrating again. 'I got to get this,' he said.

Paul called after him: 'You realise that all the king's men couldn't put him back together again, right?'

George moved the phone away from his mouth. 'Then be better, Paul. I believe in you!'

Chapter 9

Jenny still wore the same white top, the sleeves pulled up over her wound, the material frayed, singed and stained with dry blood. Her jeans were scuffed at the knees from climbing the wall and she was caught by a stab of pain in her ribs as she turned to where Anne called out to her in the kitchen. Jenny had gone to her room to tie her hair back and freshen up with some borrowed toiletries.

'Are you in pain?'

'I bumped my side. I think it's just bruised is all.'

'You really are in the wars, love, aren't you? You make sure they take you to get checked out at the hospital.'

'I will do. It could be worse.' Jenny hesitated. She thought about Joseph again, about what had happened to him, about how he hadn't stood a chance. He'd been a sitting duck. He'd had been a good man too; they'd had their problems, but he was not the type to run away when she fell pregnant and she didn't run when he moved them across the country using hotels that accepted cash only. If she was honest with herself, she had known that he was involved with *something* from the start, but she had convinced herself it wouldn't affect her. Now she wished she had asked more questions. Then at least she might have more of an idea of just how deep it ran, how much danger she was really in.

'Are you sure this is the right thing to do?' Jenny said.

'What else can you do, love? You got to put your faith in the police. There's no one else who can help you. You can't stay hidden in the loft forever, can you? Just think, you could be holding your little girl within the hour.'

'I just can't face stepping out there. Maybe they could come here?'

Anne shook her head. 'Some of the other residents are starting to get back. I can't have police attention here and I reckon there will be a lot of it when they work out who you are. I've had it before. There was just a door knock about a car accident out the front — some two-minute conversation with a bloke in uniform. Before I knew it I had three empty rooms. The government gives me a decent grant for every one of them. That grant scarpers when they do.'

'Okay.' Jenny was aware she didn't sound sure. She wasn't sure; there was nothing she could do to hide it.

'Don't worry. Look, I'll drop you right at the door. I'll come in with you. There won't be a problem. Who would do anything to you walking into a police station?'

'These people, Anne . . . broad daylight . . . people around — it didn't seem to matter to them. I know what will happen, we'll go in and they'll sit me down to wait out front. Anyone could be coming in and out. It takes a second, Anne. I've seen that.'

'I'll tell you what . . .' Anne clicked her fingers. 'We'll call ahead. Tell them we're on our way down and that we want someone waiting or we're not coming at all. It was 1-0-1, right? The number?'

'1-0-1, yeah. Okay, that sounds good.' Jenny sucked in a lungful of air. She knew this had to happen. Anne was right: she couldn't hide in the loft forever and she had to see Isobel. She just didn't want to feel scared any more. Surely at the police station she wouldn't have to.

Anne gestured at some folded clothes that were stacked on the table. 'I had a family here, they upped and left a while ago, they left a lot of their belongings. It happens a lot. The wife was about your size. I fished out some bits. They look clean to me. I figured you could do with a change.' Anne was looking her up and down. Jenny could hardly disagree. 'You know . . . before we go outside. I know you don't want to be drawing attention to yourself right now do you, love?'

'I guess you're right.' The new clothes were a slim-fitting pair of black jeans, a long-sleeved red top and a zip-up black gilet with front pockets and a grey hood. What she *really* wanted was a change of underwear — some of her *own* underwear. That would have to wait. 'Thanks, Anne . . . you know . . . for everything.'

Anne nodded. She had her phone to her ear already. Jenny took the hint and moved to the back of the kitchen to get changed. Jenny could still hear Anne on the phone.

'Hello, I'm ringing to let you know that I am bringing the girl down to the police station — the girl who ran away from the shooting yesterday.'

Jenny bit down on her lip; said out loud, the description made it sound like someone else.

'In Dover.' Anne rolled her eyes at Jenny. 'No, I won't be giving any details about me — no, you don't need to know who I am. I will be dropping her down in ten minutes but we will only come in if there is someone there to meet us. This girl has had quite a time of it, she needs to be safe.' Anne frowned into the phone, she made a gesture that suggested someone was typing. 'No, you don't need my address. We are coming to you. Look, we are on our way. Have someone meet us, okay?' Anne pressed to end the call. She spoke to Jenny, 'Honestly, they want to know the ins and outs of a duck's arse! Why can't they just listen and do their job?'

Anne was still holding the phone. It rang almost immediately. She scowled at it then lifted it to her ear.

'Hello . . . Oh, Jesus! What is the matter with you people? You need what? How does that keep us safe? Fine, look, I will be in a blue Fiat, I will pull up outside and I would like a police officer to come out and meet us. If you can't assure me of that then I won't be coming down. Yes, yes, I understand that. I agree we need to get her safe, that's why I am doing what I can.' Anne sighed, and shook her head.

Jenny felt nervous all of a sudden, she tried not to think too far ahead. She just needed to get into a car, the station was just a few minutes away and the police would be waiting to meet her. They had her daughter; they would be reunited. And they would be safe.

'I'm not telling you that,' Anne snapped down the phone. 'I said that already. We are ten minutes away and we will be coming from the sea side of the town. That's all you need to know, thank you for your help. Goodbye!'

Anne was off the phone. 'Well, the police have finally agreed to our terms!' Anne chuckled playfully. 'Let's get you safe, love.'

Jenny's new clothes were a good enough fit. The jeans were a little tight and they rubbed against her grazed knee, but she was barely aware of the discomfort. Other residents were coming in as they left through the communal front door. Jenny kept her head bent. The same car that had had its bonnet up the previous day still seemed to be the centre of two men's attention despite the persistent rain. They leaned over the engine with hoods pulled over their heads. Everyone seemed to be oblivious to the woman skulking in the passenger seat of the old, blue Fiat. The car started at the second attempt, it coughed a little and Anne wiped at the condensation on the windscreen with her sleeve.

'She's an old bird — needs a few minutes to warm up. Just like her mother.' Anne played with the heating controls. The fan was loud, and the noise filled the cabin. Jenny was glad of the layer of moisture and condensation, she felt concealed. Safer. The car bounced a little as it pulled away. The traffic was constant and slow moving. They had to turn left into a two-lane, one-way system and a roundabout was upon them immediately. Anne went all the way around it and, as they headed back towards the town of Dover, Jenny was on the side nearer to the sea. She peered out over the dull, grey waters that seemed to mirror the sky exactly. Just a few days earlier, on a far sunnier day, they had walked as a family along the promenade and been to all the seafront attractions. Both Jenny and Joseph loved the sea air and panoramic views. Isobel had slept soundly — she was such a content little girl. Jenny had thought at the time that they all seemed to be content for once, that maybe their life together would start settling down soon. Joseph had promised it often enough, he had even agreed to them looking for somewhere to rent more permanently in the area. Only a week had gone by since then, but it felt like a lifetime ago.

The traffic was still thick when they got to the next roundabout. Anne took a right and any view of the sea was gone.

'You okay, love?' Anne said. It roused Jenny from her thoughts.

'I'm okay. I just can't get my head around how everything has changed. I just don't know what I can do from here.'

'You get your baby girl back and you start all over again. The police will keep you safe. Once they do that, nothing else matters.'

'What about her dad? Does he not matter? She's not even a year old and she's lost her dad and I don't even know why. What if it turns out he's mixed up in something, what if he turns out to be a criminal or a bad man?'

'How was he to you? To your baby?'

'He was great. He was great with me and great with her. I felt really lucky, you know? We didn't plan Issy, I admit, and we definitely hadn't been together long enough for it to be the right thing to do, but he was insistent that we would make it work. It was never a consideration, you know, to not go through with it.'

'I know what you mean. You are lucky, too. Most men in that situation . . . well, you wouldn't see them for dust. Sounded like a keeper.'

'I just don't know now. I just don't know what happens next.'

'One step at a time, love. First, we get you to the police station and to your little girl. That's step one. Don't be worrying about anything beyond that right now.'

Anne tutted. She was looking down to her right, at the mirror. The Fiat had been drifting across to the right-hand lane as they approached another roundabout, but Anne suddenly jerked it back into the left.

'Some people are in such a hurry,' she said. A long, silver car flashed past them in the right lane. It had to brake hard for the roundabout and then it was gone, it moved round to the right and out of sight. Anne moved back over; there was one car in front. It pulled out so that Anne's Fiat was now on the cusp of the roundabout. Anne checked to her right. The silver car had gone all the way around and she had to wait for it. 'Bloody idiot doesn't even know where he's going.'

The silver car's headlights flashed. It had slowed to a crawl around the roundabout; now it stopped, holding up the traffic behind. It flashed again. Anne shook her head and pulled the Fiat out onto the roundabout. Jenny was still watching the silver car. Something about it wasn't right: why flash someone out at a roundabout? She didn't have time to scream, she saw the silver car hurtle forwards as if it had been kicked from behind. A split second later and the Fiat took the impact hard in the driver's side. Jenny felt herself thrown right, then hard left. She screamed, the car juddered sideways, she could hear loud engine revs from outside as the Fiat skidded and bucked sideways towards the crash barrier on the left side. Jenny was forcibly turned towards the barrier and it was getting relentlessly closer. She saw a flash of colour — a car trying to get up the inside and out of the way. It didn't make it. Jenny's side took the impact this time, the metal bent inwards, the noise was terrific. Anne cried out as Jenny's window imploded and shards of glass fell into her lap. The flash of colour was now gone. The silver car was out of sight, too. The Fiat stopped moving and rocked back onto its wheels. Jenny turned to Anne. She looked stunned and her face was ashen; she was bleeding freely from the back of her head. Then, beyond Anne, she saw it again: the silver car was backing away, its front bent in and crushed and its windscreen with a spider web pattern to it. There was the roar of an engine and the screech of tyres and then the silver car was speeding towards them again.

Anne turned to Jenny. She looked resigned. Strands of her hair were slick across her face and ran between her lips. 'Run love!' she gasped.

'ANNE!' Everything flashed white. Suddenly Jenny was staring at the sky, then the dark grey tarmac, then the sky again. She could do nothing but grimace as forces pulled and tugged at her body. Then she was aware of being upright again. Her head spun, her ears rang and everything had a pink tinge. Her door was rocking open — she couldn't be sure if she had pushed it open or not. She could see a raised curb and she felt for it with her left foot. She couldn't see Anne. What was left of the driver's side was now empty. She got out onto the curb and bumped into a sturdy metal railing. Her left hand reached out for it instinctively. People were approaching her on foot, though she couldn't make out any details. Everything seemed fuzzy and she could feel herself falling. But something kept her up. Then came a sound with which she was now familiar: a gunshot.

Still acting on instinct, Jenny ducked behind the shell of the car. Her ears were ringing loudly and when she heard the second shot it sounded distant — but she couldn't be sure and she knew the shots were meant for her. She knew she had to go. She heard voices — they might have been shouts but, regardless, she couldn't tell what they were saying. There was a gap straight ahead between the car bonnet and the railing. Her body flooded with adrenalin again, she sprang through it. As she moved clear of the wreckage, she heard another crack of gunfire.

The traffic had come to a standstill and there were a lot of cars around. As she darted between two of them, she heard a sound like falling glass from her right followed swiftly by a shout of anguish. She turned left and aimed for another two stationary cars. As she approached the gap between them, one of the doors was pushing open. Jenny screamed for them to get back in their car. She kept weaving between the gridlocked vehicles and could now see an alleyway ahead. Leading off one of the roundabout exits where she now found herself, it looked like it ran down the side of a church. At least she hoped it was an alleyway. Though her lungs felt like bursting, she made it. She hit the opening so fast she bounced off the church wall, and the sharp flints in the masonry bit into her shoulder. Jenny kept running and burst from the alleyway into a cobbled street. She turned right; it seemed a logical assumption that those chasing her would expect her to continue left, the direction she had been heading in. The cobbled street was busy with shoppers and she recognised it as the High Street. People stopped to gape at Jenny but she didn't care. They were just cover for her.

Chapter 10

George followed Whittaker's car through the gate to Langthorne House. The old man looked stressed as he stood up out of the back seat. He made straight for George.

'Major, how's your day?'

'The phrase *bad to worse* comes to mind, old boy. Are you plumbed into the grid?'

'I have my radio, but I've not been monitoring. Are there developments?'

'I'll say there are. The woman made contact — or at least we *think* it was her. There's been another incident out on the roads. More carnage. Our woman has gone back underground. And this time I don't think she'll be popping her head back out again.'

'What happened?'

'Oh, George, I have literally no idea right now. Someone is on their way here for a strategy meeting. Another damned strategy meeting. The press have made the link. I'm getting nothing but questions I can't answer. I think it's fair to say my dinner will be getting cold tonight, my friend.'

'Call ahead, sir. Forewarn the wife, soften the blow.'

'I sometimes wonder if you listen to a damned thing I say, George. I already told you my day is a stinker. The last thing I need to be doing is calling up the enemy with unacceptable news.'

'You'd rather save it all up for when you get home?'

'Who knows? Part of me is considering bringing up how I should approach the wife in this latest strategy meeting. Some of our finest tactical minds will be there, see? Someone must have an idea.'

The men chuckled. Then the chuckles subsided quickly.

'What's the story with this other job, George? No doubt I will be fielding questions on that one too.'

'It's a sad one, I'm afraid. Elderly couple robbed at home in the middle of the night. Just the old boy survived it. CSI are still there, but it's just one officer. She could do with some help to get the scene processed. Any chance you can spare her some help?'

Whittaker rubbed at his face. 'I know that what you have is far from ideal, but our situation down here just got worse. From what I hear we have yet another scene — someone else fighting for their life on the streets of Dover. I'm losing people to this job, George, if anything. I'm certainly not able to free anyone up.'

'Okay. I think she's quite happy to keep working away up there. They'll just have to stay on the scene longer. I suppose our victim isn't going anywhere. I want this one though, sir — the job, I mean. I'm going to have the bastards that did this.'

Whittaker registered a flicker of pleasure through his mask of stress. 'It's yours, George. I don't hear that enough from my officers. I could do with getting you up to speed on this other job, though. A fresh pair of eyes and a man of your experience might be able to start filling in the blanks. Or at least point out what the blanks are. Right now, that would be a start. Especially now you're sober!'

'I was always sober, sir. Now I'm just a little more sober.'

'On top form then, old boy.' Whittaker led the way back to his office. He tasked DS Richards with getting the update about this latest incident. She nodded and left them to it.

'Push the door shut, George.'

'Are you sure you don't want to be in there getting that update yourself, sir? I can stick around.'

'No. God, no. I mean . . . yes, I should, but I just wanted to push the door shut for a few minutes and organise my thoughts. I reckoned that telling you what I know might be a good way of doing that.'

'Okay. Sounds like you've had a lot going on. What's the deal?'

'Where to start? So we get a call — well, a number of calls — from members of the public reporting gunshots and car crashes on London Road, Dover shortly after 10 a.m. yesterday. Sunday of all days, the day of rest.'

'We both know criminals don't play by those rules, sir.'

'We do indeed. In fact, it seems to have become a popular day for major incidents. So, anyway, patrols are sent. There's a patrol already parked up at the Morrison's store not far from the reported incident and they hear the commotion for themselves. And then I'll be damned if they don't find a baby left on the bonnet of their car! There are more gunshots and much confusion. So we're all chasing our arses and one another's arses, then a crashed car is found on London Road with some poor bastard shot up and lying on the pavement, dead as nails in a door. Then, bugger me if we don't get more calls, more shots fired but this time in a built-up area nearby. I mean, it's walking distance, so naturally the calls are linked. Police attend where neighbours have reported the bangs and, sure enough, we find another fella with a hole where one shouldn't be.' Whittaker flicked open a blue-backed book he had been carrying. He ran his finger over the page. 'Stephen Maddocks. He's well known locally apparently.'

'Stephen Maddocks! Yeah, I know him. Everyone knows Stephen Maddocks, bless him. He's a bit simple. Got a real obsession with the police.'

'He did.'

'I see.'

'Well and truly did.'

'Jesus! How the hell did Maddocks get mixed up in this?'

'Well, you can imagine the amount of witness statements and the rest that are outstanding, we're still piecing it together. Basically it would appear our missing woman initially ran from the car on London Road.'

'Leaving a dead guy?'

'Yes, that's what we think we know. She's cut through to the car park and ditched the baby on the police car. Then she kept on running. We can only imagine she was the target for this gunman and she didn't want to be holding her baby if he caught up with her.'

'Baby?'

'Keep up, George! So she's carrying a baby girl when she runs. Six months old, tops.'

'Okay. This is getting worse.'

'I know, tell me about it. Poor girl. The baby seems fine. Now . . . the mother . . . we think she ran down the river path where she met with this Stephen Maddocks, who might have offered her his help. He's probably come out of his house to see what the fuss was about.'

'Probably heard the sirens. He's one of these people that always seem to turn up at incidents.'

'Every town has one. But, yes, he lives nearby. He was likely walking up the path and she's run right into him. He's happy to help and somehow the gunman follows her into his house.'

'He was shot at home?'

'Yes. It looks like he was shot through his own front door. There's also blood in the rear courtyard. The running theory being that this is how the woman escaped. We assume she has picked up an injury of sorts.'

'She really was having a bad day.'

'She was. And it has gotten considerably worse. We lost her from that point, but witnesses told us that the dead man, before he died, was shouting out to her and he was calling her Jenny. That's all we know about her at this point. So I did an appeal on the telly box and I called her Jenny — as if we knew a lot more than we do.'

'Makes sense.'

'You wouldn't think so. I've come in for a little flack for that from our more senior colleagues. I wanted it to be a personal appeal. I wanted her to think we know what the hell we are doing, you know?'

'And she got in touch?'

'Someone did on her behalf. We've had a few hoaxes, but a call came in to say that the girl was in Dover and the caller was bringing her to the station. On the way, the car was rammed repeatedly by a vehicle that now appears to have been stolen. Our girl's driver is killed in the impact. We have more gunshots and a female was seen running from the car towards the town. She roughly matches the description of our missing girl — and it has to be her.'

'It does, I agree. Someone's really got it in for her. What do we know about the man she left behind at the first incident?'

'White male, late thirties. Dead. That's about all we know for certain right now. The car is a hire car, no IDs found. The hire car company have provided a driving licence number — it exists on the DVLA system but for someone entirely different and the photo sure as hell doesn't match.'

'I see. So, a fake licence with a doctored image. That's not a good sign.'

'It isn't. It appears it was a good fake too. The sort professional criminals might source.'

'Did you use the lantern?' The lantern was a fingerprint scanner attached to a mobile phone, a way of identifying people on the spot. It was expensive and in most cases rendered unlawful by legislation but in circumstances like these it could be invaluable.

'We did. No match on the system. We've gone with a fast track on the DNA and dental records. But we both know they're not particularly fast. I think maybe when this is all over I might petition to have the name *fast track* changed.'

Neither man had sat down since they had entered the office. Whittaker leant on the back of his chair and George stood opposite, running over the timeline in his mind. Suddenly, it didn't quite fit.

'The last incident — where the car was rammed — how was it called in?'

'On 1-0-1.'

'Did we get details of the caller?'

'No, they refused.'

'The phone number?'

'We have a mobile phone number, yes. I'm not sure it furthers our cause though. If it's not a contract phone, there won't be anyone attached to it.'

'The vehicle was rammed on the way to the police station, right? What I don't understand is how our offenders knew she was in that car and on her way?'

'Maybe they followed her from Stephen Maddocks' place?'

'What, the day before? And then they waited for her to get into a car before they rammed her? That doesn't make sense. These people had been shooting in the street. If they saw her go into a house they'd hardly have any qualms about shooting their way in. Wouldn't have been the first time, would it?'

'So what are you saying?'

'Have you listened to the 1-0-1 call?'

'No, I don't know if anyone has. It's not been mentioned.'

George stepped to the phone on Whittaker's desk. He pressed three numbers, an internal extension.

'Jane, hey! It's George Elms down in Langthorne. I need your help.'

'Don't you always. You and everyone else today, George. If it isn't quick and it isn't urgent then I might have to turn you down for once.' Jane Adams was a team leader at the Force Control Room. She led the team who could review and provide calls to the police if they formed part of the evidence — which they often did. She was on speakerphone. Whittaker cut in.

'Jane, this is Chief Inspector John Whittaker. Can I just assure you that this phone call falls into both of those categories. I'm stood here with George. The world is falling down around our ears here, I'm sure you're busy for the same reason.'

'Yes, sir! What can I do for you, sir?'

George spoke again, 'Jane, we got a 1-0-1 call today — someone claiming to be with the woman who fled yesterday's incident. Do you know about it?'

'In Dover? I know the incident. I know there was a call today. We haven't reviewed it yet.'

'So you haven't downloaded the WAV file yet?'

'No. We've had requests for the others, but not that one. I did ask if it was needed but I was told that one can be done slow-time.'

'Okay. I'm now telling you that this one might be the most important of them all. Can you process this one and send it to Mr Whittaker direct?'

'Yes, of course. I can do it straight away. I just need a minute or two to find the call reference again — it'll be on a job form.'

'Thanks, Jane. I owe you one.'

'You owe me a lot more than one, George Elms.'

George grinned at the phone. 'Noted.'

The call ended. 'What do you think this might give us, George?'

'I don't know, sir. Maybe nothing.'

Whittaker finally flopped in his seat. George took the invitation to do the same.

'I would offer you a coffee, George, but I've run out of people to ask to make it.'

'A man of your stature, sir, and there's no one left to make you a coffee?'

'I know. Damned travesty is what it is. That will be the subject of another petition, I feel. How are you now anyway? I know this awful business with the wife was on your mind earlier. I need you up for this right now, George.'

'I'm fine. Luckily I can't deal with two things at once — so I'm more than happy for work to be the thing that consumes me for a bit.'

'Did you get to see your little girl?'

'No. I didn't, but there was positive news around that. It shouldn't be so difficult from now on. It's her birthday tomorrow, this will be the first one in three years that I'll be able to spend with her.'

'You have the day off?'

'I do, sir. Very much.'

'Well, then, you've not got long to sort all this out now, have you?'

Whittaker's machine pinged a notification that he had mail. He clicked his mouse. 'It's here already.'

George moved round. 'There are two files?' George frowned. One was labelled *Inbound 1m20s,* the other *Outbound 36s.*

Both were attachments to the email in a WAV form. Whittaker clicked on the first and a player popped up. A few seconds of buffering and a female voice could be heard through the computer's compact speakers. Both men leant in. The woman asked for the police, she told them she had the girl who had run away from the shooting. A female call-taker responded, her tone a little bored. She asked the questions George would expect. The caller wasn't very forthcoming. She sounded older, sixty plus he guessed, and with a slight accent, maybe south London. They made the arrangements for the girl to be brought to the police station. The call ended.

Whittaker was sat back in his chair shaking his head. He looked disappointed.

'That doesn't really tell us much, George, does it?'

'Not really. What's the outbound call?'

Whittaker clicked on the second attachment. This time the FCR representative was a male voice. The informant answered the call and she sounded annoyed. The FCR agent said he was concerned, that he wanted to be sure they got there safely. He said the police officer had asked what car she would be arriving in and from what direction so they could come out and meet them. The informant gave details. She still sounded irritated. The call ended.

Whittaker huffed. 'Still nothing of great importance, George.'

'With respect, sir, that's the most important thing I've heard so far.'

Whittaker straightened in his chair. 'How so?'

'Why would he need to know the type of car? And the direction they were coming from? And why did someone different call her back? That agent is a leak. He has contact with whoever rammed that vehicle off the road.'

'Well, fuck my old boots! We need to get up there. He needs nicking.'

'That would be my next move.'

'What do you have planned for the next couple of hours, George?'

George suddenly realised where this was heading. 'Investigating a murder at a farmhouse, Major. Keeping a promise to a devastated old man.'

'Anything you can put back? I need someone with your ability in front of this lad. I need answers from him, George — and immediately.'

George sighed. 'Fine. For you, Major. But remember this! I'll call Paul Bearn on the way up. He's going to FLO for my job. He's not technically trained, sir, but I figured he could handle—'

Whittaker waved him away. 'Extraordinary times, George. You do what you have to do. Call me the instant you have something from him. Nobody else. The idea of a leak suddenly makes me feel very nervous.'

'Will do. Can you hit redial and speak to Jane up there? We need to get this boy isolated. Get his personal phone off him and get him into a room.'

'I'll get him nicked, lord knows there should be enough coppers about up there.'

'I'd rather you held off on that for now, Major. I'd rather speak to him before he realises how much trouble he's in.'

'Okay, George, I'll make the call.'

George lingered deliberately until Whittaker picked up on it.

'Is there something the matter?'

'I need to speak to Emily Ryker. I could do with her shaking some trees for my job.'

'You can call her on the way, George. Or I can speak to her if you want?'

'I'd rather speak to her myself. No disrespect — I'm not sure what I need myself yet and I wanted to talk it out.'

'She's the intel lead for this shooting, George. Be careful you don't tuck her up with too much.'

'I tell you what, sir. Let me take her with me to speak with our friend at the control centre. She will still be on the phone. That gives me a car journey to talk to her. And she needs to know the outcome of this conversation anyway.'

'I don't know, George. I need her on the pulse down here.'

'You know Ryker, sir. She's on the pulse no matter where she is. Call it a payoff. I'll assist with talking to our leak and I can use your intel officer for the time it takes to get it done.'

'Fine, George. But she's there to assist you with this task and then you bring her back. I don't mind her making a few calls for you, or whatever, but that's all she can do. I need her full attention on this job.'

'That's all I need.'

George stepped out of the office. He was careful to close the door behind him. He could see a few people hovering, Whittaker had been ignoring his phone but he was still in demand. George could hear the door knocking before he had made it to the other side of the room.

Emily Ryker was in the intel office. She was leaning in close to her screen, her hand resting on her mouse. She had a desk lamp hooked over the top of her screen. George angled it so it shone in her face.

'Jesus, George! You trying to blind me?'

'Only with my beauty.'

'I see. Well, I suggest turning lights off if you want to make yourself look better. Are you sober now at least?'

'Nope.'

'Brilliant. It's not like there's anything much going on. You should just be able to find a dark corner somewhere and see this shift out.'

'That would be lovely. Instead I've already been to one murder and now I have a task for another. And you are coming with me.'

Emily backed away from her computer. She lifted her hand from her mouse and pulled her glasses off her face. 'No can do, George, I'm trying to stay available. I'm hoping there are going to be some significant calls coming in. We've got public appeals and source handlers out and about and that's just for starters. I have each of my fingers in a different pie. The answer's out there somewhere.'

'It always is, Ryker, and you've been warned about the pie thing. We've just had a look at two calls from today — the call telling us the missing girl was on her way and then an outbound one from someone at the FCR asking her what type of car she was driving and where she was coming from so he could leak the information to whoever led the ambush.'

Emily stared at him a little more intently. He could tell she was testing him. 'This is true?'

'Of course it's true. I'm on my way to speak to our leak. I want to take you with me.'

'Who is he? I'll need to get an intel package done for him.'

'Not sure yet. Come find out with me. We'll talk in the car!'

'I can't do anything in the car.'

'Exactly. You can't run away. You can assign the intel package to a minion. Do you want to be trying to find someone relevant on this loser's Facebook profile, or would you rather be sat opposite him in a room? Your choice.'

Emily stood up. 'Fine. But Whittaker might get the hump. He's been very protective of me. Anyone asking for an update has been sent in my direction. I don't think he wants to lose me. I'm like his comfort blanket.'

'I've just spoken to him. He's on board. Maybe you're not as important as you thought.' George smiled. He was relieved when Emily broke into a smile too.

Chapter 11

Jenny ran until she felt like she had left the chaos behind her: the sirens, the tooting horns, the gunshots — everything. Through a break between buildings, she had seen trees and rolling hills in the distance, stretching away from the town with Dover's famous castle dominating the backdrop. She made for it, passing the police station on her right as she did so. She kept her head down, her mind churning with so much confusion that rather than seeking sanctuary, she hurried past, convinced that someone might even spill out to continue the chase.

How had they known? The people who rammed her car had known that she was on her way to the police station; she didn't know how she could be so sure, but she had never felt more certain about anything.

The town's layout now opened up considerably. Leaving tight lines of terraced houses behind her, she was surrounded now by a broken mishmash of bigger houses and blocks of flats. She crossed a road and headed up the hill towards where she had seen the green grass. The higher she went, the bigger the houses became. Soon she saw a brown sign that pointed out a footpath. She followed it into a sparse wood, still hearing traffic through the thin layer of vegetation. When the path forked, she headed right up the slope; she needed a break from people.

By the time the wood opened up to wild grass, Jenny had left the traffic far behind her. The worn path led to a gap in a stone wall behind which was the edge of a huge graveyard. She entered cautiously. The grass was shorter, well kept; the atmosphere sombre, of the sort only a graveyard can produce. She moved through a line of tombstones until she made it to a wooden bench beneath the canopy of a mature tree. The bench was dry and, though the rain was much lighter now, she was glad of the shelter. She now had an elevated view of Dover, nestled in the valley below. The green of the lawn ran into the brown of treetops then the grey of the town far below. She felt so much safer now that she was out of the town, looking in.

Jenny checked herself over. She was damp, her clothes had a layer of moisture on the outside and she had a layer of sweat against her skin that was quickly turning cold. She shivered. She had her breath back but she knew she was just about done in. She doubted she could summon another sprint if one was needed. She was exhausted and her legs ached. Her hip and ribs were still sore from the day before. She had banged her shin badly and she had a bump on the top of her head that was tender to touch and the probable cause of her headache. Her left shoulder bled from the collision with the flint wall of the church. She pulled her legs up to hug them and rested her chin on her knees, staring out at the view. For the first time in a long while, she felt a degree of calm, like getting away from the chaos had afforded her an opportunity to think straight and work out her options. She only had one and that meant going back into the town. She could still hear sirens in the distance and see blue flashing lights. She had the impression that they didn't know what they were chasing. And neither did she.

* * *

George had already released the handbrake when Emily got into the car.

'This is a rush job then is it?'

'We need to get him secure.' George ran his fingers over a black panel, he settled on a button marked *999* and pushed it. The car was unmarked but it had blue lights concealed in the front grille and rear window. They flickered to life. The gate closed behind them and he pressed the horn to start the siren. George accelerated away from Langthorne House towards the town of Maidstone where their potential leak should be waiting for them.

'There's another reason I want to rush.'

'What's that?' Emily was battling to do up her seatbelt.

'Do you know about the other shooting?'

'Wingmore Farm?'

'That's the one.'

'What sort of an intelligence officer doesn't know about a murder on her patch?'

'How much do you know?'

'Okay, fine, so I don't know much. This Dover job is everything at the moment. I've not really kept up with Wingmore Farm. To be honest, I was told not to worry about it for now. The timing is not ideal.'

'I thought as much. I'm worried that it's going to get forgotten about. Already it's been assigned one CSI and just a few response officers holding the scene. As far as investigators go, there's me — officially. I managed to steal Paul Bearn, but he's stuck to our witness and can't really do much else. They've put out for overtime but everything that comes in seems to be sucked up by this other job.'

'It won't be forgotten about. It might just have to sit on the back burner for a day or two.'

'That's the thing . . . you can't put something like that on the back burner. Whoever shot that woman is out there right now with a smoking gun, a dirty van and his co-defendants that he can't guarantee control over. They're no professionals. They turned up with balaclavas and lumps of wood and ended up with a gun going off. We need to be putting the pressure on, that's how you force them to make mistakes or flush them out into the open.'

'Are there no clues?'

'Nothing. Robbery gone wrong. The victims targeted because they live in an expensive place in the middle of nowhere. They weren't there to murder anyone. They'll be panicking, expecting knocks on their doors. We need to keep the pressure up.'

'Sounds like sense to me. Not sure what you can do, though. This other job has more bodies. It's all over the news and a likely intended victim is still out there and at risk. You can see why it's sucked up everything we have.'

'Can you make a few calls for me? To your source handlers? See if they can get word out to see if anyone is nervous about a job. Someone out there knows who these gang members are. They might have known it was going to happen. They might know it went wrong — or if someone is trying to get rid of a gun or a van. Anything.'

Emily exhaled heavily. 'You know I'll try and help, George, but I'm the same as everyone else. I've already been in touch with the source handlers. They've all been tasked around the Dover shooting. Like I said, it's all over the news, so everyone's talking about it. If everyone's talking about it, that includes the criminal world. I'm expecting a lot back, but it will all be about Dover. I need to be sifting through it and picking out what's relevant.'

'I know. I appreciate that. Just don't forget about me like everyone else will. I met the husband this morning, Ryker. If my victim hadn't left anyone behind her then maybe I could accept that it's not the day's most important job. But you should have seen him. You're sixty-two years married to someone and then out of the blue you get a knock at the door and a gunshot. He's lost everything. I can't give any of it back, but I gave him my word I would find the bastard who took it away from him.'

'You should be careful what you promise, George. I know how you get fixated on keeping promises. I seem to remember a few very-near-death experiences linked to your word.'

'Still here though, aren't I?'

'You are.'

'Ouch, Ryker.'

'Jesus! Sorry, George. I didn't mean it quite like—'

'Yeah, you did. It's okay. You're right.'

Emily didn't speak again straight away. 'Sixty-two years . . .' she said, eventually.

'I know, that's almost two lifetimes.'

'Did you even manage sixty-two days, George?'

George laughed. He didn't feel like it but it took him over. 'Kick George while he's down day, is it? You'd better get me some sort of a result now, Ryker!'

Emily was laughing herself but she had at least pulled her phone from her pocket. She would use the rest of the car journey to make her calls back to the source team.

By the time they arrived at their destination, Emily had finished on the phone. It hadn't sounded positive. George knew what he was up against. You couldn't task too much out; you had to stick to one job at a time when you were dealing with grasses. It sounded like the Dover job was still taking precedence, but the source team had agreed that if they were offered any information they would send it back up the line. George had taken that as the best Emily was going to get. He did wonder, though, if the conversation might have ended differently if it had been him making the call.

George could see Jane Adams out and waiting in what looked like a bike shed in the Force Headquarters car park. She'd been sucking on a cigarette and now pushed it into the top of a metal post. George had worked closely with Jane in a previous life; it had been rare for a day to pass where his team didn't need copies of 999 calls. They were often used as part of the evidence: they could be very effective in identifying cries for help in the background or capturing the panic and intensity in a victim's voice when they later denied being a victim at all. Jane bustled over and stood by George's door before he had finished parking. She was a handsome woman, almost as tall as George in her heels. She had short hair brushed over to one side and black-rimmed glasses.

'Adrian Minter,' she said to George, straight off. 'He's still working at his desk. I spoke with the chief inspector and we thought that was best.'

George climbed out of the car. 'You told me you'd quit, Jane.' George gestured at the post from which blue-tinged smoke still spiralled.

'First one in four months. I guess that's what happens when you suddenly find one of your team is a murder suspect.'

'I don't think we can call him that quite yet, Jane. More likely he's been a bit silly. But we shall see. Does he have his phone?'

'No. They all have to put them in a locker before they go out onto the floor. They all have their own lockers. I've pulled phone records so you can see that he made the outbound call. It was within thirty seconds of the other operator hanging up. He's got some explaining to do, George.'

'That he does. Do you know Emily Ryker?' Emily held out her hand. Jane took it up and they exchanged pleasantries.

'Ryker, here, is an intel officer through and through. No doubt she'll want the personnel file before we leave.'

'It's all ready for you.'

'Of course it is! Let's see what he has to say then, shall we?'

On looking over his file, George discovered that Adrian Minter was in his mid-twenties and had previously worked as a phone-based sales agent for an insurance company. He had no police record of course, having been vetted as part of the force application process. His home address was a one-bed flat in Maidstone. He looked nervous. He wore black trousers and a short-sleeved shirt tucked into a belt with an oversized buckle. He had a slim build and an awkward posture. He dropped straight away into the chair George had positioned deliberately, so it that was obviously intended for him.

'I always find it respectful to ask permission to sit when you're meeting with senior officers.'

Minter flushed red, redder even than when he came in. He fidgeted, glancing to where Jane was perched on the edge of a desk in the background. Jane had checked with George that it was okay for her to sit in before she had gone to fetch Minter. George had positively encouraged it. He wanted to build the pressure, to put Minter on the back foot. The chair was part of that too. He had asked Emily to sit next to him. He deliberately didn't introduce her so that Minter wouldn't know who she was. This was his chance to get the information he needed. Once someone was arrested they became part of a slow, methodical process where the offender had time to reflect. Then a solicitor could get in their ear and the opportunity for a genuine, panicked reaction was much harder to prompt.

'S-sorry.' Minter fidgeted as if contemplating standing up again. Then he changed his mind and shuffled straighter in his seat.

'Do you know who I am?' George said.

Adrian looked back over at Jane. 'Jane . . . she said you're an inspector. She said you need to talk to me.' He turned back to George, then to Emily.

'A woman died, Adrian. Because of the phone call you made. So you need to know from the off that this is serious. Conspiracy to murder, Adrian . . . are you aware of that offence? Fifteen years in prison — minimum.'

'Consp . . . murder? What are you talking about?'

'Take your time. Get your thoughts in order and then you need to tell me how you came to make a phone call that led to a woman's death.'

'I didn't. I don't know what you mean. What call?'

'How many outbound calls have you made today?'

The red in Arian's face had run out completely, his face was suddenly whiter than looked possible. 'A few, I think. I don't know. I've been busy.'

'One.' George held a sheet of paper in his hands, he gestured with it. 'One call all day. Your job is to take emergency calls. Jane here tells me you're good at it. No problems at all. It's mostly inbound but there can be a need for you to make outbound calls, right?'

'Yeah.'

'So the one outbound call you made today . . . why was that? And give me a little credit for a second, Adrian, and pretend that I already know.'

Adrian looked at everyone again. They all stared back. He must have realised there was no one there to bat his corner for him. 'I-I didn't want to.'

'Didn't want to what?' George sat back. He wanted Adrian to know that this was his time to speak. Adrian peered back at Jane. She still stood behind him leaning on a table, her arms crossed.

'Someone called me. They said they knew where I worked. They said they needed some information, nothing that would cause any trouble. They just needed to know if someone called in and a few details of that person. That was all.'

'How much?'

'How much what? Information?'

'Money, Adrian. How much did they offer you?'

'Jesus, they made it sound like it was nothing. Like no one would care.'

'How much?'

'It was five hundred quid. They dropped it through my letterbox some time yesterday. I don't know when. I got in from work and it was there. They're supposed to do the same thing today, now I've done what they asked.'

'A grand. A thousand pounds, Adrian. Think about that. That's not a small amount of money is it? What information did they want?'

'There's a job running — the shooting in the south of the county yesterday. You know all about it right?'

'Assume I don't.'

'Okay, well there's a girl missing. She ran away from it all. We've appealed for her to get in touch. There's a set protocol when she does. I was told I just needed to text a number when she got in touch.'

'That's all?'

'That's all.'

'Just text a number to say she had got in touch with the police. Nothing more?'

'No, that was it.'

'For a thousand pounds?' George sat straighter and then leaned forward into Adrian's face. 'Do you think I'm an idiot?'

'No. No, sir.'

'After that call came in, you phoned the informant straight back. You had to get some information, what information?'

'Fine. Look, fine! But this is it . . . they said they wanted to know where she was. Failing that, where she was going and how. I called her back so I would know what car she was in. I reckoned this was the best I could do. As soon as I made the call, I knew it was a mistake. I know every call here is monitored, but these people dropped the money through my door. They know where I live. I made the call, made an excuse to get off the floor and then I sent the text. I was praying that would be the end of it. I didn't expect them to drop any more money but I didn't care. I was almost hoping they didn't. I don't want nothing more to do with them.'

'And you don't know who *them* is?'

'I don't know. I have no idea, you have to believe me.'

'What did you think they were going to use that information for? I mean, it's obvious to me, but what were you thinking?'

'I don't know. I guess I could have worked out that they were looking to find her before she got to us. But I didn't know that, they never told me that.'

'And a woman died.'

Adrian slumped forward. His mouth hung open, he snorted a sudden intake of breath. It all looked very staged. 'Am I going to prison?'

'Well, right now you're helping me. That's the right thing to do at least. What number did they contact you on?'

'My phone, it's in the locker. It wasn't hidden or anything. It will be the last number I sent a text to. I can go get it if you want?'

'We already have your phone, Adrian.'

Adrian hung his head again. 'Okay.'

'And you don't know anything more about who contacted you?'

'No.'

George nodded at Jane. She moved to the door and tugged it open. Two uniform officers were standing on the other side. They paced in, Adrian immediately looked up.

'Adrian Minter, you are under arrest for conspiracy to murder. You do not have to say anything, but it may harm your defence if you do not mention, when questioned, something you later rely on in court. Do you understand?'

Adrian snorted again. This time his anguish seemed more genuine. He looked straight at George. 'I thought I was helping you! You just said!'

George stood up. 'You were helping yourself, Adrian. A thousand pounds wasn't it? I hope it was worth it.'

George left the room as the handcuffs were being applied. Jane followed him out. Emily split off to make a phone call. She had Adrian's file open in her hand.

'Such a shame,' Jane said.

'He made his choice. I wouldn't worry about him.'

'No, I meant I literally just typed up his three-month assessment. I needn't have bothered!'

George broke into a smile. 'I hope it wasn't glowing.'

'It was actually. You'll stay for a cup of tea, George?'

'I would love to, Jane, but I have to get back to Area. It's manic down there. I don't think Mr Whittaker would appreciate me taking a break right now.'

'You work too hard, George, I've always said that.'

'I think I've always agreed with you too. I meant what I said . . . I owe you one. When everything's a bit calmer you can make me tea. I'll bring a cream cake up or something. I know you look after me, Jane.'

'It's my pleasure, George. Anytime.' She smiled and her cheeks flushed a little. George had always thought she was naturally flirty but he was beginning to think that maybe she saved a little extra for him. He smiled back, now reconsidering if he should stay for tea. His phone vibrated in his pocket. He pulled it out to see Whittaker's name on the screen. It made up his mind.

'Boss.' George waved a cheery goodbye to Jane as he made for the exit. When he turned sideways to push the door open, Jane was still watching.

'George, what news?'

'Just this second out of my meeting with our friend Adrian. The boy's an idiot. He's been very naïve but I don't put his involvement as any more than that.'

'Has he been nicked?'

'Yeah, he'll get the full treatment, he'll be formally interviewed but I don't expect anything more to come out of that. I have what I needed.'

'He was helpful then?'

'I'm pretty sure he told me everything he knew. Unfortunately, that isn't a lot. He was called out of the blue. We have the phone number but it will be a burner phone at a guess. He was offered a grand in two payments for the information he gave. He's had five hundred already. It was stuffed through his letterbox. The other five hundred is due now he's given the information.'

'I see. So he has no idea who these people are?'

'He says not. I believe him too. He got greedy and stupid.'

'So where are we? Someone sitting up on his address for this next payment?'

'I don't think so, boss. They got his number from somewhere. We have to consider it was someone else here and someone who knew him well enough to know that he might be susceptible. They may already know he has been arrested — that's if they ever intended on paying him the rest. I wouldn't, would you?'

'No, I guess I wouldn't.'

'I have his address. While I'm up here I'll do some house-to-house, see if his neighbours saw anyone dropping anything through his door. You never know, we might get lucky.'

'Okay, George. Keep in touch.'

'I will do. I was planning on dropping in on my job on the way back. I want to see the old boy again. I want him to know I'm about.'

'Understood. I'm sure Paul Bearn is very capable.'

George finished his call. He considered calling Paul straight away to get an update on how Stan was doing. He decided against it. He trusted Paul like no other; George would let him get on with his job. He could talk to him soon enough. Emily was already standing by the car.

'Did you say goodbye to your girlfriend?'

'That was Whittaker. I think you might have misunderstood the signals between us two.'

'You know what I mean, George.'

'Let's go knock some doors.'

Adrian Minter lived in a reasonable area. It was walking distance from his place of work, off Coverdale Avenue towards the town centre. It was a busy road in both directions and had a parade of shops servicing the densely populated estates close to the police headquarters. Behind these shops was an L-shaped building with two levels of flats. Adrian's was on the first floor. George walked the concrete stairwell noting the standard smell of urine. Adrian's flat was four along. The walkway was exposed to the elements, the frontages of all the flats were featureless and identical. He knocked on Adrian's door — just in case. There was no answer. The next flat along was the last one. All the front doors were the same: dull, white UPVC with three frosted panes: two squares and a semi-circle at the top. At least this one had a welcome mat. He knocked. He readied his badge in his hand.

'Hello?' an elderly female voice called through the door.

'Good afternoon. I'm sorry to bother you, my name is George Elms. I'm a police officer, ma'am.' The door scraped with chains and turning locks. The door was opened an inch — just enough for George to see half a wrinkled face looking out at him. He held his badge up to the gap. 'Nothing to worry about.' George added.

'Just a moment.' The door was pushed shut. George exchanged a smile with Emily. The door opened wider. 'Oh!' The woman exclaimed at Emily.

'This is my colleague, DC Emily Ryker.'

'I see.'

'Like I said, nothing to worry about. Do you know your neighbour? The flat next door?'

The woman stepped out of her front door to have a look, like she needed a visual reminder. 'I say hello, you know? I wouldn't say I *know* him. I mean, I keep myself to myself. You got to round here. Is he in some sort of trouble?'

'Not really, no. I'm more concerned about people that might have come up and spoken to him. Have you noticed anyone at his door in the last couple of days? Or anyone hanging around that you haven't seen before?'

'Always people hanging around here. They use the stairwell, see. We get the kids from over the estate. They come and sit in there and have a drink. I mean they don't give me any bother but I'm usually in and settled before they come out. Sometimes I see them in the summer.'

'So you haven't seen anyone new around?'

'No. Did you want to come in rather than stand out there?'

'No, thank you. I'm sorry I didn't take your name.'

'Rose. Rose Miller. Do you need my phone number?'

'I don't think so, Rose. Thanks for talking to me though. I'm really sorry to have bothered you.'

'Oh, it's no bother, officer. I like to help you lot. You know where I am if you need me!' The woman seemed to suddenly be aware of herself. She mumbled her goodbyes and stepped back into her flat. George ignored Emily's wide grin. He stepped past her to get to the front door on the other side of Adrian's flat.

'*You know where I live, Inspector Elms. You can come here anytime. Do you need my phone number?* Are you wearing a new aftershave or something?' Emily's voice was low and mocking. She was chuckling too.

'Yes, thank you, Ryker. We'll just do this one and then we'll call it a day. This is a poke in the dark.'

'I know where else you might be able to get one of those!'

George composed himself before knocking on the next door.

This one was answered quicker and by a far different animal. George stepped back. The man filled the doorway. He wore a white vest pulled taut over his chest by a protruding stomach. His head brushed against the top of the doorway and he had black football shorts straining against the size of his thighs. He had a flashing blue games console controller in one hand and a large packet of cheese and onion crisps in the other. He held the bag like a throttled chicken.

'What you want?'

'Sorry to disturb you, mate. I'm George Elms and this is Emily Ryker.' George held up his badge and the man's gaze stayed fixed on him.

'So?'

'We're doing some enquiries around someone that might have been to your neighbour's house. There's been a rather serious incident and we think someone involved might have been here. Have you seen anyone knocking at his door?'

'Nah, mate. I don't really take much notice. You get people up here knocking at doors an' that, but they don't bother me. They wouldn't fucking dare, you know what I mean?'

'I think I do, yeah. So you haven't seen anyone out of place or that you haven't seen before?'

The man shook his head. 'I got a leaflet. That was it. I don't get much post. People don't know I live here. Soon as they do, they start asking for money. I'm still on the run from Brighthouse. Them people need to get their house in order before they start coming to mine, you know what I mean?'

George had absolutely no idea. 'Okay, so just a leaflet. No problem. Thanks for your time.'

'Yeah. One of these restaurant ones — kebab house. I called them up too. I like a kebab and I thought it was a new place — but it weren't. It was some setup on the other side of the town. They don't even deliver out here. I said to them on the phone, 'why the fuck did you stick it through my letterbox then, you cunt!' They never had no answer to that.'

'What leaflet?' Emily cut in. George was moving away, looking to leave.

'Wassat, babe?' he said.

'Have you still got the leaflet?'

'I don't fuckin' . . .' The man was half-turned as he spoke, he was inspecting the floor. He bent down behind

106

the door. He handed the leaflet to Emily. 'No good to me, babe. You can have it.'

He shut the door.

'Babe?' George said.

'I still got it, too, George.'

'Do you want to knock again? He might be single?'

'Oh, he's definitely single.' Emily lifted the leaflet. '*Best Kebab*,' she read. 'Go knock on your girlfriend's door, see if she got one of these too.' George did as he was told. She confirmed that she had.

'You're thinking the leaflets are linked?'

'I don't know. It's a common tactic, right?'

George nodded. He'd used it himself. If he needed to get close to an address for a peak through a window or to work out the easiest way to force entry, he would scoop up some menus from a local takeaway and drop some through the letterboxes of the target address and a few houses either side. No one would look at you twice. It was also a tactic used by some burglars or con artists. It would be a good way of getting an envelope through someone's door if you wanted to be certain of blending in.

'You fancy a kebab?'

Emily screwed her face up at the menu printed on the flip-side. 'Definitely not.'

George checked his watch. 'We'll do this one last enquiry and then I've got to get back.'

Best Kebabs was already looking to be a bold claim before George and Emily stepped in. It was part of a drab, concrete square that sat between a launderette and a betting shop and boasted two-for-one pizzas on a handwritten cardboard star. The front of the shop was empty. George guessed they hadn't been open long. The displays were largely empty too. A man appeared carrying a tray in each hand, both were loaded with long metal skewers through clumps of sandy coloured meat.

'Hello!' The man was immediately cheerful. 'One moment.' A thick accent, maybe Middle Eastern. George scanned the counter. Sure enough, he could see a stack of the same menus that had been posted through the addresses either side of Adrian. The man positioned the trays under the counter and they were visible behind glass. A fly had settled already. The man straightened up.

'How can I help?'

'Who does your leafleting?'

'Leaflet?' the man scowled, his smile dropping away in an instant.

'You have a stack of menus there, who takes them out and drops them through the doors? Do you do it?'

'Ah. You want job?' The man still looked confused as he looked George up and down. He probably didn't look like their average candidate.

'No, not exactly.' George showed his badge. 'I'm investigating a serious incident. I need to know who's been out delivering your menus and where they go. No one's in any trouble, I'm sure. We're trying to piece together what happened and you guys might be able to help.'

'I'll . . . you wait. I go see the boss.'

The man left in a hurry. George had already noted the darkness of the back room had suddenly been flooded with daylight in the last minute. He reckoned they had lost at least one employee out the back. George didn't need to be reacting to that: more than likely he would end up chasing someone down on foot who would turn out to be an over-stayer. Immigration certainly wouldn't thank him for that.

An older man with a shirt tucked into heavy-looking brown trousers emerged from the back. He was overweight, his shirt was open enough to reveal a tight-fitting white vest underneath and his sleeves were rolled up. He was chewing on something. He finished it before he spoke.

'Problem?'

'I don't think so. I'm just here asking a few questions. I'm trying to piece together a serious incident some distance from here.'

'We don't get involved in things like that here. This is a good place.'

'Things like what?'

'Like what you investigate. We don't have police come here. We have no trouble. This is a good place.'

'Someone who did have some trouble had your menu delivered. We just wanted to speak to the person who delivers your menus. Maybe he saw something.'

'Our menus? No, we do not deliver these. Not for a long time. No one is reliable, yes?'

'You don't put them out through people's doors?'

'No. But people, sometimes they take. A lot at once maybe?' The man shrugged.

'Who did?'

'I not know, but maybe another of our men. Maybe somebody knows. I will talk tonight, okay?'

'Do you have CCTV?' George looked up at the ceiling. He could see a plastic dome that looked like it had a camera inside.

'This? This does not work. Not now. It is broken.'

'That is a shame.' In George's experience, takeaway shops rarely had working CCTV if they were asked by the police. George scribbled out his details. The man thanked him for them and pocketed the piece of paper without looking at it. George took his name, he was hesitant at first but he gave it. George thanked him and they left.

'We're not expecting any assistance from in there, are we?' Emily asked.

'No. It's a tentative enquiry anyway. Not that it's my problem. I'll update Whittaker on the way back and then I'm going to see my victim.'

'You want me to come with you?'

'If you don't mind. It's on the way. I only want to drop in and see him for a few minutes for an update. I want him to know that I'm still about.'

'Do you have an update to give him?'

'No. But I'll think of something.' They made it back to the car. Emily seemed to be studying him with an air of suspicion. She was right to. There was nothing new to tell Stanley Wingmore about who had murdered his wife. But he wanted Emily to see him for herself, maybe then she would lean a little harder on her source handlers, dig a little deeper. He reckoned she knew exactly what he was doing.

Chapter 12

The rain was now heavier. Jenny was still under the cover of the tree but now the moisture was simply gathering on the leaves and falling in bigger drops. Her whole body shivered as she pulled the hood of the gilet in tighter and peered around for better shelter. The cemetery was vast, the size of twenty football pitches or more. She couldn't see any buildings in the grounds, despite her elevated view. She presumed there must be a church or chapel somewhere at least. She gradually became aware of the distant whir of an engine. The sound was intermittent and somewhere in front of her, but the breeze rolling down the slope towards the town made it difficult for her to identify it specifically or to pinpoint where it was coming from. She stood up; her legs were stiff with the lack of movement, her back and hips the same. There was a line of trees to the west that looked like a good source of cover. Once she reached it and dropped down the slope a little, the tree line curved away sharply to reveal a sheltered clearing. In the middle of the clearing stood a cabin. She moved closer to investigate. The curvature of the woodland meant it couldn't be seen by anyone looking up the slope. The cabin was made largely of wood and was shaped like a miniature house or some small-scale model. It had clearly been there a while; the wood was weathered and the grass around it well trampled. It had a solid-looking chimneystack of different coloured, flat stones, pushing up to the edge of the roof on the side closest to her.

The door was made of thick wooden slats that likewise differed slightly in shade. A porch hung over it, held up by four wooden poles. There were no signs of life. She walked around it once, careful not to stand on any of the thin sticks or crunchy brown leaves that littered the ground. It had a wooden lean-to on the far side. Its double doors hung open to reveal a sit-on lawn mower. It smelled strongly of freshly cut grass and, when Jenny felt its flat nose, it was still warm. She started to move away.

'Can I help you, love?'

She grimaced. She was going to have to interact with someone — and he had called her 'love.' Visions of Anne flashed through her mind — that last look she had given her: *Run, love!*

Jenny stopped and turned. A man stood out on the wooden porch, the door behind him open. She saw a puff of white smoke from the chimney and its movement drew her eye. She was pretty certain it hadn't been smoking just a few seconds ago. The man was tall, despite an apparent stoop. His right palm rested on his hip as if he might have a back complaint. He had dark trousers tucked into welly boots and a lumberjack-style jacket. His grey hair and beard were topped by a wax hat with a rim to keep the rain off his face.

'No. Sorry, I was just trying to find somewhere dry.'

'You found somewhere then. Do you want to rest up? This rain will pass. It even stopped my mowing.'

'No. Thank you.' But she didn't step away. She didn't know where else she was going to go. If she got thoroughly wet, she didn't know where she might get dry again.

'I've just lit the stove. I can do a cup of tea. By the time we've drunk it, I reckon you might have a window.' The man leaned forward a little and stuck his hand out from under the porch roof. 'No point soaking you to your skin, love. It's up to you, mind.' He moved back into the cabin. Jenny looked around her. She couldn't see anyone else moving. Everyone else was out of the rain, comfortable in their warm homes, drinking tea. She walked to the door.

The smell dominated her senses as she walked in. It was wonderful, a combination of split timber, smoke from the burner and cut grass. It was bigger inside than she had imagined. To the right side of the door was a camp bed along the wall faced by two chairs. To the left was the wood burner with a wooden bench that held a tall flask and some pots. The man sat on a chair at the bench. A black, iron kettle was balanced on top of the burner. It was already fizzing steam from its nozzle. She could hear the rain bouncing off the tiles.

'You decided you'd like a tea after all, then! A good choice. You can pull up one of those chairs over there if you want, sit closer to the heat. You look a little cold, love.'

Jenny did as she was told. Gladly. She sat down. She stretched her hands out towards the flames — the fire was already roaring. 'Thanks,' she said.

'No bother. I'm Mike. I do the upkeep around here. This is kind of my work place, I suppose.'

Jenny peered around again. 'You could do worse.'

'I could at that.'

'Did you build it?'

'No, love. I added to it a bit. I put the burner in, see? But this has been up here a long time in some form or another. How do you take your tea?'

'Just white, please. Thanks again, I could really do with a cup of tea.'

'I can see that.'

Jenny was suddenly conscious again of her appearance and of her injuries. She knew she was drawing attention to herself. There wasn't much she could do about it. Mike put a tin cup down in front of her. He topped it up with milk from the flask. 'So, you up here with a loved one?' Jenny was puzzled; he must have picked up on it. 'Do you have a relative buried up here?'

'Oh, no. I just needed the peace and quiet. That is okay, isn't it?' She was suddenly a little panicked, like she had broken some law.

Mike chuckled. 'That's just fine. There's nothing like the peace and quiet you get in a place for the dead. They tend to keep themselves to themselves.'

'I guess they do. I'm a little jealous. You ever have the feeling that the world is just chaos everywhere and you just need to get away from it all?'

'Oh, yes. Now you are preaching to the converted, love. I used to chase chaos for a living but it was always one step ahead of me. I was a medic for over thirty years. I worked the wards and the ambulances — always accident and emergency work. This is the perfect job for me, now. That was all noise and chaos. This is making sure the lawn is neat for the eternal rest. I've never been happier to come to work.'

'A retired medic. Sounds like you earned your retirement.'

'Well, everyone does, really. The thing with being a medic for so long is that you get good at spotting people that need help. Even those who are trying to hide it.' He lingered on her, holding his smile.

'I reckon this tea is giving me all the help I need.'

'You'd be surprised just how often I prescribed it. A good cup of tea. You really can't go wrong.'

'You really can't.' Jenny took a sip. It was hot as hell.

'You sure there's nothing more I can do to help? I got a car just down the hill if you want driving somewhere through the rain? After we've finished our tea, of course.'

Jenny was back to thinking about where she could go next. It was still too soon to go back into the town. She would surely be better off waiting until it got dark.

'Thanks, but I've got nowhere I can go.'

'Really? A bright young thing like you? Not got friends or family nearby? I don't mind a bit further afield or a train station? You shouldn't be sat out here in the rain.'

'No, my family are a long way from here. I was just looking to find somewhere to wait for an hour or a little more. In the dry. Can you help with that?'

'Oh. Well, I don't know about that — I mean, the wife's at home. I don't know if I could make her underst—'

'Mike, I don't need you to take me home with you! I meant here. I can't think of anywhere I would rather be right now. You really do have a beautiful place to while away the hours. I was hoping to be able to watch the sunset maybe. Then I'll be gone.'

Mike peered around now. He settled back on Jenny. 'Sure, I guess you can stay in here for a couple of hours. My shift's just about done. I just fired up the stove for the last tea of the day. You can stick around. I'll leave the flask and there's some milk in there if you want some more tea. Just push the door shut when you're done, okay? There's a padlock.'

'Sure. Thanks so much, Mike. I can't tell you how much it means.'

Mike waved her away. 'We gotta help each other out. You take that from a thirty-year paramedic. The main thing I learnt in all that time is that we all need someone sometimes.'

'I think you're right.'

Jenny made small talk for another fifteen minutes or so. Maybe it was the sudden rush of warmth, the soothing crackling of the burning logs and the knowledge that there was a camp bed directly behind, but she suddenly realised just how tired she was. Mike was true to his word. He finished his tea, tidied a few bits and locked up his mower before saying his goodbyes. Jenny promised to drop back in for a cup of tea on another day. He stoked the burner for her and plied it with two fresh logs before he went. Jenny moved the chairs out of the way and dragged the camp bed over the uneven stone floor. She positioned it so it was close enough to the fire. She lay on her left side. Her head was still tender to lie on but it didn't seem to matter. She forgot her pain quickly and was overcome by sleep.

* * *

'Hey, Paul. Good to see you.' Paul Bearn stepped out of the grand front door of Wingmore Farm to greet George and Emily as they pulled up in the car. George hadn't called ahead. Paul must have been in the front room. George could picture Stan sat in the same place he had left him. Paul would have heard his approach on the gravel drive.

'Good to see you too, George.'

'How's it been? Hard going I bet?'

'It's been okay. We know he's taken it hard, but I'm struggling to get through to him. There's certainly no sign of improvement yet.'

'It's still early. And, trust me Paul, you will be making a massive difference just by being here with him.'

'I know that. It's like he's missed out a step though. We've seen enough people a few hours after something like this and they always seem to be a bit numb, you know? But you can spend the day talking with them and they start to make sense and you can get things done. Then you'll come back the next day and you might get nothing. Like they've realised just what has happened and you can't even get two words. It feels like that's where Stan is right now.'

'Is he talking to you at all?'

'Yeah, he is. He's a nice old fella. He told me about Janice, about how they met and where they've been.

They're quite the travelled couple. We've talked a bit about what needs to happen, about funeral arrangements and getting people here, but he's struggled with that. I can't really get him to engage.'

'Have you spoken to the daughter? He wouldn't let me call her.'

'No. But I'm told a neighbour has. I can't get any details to confirm that either way.'

'So we don't know what she knows?'

'I can't be sure she knows anything. He's a wily old bastard, George. I get the impression he wouldn't hesitate to pull the wool if he wanted to.'

'Where are we with CSI? I see Ali's van is still here.'

'She's still here too. She'll be back tomorrow for certain. It might roll into day three if they can't get any help for her. But the body is leaving today. Another hour or so.'

'Oh, that's good.'

'It is for Stan. I think he needs her to go now. He's been preparing himself for that. It needs to happen.'

'It does. Let's go talk to him.' George moved to the front door, Emily and Paul followed just behind him. Sure enough Stan was in the same armchair he had been in earlier in the day. He looked even smaller and his head was still slumped forward. He did look up and managed a weak smile.

'George.'

'How's it going, Stan?'

'How do you think?'

'You're right — one of my stupider questions. I hear Janice is going to be leaving shortly. Did you know that?'

'I did. Paul told me they would be taking her away. She's got another ordeal in front of her, George — they need to do an autopsy. I don't see why. She was shot in the stomach, she lost a lot of blood and she died. Surely they don't need to go chopping her up to tell that?'

George knelt back down in front of Stan. 'Janice is gone, Stan, there's nothing of her left now. The autopsy, that's the bit where we get our evidence. That's the bit where we get a report from an expert that says your wife was fatally injured by a gunshot. That's the bit where I can be sure that no sleazy barrister further down the line can't argue that your wife was murdered in cold blood so he can try and get his bastard client off the hook. You understand me? You and I both know what happened and the court will know what happened because we will be there to tell them. But I don't want a single thing left to chance. When I present a case, especially one like this, I want to be sure that there's nothing anyone can do but send them down for life. I know what you mean — I know it's not a nice thought, Stan — but that's not Janice anymore. Okay?'

'Okay, George, if you say so. Do you know how long? Until they take her away?'

'I don't. Not for sure. Let me ask.'

George swapped out with Paul who moved forward to sit with Stan. Emily stayed in the background. George moved through to the kitchen. Ali was still in there, still in her forensic suit. She was on her hands and knees in the middle of the kitchen.

'Ali!' George called out.

'I thought I told you not to go into any other rooms!'

'Sorry. I'm not technically in.'

'You're not technically out either, are you?'

'Well, no.'

He could hear Ali chuckling from behind her mask. 'I'm pretty much done with this room. I've not even started with the hall where the gun cabinet is yet, or anywhere else in the house. I haven't done much outside either.'

'So I can be in here?'

'You can be that close.'

George could see all he needed to from where he stood. He could see the splatter too. He was always surprised just how much of a mess the human body could make. 'Are we getting the clean team in?'

'No. We don't do that anymore, George.'

'Since when?'

'Since the cuts, I suppose.'

'So you get to clean up your own family member's insides now?'

'Welcome to the new regime.'

'That's awful. Have you still got the contact details for them? It's the council that do it, right?'

'I used to call the council — the hygiene people. They had a contact — a private company, and basically that is what they do. They clean up the stuff that nobody else will touch.'

'Do you still have the number?'

'I actually have the company owner's number. I should be able to dig it out. But they won't do it. Nobody does anything for free these days, George, no matter how sad your story.'

'I wasn't expecting it for free.'

Ali dug around in her suit and produced a phone. She slid a finger out of her glove to operate it. George felt his phone vibrate. 'I've sent you the number for the council. You'll need to speak to them before 5 p.m., though. They work office hours.'

'Thanks, Ali. Let Paul know first — when you're ready to move Janice, I mean.'

'Will do.'

George moved back through to where Stan was sitting. He looked up at George. 'It's not going to be long, Stan, I can't give you an exact time, but I reckon within the hour. Ali will pop through and talk to you and Paul here when it's time. I'm going to head back to carry on with my bit. I'll talk to you regularly Stan and you can speak to me any time of day. You have my number.'

'Thanks, George.'

George turned to where Emily stood behind him. 'Stan, this is DC Emily Ryker. She's our finest intelligence officer. She's going to be helping with the investigation too. We've got our best people on this, Stan — trust me on that.'

Stan lifted up watery eyes to take in Emily, then he slumped back to stare at the floor again.

George returned to the car and Emily walked out with him. She slid into the passenger seat as he fiddled with his phone. It started ringing through the speakers as he turned the car around on the gravel.

'KMS cleaning services, Kerry speaking, how can I help you?' The voice sounded distant through the tinny speakers.

'Good afternoon. My name is George Elms. I'm a police inspector in Langthorne. I understand you provide a specialist cleaning service for us when a crime scene demands it. Is that right?'

'Oh. Well . . . yes. We have done in the past, Mr Elms, but that contract has run its course. We no longer work with the police. We were informed there was no funding for this sort of thing anymore.'

'I see. I know I've used you people in the past, Kerry, and I couldn't put a price on what you guys do. I'm faced with an elderly gent who in a short time will be asked to mop up what is left of his wife from his kitchen floor. That just doesn't sit right with me.'

'I see. I mean, I agree, of course. That isn't right.'

'Can I ask . . . are you the K in KMS, Kerry?'

'I'm the whole thing. My initials. Not very original, eh?'

George chuckled, 'Well, no. What can I say? I can't even pretend I'm impressed with the creativity there!'

'I picked it out of a shortlist. It was either that or Guts R Us. This isn't an easy business to brand.'

George laughed harder. 'I like it! I think maybe you should have stayed with the guts name. Just my personal opinion.'

'I'll bear it in mind. Look, I'm very sorry we can't help. Obviously you can pass our details on to your man who's facing the clean-up. We'll be more than happy to come out.'

'I honestly don't think he would even be capable right now. I was hoping to get it arranged without involving him to be honest. What sort of cost would he be looking at?'

'We would come out and quote you. But if it's one room, for example, our prices would start at six hundred. Depends if you need anything specialist or deep cleaned.'

'Six hundred! I see. Look, I'd like to put this through us. I know there's no contract or relationship with us anymore but if you could do it for a more palatable price you could invoice me direct. I'll make sure the bill is met.'

'I don't think that's going to be possible, Mr Elms. I'm really sorry. Your police force were not very quick payers historically, and that was when there was a system in place. I can't afford to be waiting on jobs.'

'I appreciate that. This would be a direct invoice to me. If I can't turn it round in three working days you can bill my own credit card. You have my word. That's the word of a police officer right there, Kerry!'

'I've worked with plenty of police officers, Mr Elms.'

'Shit!' George laughed. 'In that case, I shouldn't have said that.'

'No you shouldn't.' George detected laughter on the other end of the phone.

'How about three hundred and you can take card details from me now. I'll try and get it back on expenses, but that will be my problem. You'll have your money.'

'I'll have half my money, Mr Elms.'

'George, please. Call me George.'

'Thank you. So I'd have half of my money, George.'

'Three-fifty.'

'Five hundred, George. I'll give you a discount for bare-faced cheek.'

'Come on, Kerry! This is my money here. I'm trying to look out for my victim. Sixty-two years married. I won't have him cleaning up her blood. I can't have that. I will do it myself, but I've seen what you people do and I know how good you are. What you may not know is just how important you are in that person's recovery.'

'Flattery will get you nowhere.'

'I was already getting nowhere! Four hundred and you have my word that I will get you back at the table for a renewed contract.'

'We've already talked about policemen and their word!'

'Not me, Kerry. You've never dealt with me.'

'No offence if I say I don't want to again.'

George was back to laughing again. He fidgeted to pull his wallet out of his back pocket. 'Kerry, I'm going to hand over to my glamorous assistant. She'll give you address details and a contact number for the CSI. She'll also give you the payment details for the three-hundred-and-fifty-pound payment. This has been an expensive shift, Kerry . . .'

'Fine. Pass her over and I will take the details for your four-hundred-pound payment. And that's before inspection. Best I can do.'

'You're a wonderful person, Kerry. And that's exactly what I'm going to say when I get back to head office. I look forward to working with you in the future.'

'I'm sure you do.'

George grinned over at Emily. He was gesturing with his wallet. She took it out of his hand and introduced herself. A few minutes later and the call was completed.

'That was good of you,' Emily said. 'You know you won't see that money again, George — not with our finance department.'

'This man's already destroyed. I can't imagine what happens to him if we leave him to clean that up. I'm going to have the bastards that did this. I need your help, Emily.'

'I said I would.'

'You did, but around this other job. I know that's the force priority but it needn't necessarily be ours. You saw him back there . . .'

'I did. You made sure I did. You made sure he knew I was on board and you put me in a front row seat to listen to you begging for a clean-up. I get it. I get that you've taken this one personal. I will do what I can, George, just like I always do when you ask me to.'

'I know you will. Sorry, Emily, I didn't mean to rub your nose in it. I just know that when you put your effort into something you always get a result. I need a result.'

'What did you just get told about flattery?'

'A lie, Emily. I just got told a big, fat lie.'

Emily grinned. George was relieved. She had seen straight through him, just like she always did. But she was still on board and that would bring results.

Chapter 13

George didn't sleep well. A few years before he had been stood too close to an explosion and suffered damage to his ears that he'd been told might be permanent. That damage currently took the form of a constant whooshing in his ears — or tinnitus, to give it its medical name. This wasn't the only hindrance to a good night's sleep. The last few years of worrying and wondering about his wife and child had added to his difficulties. Now he was quite accepting of his condition. It was amazing how you could adapt when you needed to. George had once been someone desperately in need of his eight hours' sleep and now he seemed to manage well enough on just a couple per night.

He was awake when his phone went off. It was plugged into its charging cable on the kitchen side. George didn't always make it to bed; often he would fall asleep in front of whatever was on television. The noise of inane chatter or mocked up explosions was far more relaxing than the whooshing and whirring of his tinnitus. He was still lying out on the sofa. It was just a few minutes after dawn and he was considering how long he should wait before having his first cup of tea of the day.

He moved quickly across the room to his phone. The screen said RYKER and he frowned.

'What the hell are you doing up at this time of day?' he said.

'Who said I was up?' Emily sounded tired. Her voice was lower than normal and her words were breathy.

'I guessed you would have to be up to call me. I can't imagine you would have anything new to tell me from your bed.'

'That's how good I am, see? I put the word out about your farm shooting like I said I would. I got woken up by a text from one of the source handlers. They've been offered some information. And if I'm awake because of you then I'm definitely waking you up.'

George snatched the phone away from the wire. He walked over to the large window at the far side of the lounge. It looked out over the English Channel. The sea was calm and blue and the sky matched it. 'What information?'

'That was all the message said—'

'You didn't call me at 5 a.m. to tell me someone had sent you a text message, Ryker—'

'If you'll let me finish! I don't function too well this time of the morning, George. I called him back.'

'Who? The source handler?'

'Yes, the source handler. I called him back and he apologised for waking me up, but he had just got off the phone from one of his sources. He was asking to meet. The handler asked what it was all about and he gave him enough to know that it was about the farm shooting.'

'What did he give?' George bit down on his lip; he was struggling to stop himself from jumping in.

'Jesus, George! Give me a chance. He said he knew about a crew. They go out and do rural breaks. They've been working in Sussex mainly, but he reckons they crossed the border to do your job. They target wealthy people who live out in isolated areas.'

'That would fit.'

'It would. The source reckons there's a bit more to it than chance. He said something about one of the crew working off a debt — maybe he was borrowing against their takings. Whatever the reason, he chose the venue and he promised them they would get their money back and then some.'

'From Stan Wingmore?'

'From that house, yeah.'

'So what, this crew member knows there's money there?'

'That's what it sounds like.'

'Your source handler, is he going out to get more information?'

'Yeah. But George — you're not going to like it — they're all out meeting their regulars over the next two or three days over this other job. He's arranged to talk to him by the end of the week. He's hoping to set something up by Friday. In Dover somewhere. He said he would give me an update as soon as there is one, but—'

'Friday's no good, Emily! He needs to speak to him before then — like, today!'

'I knew you'd say that. I said the same. He said there was no way that was going to happen. They've got direction from up on high. There's a lot of pressure to clean this other mess up, George. The media don't even know about Stanley Wingmore's night.'

'You know I can't accept that.'

'I knew you wouldn't want to.'

'Can you go back to him?'

'And say what?'

'I'll speak to Whittaker, get him to put his weight about. He can clear the way for the handler to go and meet him today.'

'I don't know if that will do any good. I think Whittaker might even prefer him to be trying to get results for the Dover shooting. No one's under more pressure than he is around that.'

'Who was it, Ryker?'

'Who was what?'

'The handler you spoke to?'

'You know I can't tell you that, George. I did you a favour going to them in the first place — it was all off the record.'

'And he told you off the record, but why would he do that? He would know that you would go to the investigator with the information, otherwise what is the point of it? I just want to know who it is so I can sound it out with them. Make sure there isn't anything more that he missed out.'

'Give me some credit, George.'

'I'm not mugging you off, Ryker. I know you don't miss a trick. But that's my excuse to call him.'

'I can't do any more, George, I've already done too much.'

'I know where they're based, Ryker. I'll go over there and ask everyone if they spoke to you.'

'You can't do that! Why are you being an arsehole? I'm trying to help you out. He shouldn't be calling me direct with that information — it all needs to go through a controller. You'll get him into all sorts of trouble.'

'He might get booted off the team, Ryker. I don't want to do that, I don't want him in trouble and I definitely don't want to be stitching you up. But he knows something, or at least he knows *someone* who might be able to get me a little closer to these bastards. It's even more important now — if these people are out of the county, they'll disappear. You know I'm right. Just tell me who you spoke to. I'll go to him direct. I'll be subtle and I'll ask him to help me. I'll tell him that I ordered you to tell me his details.'

'You're an arsehole, George.' The phone fell silent.

'Ryker? RYKER? Dammit!' George threw the phone over onto his sofa. He turned back to the view. His mind rushed through all the options. He didn't have many. The source handling team were a closed bunch with a very clear structure for gaining information and feeding it back up the line, just a few officers and a sergeant covering the whole of the south side of the division. Their roles were to effectively form relationships with CHIS — Covert Human Intelligence Sources. More often than not, these were petty criminals, drug addicts or low-level gang members who were willing to meet with undercover officers and trade information. Their reward varied from having their gas bill paid to a free McDonalds or cash in their pocket. It was controversial, but effective. Such was the risk to the sources that every interaction had a strict set of rules. Just as strict were the rules around how the information gleaned was recorded and passed on. To step outside of protocol was to risk everything — it was the same for any of the officers. George was trying to think of a way he could use that to his advantage. Turning up and applying some pressure wouldn't work; they would shut up shop and he would never get what he needed. But he couldn't just do nothing, just accept that there was a way of getting closer to this gang but that it would have to wait until the end of the week. George was back to peering out at the sea when his phone pinged. He walked over to it. It was a text message from Emily: *Andy McGuiness.*

George punched the air. He knew McGuiness. He hadn't known he was a source handler. He had been a response copper when George had been a sergeant running a team of detectives investigating burglaries. He had been good, too — pro-active. He liked to get in the faces of the bad guys. George's kind of copper.

His phone beeped again from Emily. It was a row of digits — a mobile phone number. George was in cotton trousers and an old jumper. He needed a shower and then he would make the call from the car. He didn't know where he was going to be going but he was determined it would be somewhere. He threw the phone back onto the sofa. He was nearly to the bathroom when it pinged again and he had to double back. Another message from Emily: *Arsehole.*

George smirked. He couldn't disagree.

Chapter 14

Jenny woke in panic. She had been dreaming and it had been vivid. Joseph had their daughter. He was saying that they needed to go, and that they needed to go now. He'd said they couldn't take Isobel with them. Jenny had been frantic. She was trying to get Isobel off Joseph and then, suddenly, she was leaving and Isobel was sat up in bed crying hard, her arms jutting forward — crying for her mother. Jenny was still panicked and stricken as she jolted awake, and it took her some time to calm down enough to recognise where she was: a wood cabin, bright with light, the air thick with a scented layer of smoke. It all came rushing back. She felt cold, so cold. She swung her legs around so that the wood burner was almost between them. The cast iron was still warm to the touch, but the heat was nothing like it had been. She opened the door, it was heavy and it creaked. The stove bottom had a layer of white embers, some two inches deep, that still glowed red in its centre when she prodded it with some kindling. Sure enough, the small pieces of fresh wood caught straight away. She stacked it up with bigger pieces on top and finally a couple of logs. Within a couple of minutes it was roaring again.

There was water for the kettle in a clear bottle on the floor and just enough milk in the flask for a cup of tea. She needed one. She also needed to pee. She left the kettle warming on top of the wood burner. Outside, she could see a patch of frost sparkling in the sunlight that arrowed through the trees. The sky was perfectly clear, the rain clouds completely gone, and there was a freshness that only came first thing in the morning. She'd meant to sleep only for a few hours and then head out when darkness fell. Instead, she had slept all night. She knew she had been exhausted, how she had yearned to sleep a full night in the last few months, but she'd never considered that a put-up camp bed in a wooden hut would provide her next opportunity to do so. Jenny walked over to the trees to pee. Nobody was about. The sun was low and, from her recent nights with Isobel and having seen the sun rise the previous morning, she reckoned it had to be around 5 a.m.

She pulled up her trousers and stepped back out. The silence was beautiful. Her elevated position was crisp and clear, but a thin mist hugged the ground further down the hill towards the town like it was trying to hide it. Jenny could almost pretend it wasn't there. She didn't mind that she had missed the darkness. She suddenly felt better. Safer. Maybe it was the decent night's sleep or the bright sunshine and the stillness, with gentle birdsong the only sound. She walked back into the cabin just as the kettle began to whistle. She poured out her tea. While she waited for it to cool, she tidied the camp bed away and anything else that was out of place. She pulled out some of the smaller kindling twigs and arranged them on the floor. She swigged at her tea and surveyed her work. The sticks read: *THANKS*. It was simple but it did the trick. Mike the paramedic had spent his life helping people; old habits died hard, it seemed. He would never know just how much he'd helped her.

Jenny finished her tea. The mist was clearing a little, the sun burning it away as it got stronger. The town of Dover was revealed slowly. It was still early, but the traffic was moving and Jenny knew the risks of heading back down there. She had just one place to go and then she would leave. And she didn't intend on ever going back.

She took a more direct route back to the town. The road and the wooded path that she had come up was on her right. She hugged the tree line that ran down the left side of the cemetery for as far as she could, but then had to break away and walk back to the centre of the lawn so she could make for the gate at the bottom. The mist was all around her now. It was thinning out all the time but it was noticeably cooler. She pulled the sleeves on her top over her hands.

Jenny made it back to the wide road. It had been choked with traffic when she had made her way up in the middle of the afternoon. Now a solitary car passed. She crossed and turned left, away from the police station. She walked past a doctor's surgery on the right and then up a street that took her towards the town centre. She could see a large park on her left side as she walked. Already a couple of drinkers were sitting out in the early sunshine. They rested on some steps up to a platform that seemed to mark the centre of the park. One of them gestured at her with his bottle. Jenny was horrified to think that they might have looked at the state of her and assumed instantly she was in the same situation as them. To the seasoned, homeless drunk, she must look like another seasoned, homeless drunk. Jenny picked up her pace.

She walked across the High Street and kept going. She turned right at a large roundabout past a café with delicious breakfast smells blanketing the pavement. She continued past and rounded a corner to find herself back on Dover Road. The traffic was still light. The confidence and self-assurance of early morning that had come with the warm sun on the calm hills was starting to evaporate like the early morning mist. Jenny continued along the road, across the forecourt of a petrol station and towards the train station. She knew she was coming to her hotel. She knew she had to go back in there. She knew there could be people waiting for her.

She stayed on the opposite pavement to the hotel. Her head was up; she was looking for any movement, checking every parked car for seated occupants, every window of every shop, house and flat. Trying to be careful. If the people that were after her — who'd come after Joseph — if they had known about that place, then why hadn't they come to the room? When they'd all been asleep, maybe? Jenny was still trying to piece together the events of the previous forty-eight hours, but she was sure of one thing: nobody had tried to hurt them until they'd left the hotel. The more she'd thought about it over the last couple of days, the more she'd convinced herself that they'd been watching the car. That was the first sign of trouble: when Joseph had moved it. Whoever it was knew about the car; they didn't know about the room. That meant she had a chance at least. The room was booked out until the end of the week. That gave her another night and a day. She didn't intend on staying there, it was too close to where it had all begun, but she needed her phone. It had all her contacts, people who could help, who could finally take her and Isobel away from here. And she might find some answers. Joseph's stuff was still in there, too — including the things she had never been able to look at before and that had never been any of her business. The bits that when she had asked Joseph about them had always invoked the same reply: *You trust me, Jenny, right? It's best that you don't know. You just have to trust me.*

Well, now there was nothing left to trust in.

The Dovorian Hotel was opposite her. She ducked into the frontage of a large townhouse and peered out. There was nobody on foot, no cars at that point and all the curtains on the hotel looked closed. It was deceiving from the outside: a square of dull grey with bits cut out for windows and with no redeeming features, made all the more drab by the layer of grime from the typically busy road in front. But Jenny had liked it inside: it was neutrally decorated but colourful; the rooms were spacious, the beds huge and comfortable. She could see the window to her room from where she stood. The blackout curtains were drawn across. She couldn't remember if she or Joseph had opened them, or if he had just turned on the light. She couldn't be sure. It didn't matter. She was going to have to go in anyway. What else could she do?

She stepped back out onto the pavement and moved further up the road, past the steps that led down to the train station; far enough until she felt she could cross without anyone from any of the other hotel windows being able to see her. She reached the other pavement and turned back on herself. She brought her chin down onto her chest, her eyes lifting so that she was still looking forward, out from under the curve of her hood. She had to cross a junction; a road rose steeply up to her right, past the side of the hotel and beyond. The side entrance to the hotel was halfway up. She pushed the door open. A long carpeted hall with a repeating pattern was laid out in front of her. She strode along it. The lifts were right next to reception. It was manned twenty-four-seven but there was a back office. Whoever was working that morning had to be in there. The desk was empty. Jenny was glad, she pressed the button to call the lift and the doors parted immediately. The three back walls were mirrored. She selected the third floor. The door shut and she took a moment to take in her reflection. Suddenly it made sense that she might be beckoned over by street bums. She turned away from herself in disgust. The doors parted. She stood still for a second or two, trying to use the two mirrored sidewalls to see out, to see if anyone was hiding just outside the doors. The angle was wrong; she had to step out.

The hallway was empty. She turned right. She felt in her pocket for the key card, it was still there. She pushed it into the slot below the handle. She pulled it straight out. A light flashed green and it clicked. The door pushed away from her. She knew the room layout: there was a short hall; the bathroom was off to the left; the main room opened up beyond that, a large window on the far side, the wardrobe and TV units down the right side. The door opened enough that she could see the bathroom door. It was pulled closed. Again, she couldn't remember if she had done that or if it had been like that when she left. She stepped over the threshold and pushed the door a little more. She could see a pair of Joseph's shoes left untidily in the middle of the floor. She remembered vaguely that he had been fiddling with them, as if considering changing the ones he had on. The blackout blinds were pulled right across and the room was dark. She could see more shapes and bundles littering the floor. As she pushed the door completely open she could see through to the big bed — it had been made. There was a fresh set of towels on the end of it. The maids had been in and had done their bit. They'd left assuming the occupants were out. Jenny's confidence was back. No one knew she was here. Not the police; not the people who were after her. No one.

The door pushed itself shut behind her. She moved through to the body of the room, reached for the curtains and pulled them apart. Light flooded in.

'Get on your fucking knees!'

Jenny spun like she had been stung. A dark clad figure leant on the TV unit. Even the balaclava covering his face was a thick black material. Jenny attempted to speak but all that came from her was a rushed whimper.

'I said, get on your fucking *knees*.' The voice was a suppressed growl, full of strength and menace.

Jenny dropped to her knees. She raised her arms, pushing her palms out towards the figure, fighting with herself to speak.

'Put your hands on your head. And face away.'

Jenny took a few moments. The instructions weren't sinking in straight away. She turned round and dropped to her knees. She faced the window. The sunlight was strong in her face. 'Put your hands on your head.' She could feel her own pulse pounding in her ears. She lifted her hands to the back of her head. She heard the man step closer and felt something solid on the back of her head, pushing firmly enough to nudge her head forward.

'Please . . .' she managed. There was so much more she wanted to say: how unfair this was; how she knew nothing at all about how she had got there; about how she had a daughter that she wanted to hold tight. Oh God, Isobel! What she wouldn't do to hold her just one more time.

'Please . . .' she uttered again. Her chest was so tight that she struggled to take a breath. The object was pushed firmer into the back of her head. She knew it was the barrel of a gun. She hadn't seen it; she had been too busy staring at the dark eyes peering out from the balaclava. But she knew.

'Begging isn't going to be enough, Jenny.' His voice was closer to her ear. His mouth was so close she felt her hair move as he spoke. She screwed her eyes tightly shut and held in her breath. This was it. This was how it ended. She didn't think it would hurt, she felt almost thankful for that.

'Are you ready to die?' The voice was a little further away; the barrel was now pressed hard enough to hurt. She rocked forward on her knees. He kept the pressure on her head. She felt a warmth and a dampness between her legs.

'You remember how scared you feel. You remember that, you understand?' The voice was back in her ear. She heard footfalls, they were moving away. She heard something bump against the wooden unit. She still leant forward, her eyes clamped shut. She didn't know what was going on, she didn't want to antagonise him.

'You can get up.'

The same man's voice. He was much further away. Jenny dared to open her eyes. She stared down at the carpet and moved her head slightly to one side. She couldn't see the man, couldn't see anyone. She took in a rushed breath where it had been held for so long. 'Why?' It was all she could manage.

'Why aren't you dead?' The man called out. 'Because I don't want you dead. You remember that. You do as you're told and that might not change. Step out of line and I won't hesitate. Do you understand?'

'Yes.' She sobbed the word, her body slumped forward as the tension ran out of her.

'Now, get up.'

Jenny took her hands off her head. She put a palm flat on the ground and shifted her weight to stand. Her legs were numb and shaky, and she struggled to get to her feet, but then she stood straight, still facing away from where the man was.

'You can turn around.'

She turned slowly. The man sat back on the television unit. His hands were in his lap, his right hand held an evil-looking black pistol pointing casually towards the floor. He swung his legs like a sixth former in a common room. He'd taken his face covering off. She immediately snatched her head away.

'I don't want to! I don't want to know who you are. I don't care.'

'Too late for that, Jenny. Now you've seen me.'

'I haven't — I mean, I didn't.'

'Come on, Jenny. Let's not be silly. I need to know that you understand your position. I know you've had a rough couple of days. That wasn't supposed to happen. You were supposed to be dead a long time ago. But you're not. Unfortunately your death was in the hands of a bunch of amateurs who somehow thought real life should be more like a spaghetti western. You can't roll up into a town and start shooting off guns — or, if you do, you need to make it count quickly and you need to get out. And yet, here you are.'

'So you're here to do it?'

'I was. Plans change. Seems you've had yet another escape, Jenny. Seems you have another job besides dying.'

'What? What could you possibly need from me?'

'I don't know too much, Jenny. I get paid to kill people. Taking people is not really my thing.'

'So you're kidnapping me?'

'No. But you are coming with me and if you don't then I will kill you. If you make a noise or a scene, I will kill you. If you try to escape from me, I will kill you. If you make me run, I will kill you twice. But you can change out of those wet trousers, use your shower, take what you want of your things. I assume that's why you came back?'

Jenny shrugged.

'You came back for something.'

'I had nowhere else to go.'

'I'm very good at working out when people are lying, Jenny — no, that's not right . . . I'm very good at *making* people *bad* at lying. I think it's the gun, Jenny. What do you think? Do you think you could lie to this?' He lifted the gun, pointed it directly down her line of sight. She stared back. The eyes beyond were cold.

'No.' She was aware she sounded weak. She didn't care.

'Get your shit together. You can shower and change. I don't want to take you out like that. You'll draw too much attention. You don't have long.'

The man lowered the gun. Jenny found she could breathe again. He moved to the bed and picked up the television remote. The television switched on. He suddenly turned to look at her.

'Tick-tock,' he said.

Chapter 15

'Andy, thanks for coming out,' George said.

'I don't recall you giving me much of a choice, George.' Andy McGuiness looked slimmer than George remembered. Slim enough to verge on unwell perhaps. His face was gaunt, his cheeks more sucked in, tighter against his cheekbones. He had bags under his eyes — eyes that looked red and tired.

'There's always a choice, Andy.'

'I'll definitely be remembering that the next time Emily Ryker phones me up and asks me to do her a favour.'

'Ryker? She's one of the best, Andy. If this force was full of Rykers I reckon the criminals would all up and leave.'

'I get a source compromised — or worse — killed, George, and all our snouts will get up and leave. You have any idea how damaging that might be?' Andy's voice was a whisper but it was forceful and it carried genuine anger. He leaned back suddenly as someone walked past their table. It was a short man with slick, dark hair. He was gliding a mop over the tiled floor and he greeted both men with a smile and a 'good morning' in a heavy Eastern European accent.

George had called Andy and asked to meet him. He had given him a choice: meet him at a motorway services on the outskirts of Canterbury or George's next call would be to Andy's sergeant, when he would request the information he needed via formal channels. The sergeant would know that Andy was giving out information against their strict protocols and he would immediately lose his place on the team — maybe worse. It wasn't much of a choice, if George was honest, and Andy was right too: ultimately the protocols were in place to stop people getting killed.

George had ordered them both a strong coffee. They sat at a table that was far enough from the counter. The rest were empty. There was a trickle of foot traffic already, but they were generally tradesmen joining the queue for McDonalds. All of them had their heads down, as was to be expected at 6 a.m. The cheerful man with the mop had moved far enough away.

'The only dead person I'm concerned about is some pensioner lying in her own kitchen who answered her door to help somebody and got a shotgun emptied into her stomach for her trouble. I want the bastards that did that, Andy. I want them bad enough to fall out with Emily Ryker and to fall out with you too. But I don't need to. I came here to explain why you *should* help. This is why you're in the source unit. You and I both know there are plenty of serious crimes out there — murders, rapes, robberies — that would go nowhere if it weren't for you and your team. This is your opportunity to be the key part in putting another job to bed. I've been up and met the husband, Andy. Let me tell you, mate . . . this fella deserves us to bend a few rules.'

Andy was already shaking his head. 'I joined this unit because the hours are eight to four, Monday to Friday. Most weeks, at least. I joined this unit because I got serious health problems — serious enough that I couldn't be doing the shift work no more. I couldn't be out rolling around on the floor outside the nightclubs at 1 a.m. This job is perfect for me. I've really picked up. And I still get to do the job . . . I still get to work. I can't lose my place on this team, George. Please don't be a part of that.'

'Andy, I need your help. Just a few words. I'm sensible, one thing I do know is how to keep people out of trouble—'

'With respect, George, your reputation says different.'

George laughed; he couldn't help it. 'Yeah, I suppose it might. So you're just going to have to trust me on face value, Andy, and hope I don't fuck it up.'

'What do you need?'

'The name of your source — so I can go and talk to him.'

'No chance! I can't be telling you who we're talking to. You know that just as well as I do. And don't think rank plays any part either. I've seen higher-ranking officers than you get smacked down trying to circumnavigate our processes. It doesn't happen.'

'I'm not here to pull rank, Andy. I know how far that would get me. Just hear me out. You can't go and talk to this bloke because they want you focussed on this other job. So you give me the name and I go and talk to him. But, where you can just call him up and arrange a meet, I need to be a bit more creative. I'll bump him on the street, get him to talk to me about what he knows without him knowing that I've spoken to you.'

'How are you going to do that?'

George didn't know. He hadn't thought that bit through yet. 'It depends on who our friend is, Andy. There's always an in. You can tell me a bit about him and we can come up with an idea from there.'

Andy was back to shaking his head. 'It won't work, George. There's no way. What are you suggesting? You start a casual conversation on the street and then suddenly ask if he knows anything about some shooting in the arse-end of nowhere that no one else knows a thing about? He'd see through that in a heartbeat.'

George stroked his chin. 'It will be tricky, Andy, I agree. But you have to trust that I can do it. I know you can't visit him, because you're tasked elsewhere and you couldn't justify being out talking with him rather than where you should be. You could pick up the phone and ask him direct. That wouldn't look out of place coming from you, would it?'

'I told you . . . I can't do that. There's risks with asking too much over the phone. You never know who's in the background, who he's with or even if the voice is your source. We don't conduct our business over the phone.'

'You're right. So all that's left is for me to bump him in the street. Tell me his name and we can talk about a plan.'

'I know what you're doing, George. You're backing me into a corner. You think I'll decide the only option is for me to visit him. I can't do that.'

George took a few seconds to swig at his coffee. It was strong and bitter. 'That is the only option though, right? I mean, when you think about it?'

'Fuck's sake, George! Look, I'll see what I can do, okay? I've got your number now. I'll let you know if I can get the time to call on him later.'

'Now.' George said. He gestured at Andy's phone that was laid out on the table.

'What do you mean now? It's six in the morning!'

'And you got a call at what? Half four? My guess is this guy's a crackhead, or hard on the heroin for sure. So he wakes up with the sun in some hovel and he's clucking for his score. He's had your call and he knows a bit. Just enough that you might give him the twenty quid he needs for his hit. We both know he's up now, probably waiting for a shop to open so he can go out with his foil-lined bag and start grafting for the day. Call him now.'

'And offer him what? These people want their payment. Especially if he's who you just described. He won't give me anything unless I'm sat opposite with a wallet.'

'I'll drop the money in.'

'This again! I told you, he can't know I've spoken to anyone else! If he knows I'm telling people he's a grass, even other coppers, he'll walk. He gives good information. We've had results off the back of his intel. And if I lose him it's a butterfly effect, he's got at least two people linked to him who are in the same business, George, and who knows who else. Suddenly we lose a lot of snouts that are doing good work. They're gonna know it started with me — the other handlers, I mean — and I'm back on nights. Or worse, I'm out of a job.'

'Think, Andy! I don't have to meet with someone to give them money. Be creative. I just need a door number and an envelope, right?'

Andy downed his coffee. His face creased like he hadn't exactly enjoyed the taste. 'I don't appreciate being put in this position, George. I don't appreciate it at all.'

'I don't appreciate promising an elderly man that I will find the bastards who ended his sixty-two-year marriage by pulling a trigger, who sucked every ounce of joy out of his life in that one action, and then having to go back to him and tell him that I wasn't able to do it because one of the other lads in the force is shit scared of having to buy a torch. I know you, Andy, I know you well enough to remember what you were like when you were uniform. You were my sort of bloke, a thief-taker. You hate these bastards just as much as I do. You might have forgotten it but, I promise, a minute with what's left of Stanley Wingmore and it will all come rushing back. I've got to speak to Stan later today. I want to tell him that we've got some idea, because right now I've got none — none at all.

Get on the phone to your snout. I need to know what he knows about who did this. I'll be clever with the information. I'm getting good at making it look like I've stumbled over something I knew was there. You have to trust me, Andy.'

'You're still not giving me much of a choice, are you?'

George did nothing to hide his frustration, it came out in a sort of growl. 'Fine! You want a choice, Andy? I'll give you a choice. I will walk out of here and I will crack on with my investigation as best I can. While the rest of the county's resources are out looking for a gang who shot up a car in Dover, I will do what I can to find the people who went to Stan's house and left his kitchen covered in his wife's blood. I will look Stan in the eye and I will tell him that I'm doing all I can. And I will not make any trouble for you with your sergeant, with your team. No one will know that you offered some information to Emily outside of your processes. So that's your first option. Your second option is that you make a phone call to your source. You find out what he knows by asking all the questions that you were saving for your face-to-face in a few days' time. Then you call me. You give me an update and you tell me his address. I'll drop off his payment — whatever you agree. I'll handle that so it's off the books. The choice is yours, Andy.'

George stood up. He dropped a fiver on the table. Andy had been staring at his phone, as if hoping it might provide inspiration. He looked up at George. 'I'm not being difficult, you know. I want to help.'

'I believe that, Andy. I know you're one of the good ones. And you *can* help. Right now, you're all I've got. You have my number.'

George made his way to the exit. He started his car and moved away. He turned off the main road into a housing estate as soon as he could and parked up. He didn't want to risk Andy driving past him. He looked at the clock on the dash. The time was 06:40 hours. He would give it until 07:00. If he hadn't heard anything by then he would have to start moving towards the police office where he knew the source team was based. He knew they started at 8 a.m. but that the sergeant was often there at least half an hour earlier. George could be there at the same time. He was going to threaten him the same way as he had hinted with Andy: that his whole team would be exposed if he didn't allow Andy to make that visit. If all went well he would be away before the team arrived and the job could still be done under the radar. Who was he kidding? Once he entered that building, none of it would be under the radar — that much was for certain.

George peered out of the window. The distant *thump* of a car door drew his attention. A man in a suit got into a saloon car over the road. Starting his daily commute, George thought. His phone pinged with a message. It was surely too soon to be from Andy. It was from Paul Bearn. *I've picked up the daughter from the airport. We're not far from the address. She's keen to talk to you. Call me when you're up. Sorry if this woke you!*

George went to staring back out of the window as the car with the suit moved off. 'Woke me!' George scoffed. It was good news though. Paul had done some sound work tracking down the daughter, who lived in Italy with her husband. She'd dropped everything to come home. If the daughter was sensible she could be a good conduit; they could start getting things done. George would try and get to see her this morning. This afternoon was his daughter's birthday and nothing was important enough to get in the way of that.

Three minutes to seven and George's phone rang. George recognised the code — it was local.

'Hello.'

'George.'

'Andy? Thanks for calling.'

'Don't be too quick to thank me.'

George grimaced. The call came through the speakers on George's phone. He moved his hand to the car keys that hung from the ignition. 'Okay, then. Andy, what are you thinking?'

'We've got taskings on our email already. I've just checked on my secure phone. They've got us out on meetings from the off — they're all for this other job. I can't get to talk to your man.'

'That's disappointing, Andy.'

'I know, I guessed as much. Look, George, you said you could bump this bloke, make it so he had no idea you had spoken to me. I don't know how that'd play out, I don't see a way of doing it if I'm honest. I could trust you with it, but this is my job — my life, George. I mean, shit, you've got me pulling over at a roadside and using a phone box!'

'I didn't even know they still did phone boxes, Andy.' George fired up the car. Andy wouldn't help him; he would head to Andy's office himself and drop in on his sergeant. He had no choice. No other options. Andy would never forgive him, of course. George would have time to be sorry for that later.

'Me neither. I know I'm letting you down, but you have to understand that we protect our sources above all else. It's an absolute basic.'

George shuffled forward in his car seat, struck by a sudden revelation. 'So, you stopped to call me from a phone box to tell me you can't help, is that right?'

'That's right, George. I stopped to tell you that I can't tell you about Nicholas Yarney. I can't go and speak to him on your behalf and I certainly can't tell you who he is, so you can talk to him yourself. And like I say, the reason for that is because he *cannot* know that I have spoken to anyone about him. Sorry, George. If I can help in the future, you know I will.'

The line went dead. George beamed at the car's display as it confirmed the call had ended. 'Bless you,

Andy.' He dialled out immediately and the car's speakers made a ringing sound.

'What the hell do you want now?'

'At 5 a.m. you had the right to be grumpy, Ryker. What's your excuse now?'

'I just know that you're about to ask me something that will either get me sacked, my card marked or my fingers burnt. Out with it, George Elms.'

George could still feel himself grinning. 'You know me so well, Ryker. What do you know about Nicholas Yarney?'

'Where did that name come from?'

'Do you know it?'

'Is that what you bullied out of our source handler?'

'Not at all, Ryker. I've never heard it before. Just call it a hunch. Us coppers are famous for them, right?'

'You have a hunch about someone you've never heard of?'

'Some of us are that good. Now, are you going to help me or not?'

'It's 7 a.m., George. I'm not due in for another hour. I'll find out what I can when I get there. Do you know anything more about him?'

'You said Andy was originally planning on meeting with him in Dover. I guess that means he's local to there.'

'So it is a name you've bullied. I'll see what I can find out. You be careful round him though, George. You know all about source information, right?'

'Of course. In an hour?' George pushed.

'Yes, George. In an hour.'

'Only I'm sat in a car that's ticking over. I need to catch him going out or coming in. I need it to look like I was just casually asking about something he might know something about.'

'Really? How the hell are you going to make that believable?'

'That's similar to what Andy said. He trusts me, though.'

'Did you give him a choice?'

'There's always a choice.'

'Then he's a fool.'

'Thanks for the support. Can you get in any earlier? I know you could, Ryker, if you wanted to.'

'There are a lot of things I could do if I wanted to, George. I'm pretty much on my way. You're lucky. Seeing as how I got woken up at fuck-o'clock in the morning to take a call for you, then you made me so angry I couldn't get back to sleep. I'm up and sorted early. I don't owe you any favours, though, George, I genuinely have no idea why I am helping you.'

'Don't think of it as helping me, Ryker. Think of that poor fella up at that farmhouse. You can still pretend you're not helping out an arsehole.'

'I really don't like your tactics sometimes, George. You get what you want and to hell with everyone else. You need to be aware of that, of how it comes across to people around you. People who care about you.'

'I get that. I'm sorry, Ryker. You know I care about you, too. I don't want to upset you. Not ever. But it's only ever for the right reasons. Our friend Stan quite literally needs putting back together. We're all a part of that now.'

'Don't I know it. I should have something in twenty minutes.'

'I love you, Emily Ryker.'

'It'll be thirty minutes then.'

George moved off. He hadn't finished his coffee at the services. He moved towards where he knew there was a place nearby. He could get a coffee and maybe a hot roll. He had no idea how long he might need to sit waiting on Nicholas Yarney. George also needed to think of some sort of plan — a pretext for speaking to Yarney so that he'd have no idea that Andy had named him as a grass. And bearing in mind that he'd last offered information just a few hours before, Andy had been right to be wary: George wasn't sure that it was going to be possible at all.

Chapter 16

Stanley Wingmore walked towards his house. The drive needed a little TLC. It was mostly compressed shingle and gravel but it was starting to show up a little bare in places. There were some parts that needed repairs, some dips and holes that collected water whenever it rained. They were on his list for jobs in the spring. Janice had nagged him every time they drove on it. He carried a coffee in a thermal travel mug. It was borrowed from where he had stayed the night with his closest neighbour, who had moved in around twenty years before. Since then, they'd become good friends, despite the fact that they were still a fair distance away. Stanley had always liked the fact that no matter where he stood in his house, he couldn't see any another buildings. Sometimes, on those rare occasions when his own family members were out, it could be nice to pretend that he was the only man left in the world.

This morning was one of those times. Unfortunately this daydream was quickly ruined as he rounded the natural curve in his drive to be met with a marked patrol car parked across it. There was blue and white tape, too, that stated: POLICE DO NOT CROSS. It wrapped around the wing mirror of the car then ran out until it was tied off on his fence. The car was covered with a layer of moisture as if it had been there all night. The driver's door pushed open. An officer stood up and pulled his black jacket tighter. He was bleary-eyed and offered a weak smile. He fixed his hat. He looked like he had been there all night too.

'Good morning, Mr Wingmore. Early start today, sir?'

'I couldn't sleep.' Stan stood still while the officer wrote his details in a white book. He checked his watch; it was just before seven.

'I'm sure you couldn't. We are expecting the CSI officer back this morning, sir. She'll be here around eight. I'm supposed to accompany you unt—'

'There's no need for that, son. I came to be in the barn. I have a kitchen in there at least. I wanted to be nearer to home. It makes me feel closer to my wife. I'm sure you understand, son. The nice CSI lady, she said she didn't have a problem with me being in there.' He let his eyes drop to the ground. He could see the officer shuffling from one foot to another.

'Of course. But I'll come find you around quarter to eight if that's okay. If CSI get here and I'm still sat in the car I might get myself in trouble. Does that sound reasonable?'

'Sounds reasonable to me, son. I will behave. I promise.'

The officer chuckled. 'This whole conversation feels ridiculous! I really don't like telling you where to go on your own land, sir. We just don't want anything lost down there that might help us find who did this.'

'I know that. I've been told that a lot. I'll see you in a little while. I can offer you a cup of tea when you come down. You look like you could do with one.'

'I look forward to that!' the officer called after him.

Stan carried on walking towards the house following the track left to his nearest barn and a side entrance to the estate that led off to a country lane. The cowards had driven away down there that night. Another marked car was parked straight ahead in the gravel clearing in front of his home. It, too, had a layer of moisture and he guessed there would be another officer inside. He could see the side of his house, but from a short distance.

The barn was another on his list of repair jobs. It had once been the hub of a working farm, sheltering livestock, young and old. It had been a grain store, a garage for farm machinery and, more recently, a tack store when the stable block had been rented out. When his wife had insisted on changing the kitchen units in the house, he had recycled them and put them in here. It had been an easy fit; the units ran down the right side of the barn as he walked in. The kitchen area was separated from the rest of the building by a plywood wall. There was still some hay stored at the back; it was bundled up and starting to rot. Next to it were three bundles of wire that he used to make fences. He let other farmers use the barn for storage now and there were two modern-looking tractors that didn't belong to him backed against the far wall. In the top left corner was Stan's first ever tractor, the one he could never scrap despite its decrepit state and leaking pipes. It had been all he had used when he first started out in farming. He'd built his whole world around it. Now it was broken down in the corner, looking small, vulnerable and out of place against its modern counterparts. Stan suddenly felt as if he and his tractor had a lot in common.

He moved to the right side of the barn, through the door and into the kitchen. He abandoned his flask and filled the kettle. The plumbing was noisy. It thumped into action and knocked continuously as the water flowed. He had been here late last night to put some milk in the fridge. Some food too. He hadn't touched it then and he didn't feel like touching it now. He opted to remove the milk only. He put it on the side while the kettle boiled. At the same time as he'd installed the kitchen, he'd also fitted some cheap, wooden framed windows. He pushed one of them open, upsetting a spider that shook frenetically in its web. He could see across to the marked police car, to the police tape that circled his home and to the side door where his wife had been removed in a black body bag. He turned away. The kettle clicked off but he stepped out of the kitchen and made his way across the barn. The aged suspension of his old tractor creaked and hissed as he stepped up into the cracked seat. He rested his hands on the oversized steering wheel. The rock-solid seat, the spindly steering wheel in his grasp, the smell of hay, mud and dust . . . he was transported back fifty years to a time when he was young and strong, with his whole life in front of him and his wife beside him.

For just a second he closed his eyes and he wasn't a widowed old man in a big empty barn.

Chapter 17

Jenny pushed her face into the warm water and let it run over her skin, through her hair and down her body. Her eyes were shut and the sound of the rushing water blocked her hearing. In the all-encompassing warmth of the shower she could almost forget that she was being held captive by a man with a gun. He had insisted she kept the door open, but she had been able to pull the curtain across. The bathroom had been stripped bare of their belongings. Everything that had been in there had been grouped together and dumped under the desk in the bedroom. She guessed this was to stop her using anything against him, though she wasn't sure what she was supposed to do with a toothbrush or a bar of soap. Forming an escape plan was a long way from her mind. If this man was of the same mind-set as the people she had been running from in the course of the previous forty-eight hours, he would have killed her the second she stepped through that door. She couldn't say she wasn't scared — quite the opposite — but standing under the warm shower and with the option of putting her own clothes back on, she knew he wasn't going to hurt her. Not here anyway.

Jenny didn't know how long she had been under the shower when he called to say she'd had long enough. She stopped the taps and reached for the solitary small towel that hung on a lukewarm radiator. It wasn't going to cover much of her.

'Are there any more towels?' she called out. She stood still for the reply. Her hair and body still ran with water.

'No.'

'I need to dry my hair.'

'You understand this isn't a holiday, right? You need to get dry and you need to get dressed. You have a towel and some clothes.'

'Are you going to watch me?' she called through the shower curtain. The bathroom didn't have any windows; even in the daylight the overhead light was on. She heard someone step into the bathroom and wrapped the towel tightly around herself. She could see him as a shadow on the curtain.

'Do you want me to?'

'No,' she snapped.

'You need to speed up. We've already been here too long. We leave in ten minutes.'

'Can I use my hairdryer?'

'FUCK, JENNY!' The fury came from nowhere and filled the bathroom, startling her. 'I'm not taking the piss. Do not mistake me for someone with any patience at all. Now GET moving!'

The shadow moved away. Jenny snatched at the towel and rubbed her body. She couldn't reach the bundle of her clothes she had picked out. She leaned out, enough to be able to see through the open door. The man stared back at her. She moved back behind the curtain to fix the towel back over her body and stepped onto the damp floor.

'Can you at least turn away?'

'You do as I say. That's how this goes.'

'I have to get dressed with you watching me?'

'Eight minutes,' he said.

Jenny arranged the bundle of clothes so that her knickers were on top. Still clutching the towel to herself, she picked them up and stepped into them with one leg.

'With the towel off,' the man said.

Jenny stopped and removed the leg from her knickers. 'What do you mean?'

'You know what I mean, Jenny. You get dressed with the towel off.'

'I thought you were just here to take me with you? You're not supposed to be getting off on it.'

'I'm here to make sure you've got nothing on you that might cause me problems down the line. You either drop the towel and get dressed in front of me or I search you when you are dressed. And if you feel violated with me watching you, you should ponder my likely search methods.'

Jenny's latent anger flashed suddenly. 'You're a real piece of shit, you know that?'

'I can be. I promise you that, Jenny. Drop the towel.'

Jenny dropped the towel. She didn't put her knickers on straight away. She straightened up and stared at the man stood in the doorway.

'You happy now?'

'Get dressed. One item at a time. Don't rush. Pull the pockets out on your jeans when you put them on.'

'You enjoying this?'

'Not really. Naked women aren't my thing, actually. What really turns me on is extreme violence. Seven minutes.'

Chapter 18

George got back to the car with his food. A brown cardboard bag hung from his mouth, the coffee bubbled up through the lid as he concentrated on keeping it straight while he searched his pocket for the keys. He cursed through his teeth. Why was it always times like this when the phone rang? He balanced the cup on the roof of the car and grabbed his phone. It was Emily Ryker.

'Ryker?'

'I have some details. Not much, admittedly, but all I can get my hands on. Are you ready?'

'Yeah. Just give me a minute.' George found his keys. He tugged the door open and threw the phone on the passenger seat. He moved in his drink and started the car. The phone connected to the system and he could hear Emily humming impatiently down the phone.

'Sorry, Ryker, I'm getting there. Just let me get my book out.'

'What the hell are you up to? I thought you wanted this information, like, pronto.'

'I'm trying to do more than one thing at once here, Ryker. Just let me get a pen.'

'That's not generally an ability that you men are born with, is it?'

'It doesn't come natural, Ryker. We have to really work at it.' George was finally sorted. He flicked open his pocket book. 'What have you got?'

'There's not much. Nicholas Yarney is a bottom feeder, a class-A addict it would seem. His choice, if you're asking, is heroin. He seems to pop up on the fringes of the Dover scene a lot. He was staying in a sort of house-share situation and the house got raided a couple of times in a short space of time. He was there each time. I guess that makes sense — knowing he's a CHIS.'

'It would, yeah. He's been squealing on his mates. Where's he living?'

'Not there. He's moved out. He now has a place all to himself. I guess that might have been his reward for telling tales. He's in a basement flat. Number thirty-seven Larendon Place, Dover. I don't know it, but I've been on Google Maps and it would appear to make sense.'

George knew what Ryker meant by *appears to make sense*. She meant that, even as a 2D image on a computer screen, it still looked like a shit hole. 'So he's there alone?'

'The intelligence says that he lives there alone, but he has the typical lifestyle. Who knows who else will be crashed out there? You can almost always guarantee someone, right?'

'Yeah, it's a fair assumption.'

'I'll send you a picture over. It's his last custody photo. He's known to us for a bit of shoplifting, possession of class A and B — they were separate incidents. He's been nicked for supply, too, but it's never stuck. Apart from that, he's got some historic driving stuff. He's never had a licence but it appears that didn't stop him from driving when he was younger.'

'Any violence?'

'Nothing we know about. There are some intelligence reports from last summer that he was dealing for a

Liverpudlian gang in Dover and he was carrying a knife as part of that. He was never found in possession of one. From his picture, I'd say he looks like a soppy twat.'

'I'll be sure to mention it to him.'

'You're going to speak to him then?'

'Of course.' George looked longingly at his bag of delicious smelling food. He pulled the car out and headed towards the address. 'I need to know what he knows.'

'I still don't get how you reach that point without him immediately knowing that his handler has stitched him up. You're going to burn him forever.'

'I'll need to be creative, that much is true.'

'Creative? I think I remember the last time you talked about being creative. It involved a brick and a victim's window. Try to be a bit more subtle this time, George. You might not care if some of your colleagues continue to dislike you, but I don't have quite the same attitude to people's impressions of me. Or the same thickness of skin.'

'Oh, come on, Ryker! Since when have you cared what people think?'

'Since I realised I was staying in this half of the county. A lot of these people still don't know me. And a lot of them don't owe me anything. In the northern half everyone owes me something, that's the way I like it.'

'Understood. I owe you, Ryker. That much I do know.'

'Too right you do. Let me know how it goes.'

'You know I will.' George tapped the screen to end the call.

Larendon Place was in the centre of Dover, not far from the main train station. It was up a steep hill, so steep that he had to take it easy so the car didn't ground out. He pushed up the hill in first gear and rounded the second corner onto the target road. He looked at the door numbers; they were in the hundreds. His address was down the other end. His phone beeped. He guessed it would be Yarney's mugshot. There still weren't many people out and about on foot but he wanted to check the image straight away, just in case he walked past him. Heroin addicts were notoriously early risers. He picked up his phone. He had a text message from his wife on the screen. It said simply: *Are you awake? Can we talk?*

George pulled over into a gap between the lines of parked cars either side of the road. He typed out a reply. *Of course.*

The phone rang through the speakers almost immediately.

'Sarah,' George said. He tried to sound cheery.

'I should have known you would be awake. I don't even know why I asked.'

'I've been up for hours. I'm at work already, actually. We've got a lot going on.'

'So I've seen on the news. Are you working that awful shooting incident down in Dover?'

'It's one of those jobs, Sarah. Everyone's involved.'

'Are you going to be able to do this afternoon? I thought you had the day off today.'

'Yes. Don't you worry about that. I came in this morning to help out, but I've just got a few bits to do and then I'll be heading home. That's why I was up and out so early — so I could have plenty of time to get sorted.'

'Good. Charley's really excited, George. I told her she was seeing you today. She's already been in this morning for her birthday presents. I had to send her away. Anything before eight just isn't acceptable during half term.'

'Of course. I forgot it was half term. Is that what you called for? To make sure I wasn't going to be kept late?'

'Well, it did cross my mind to check. But no, actually.'

George's phone pinged through the speakers. It was a WhatsApp message from Emily. 'I wanted to talk to you about something, but . . . you know . . . it's a bit difficult.'

'I seem to remember you had to do the same thing last time and you managed quite well. You hit me with it when I had a mouthful of coffee. Oddly enough I've got a takeaway on the go in here, do you want me to let you know when I'm about to take a swig?' George heard a chuckle, but it sounded nervous.

'No, you're okay. There's no need to pick Charley up. We're going to use it as an opportunity to go shopping in Maidstone. We'll meet you at the Junction Eight services. You can pick her up from there.'

'We?'

'Yes, George. Ronnie will be with me.'

'Ronnie?'

'Yes. He wants to meet you. Just briefly if you want, but it might be nice to sit down, all of us, and have a cup of coffee there. I want Charley to see that this can work out. She's been kicking back a little with Ronnie recently — well, since we came back here, really. I think if she sees you there — if she sees us all there, I think she might be a bit more accepting.'

'I see.' George took a swig of his coffee. It stopped him biting back immediately.

'If she sees you are okay with it all, then I think she will be a lot better with it too. That just seems logical, doesn't it? I don't want her confused and hurting anymore. I want her to see that she needs to move on — like we all have.'

'The last conversation we had, you were giving me some more time to get my head around the divorce. Now you're assuming I've *moved on*. Do you think two days is long enough for that? There seems to be a lot of assuming going on here, Sarah. That I am comfortable with all this. That I've accepted this whole situation. I don't even know this *Ronnie*, and why on earth would I want to? My daughter is kicking back against him? Well, I say *good!* Why would I want her to move on, to accept that she has a new dad?'

'He's not a new dad—'

'You're damned right he isn't! So let's not start by talking like he is and talking about how I should help with the transition. What transition?'

'I thought you would have got your head sorted by now. I thought you would be able to understand the logic. Your daughter is confused, she can't move on and it's making her miserable. I'm just asking for a coffee where she sees us all behaving like adults. That isn't too difficult is it?'

George's phone pinged with another message from Emily. He scooped it up. Yarney's mugshot had been taken too close; his pale skin reflected the harsh light of the custody camera. He looked painfully thin and had long mousey hair that hung over his face in greasy-looking clumps. His eyes were a washed out blue and stood out as the only dabs of colour.

'I've got another call. I've got to go.'

'What? Isn't that just like—?'

George ended the call. He'd had enough of her voice, enough of her trying to make it all sound so normal. The breaking up of his family . . . and all she needed to complete it was his endorsement. Well, she wasn't having it and he wouldn't be made to feel like it was something he should do for Charley either. Like it was the best thing for her. The best thing for her was her family back together. Her *real* family.

He pulled away, suddenly aware that he would have been drawing attention to himself sat in a car ticking over in front of the tightly packed terraced houses. The people around here had a sixth sense for coppers. He drove the length of the road. It dipped in the middle and the target address was just up the other side of the dip. There was a space almost outside on the opposite side of the road. He pulled up and turned off the engine. He picked up his phone and looked back at the message from Sarah: *Can we talk?* She didn't want him to talk; she wanted him to listen then agree.

He peered out across the road. The house was near to a junction. Larendon Road carried on after. There was movement, someone had walked up the hill and turned left towards the target property. Shit! It was him!

George froze. He had planned on intercepting Yarney going out. He knew he would have to go out and score his heroin. Any addict would start their day with a hit. He'd had a vague plan of waiting for Yarney to score and then stopping him when he knew he was in possession. That way he could use the drugs as leverage somehow, get him talking at least, offer him a deal when he found the drugs. Yarney walked right up to his door and continued through. George watched the door thud shut. His opportunity was gone.

The phone pinged again. Sarah. Another message: *You need to start getting your head around all this, George. Not for my sake, not for yours. We'll talk later. Ronnie thinks it best that he stays away, for today at least.*

Well, good for Ronnie. George was up and out of the car before he even knew it. The air was crisp and cool and he sucked a great lungful of it in as he stormed across the road. George wasn't thinking about options, he wasn't thinking about how to play it now and he certainly wasn't thinking about subtleties. He used his momentum and his rage. His boot met with the door around the handle and it flew in on the first kick. The sound had an impact on George, like being jolted awake from a bad dream — *what the hell was he doing?* Too late now. House entries were dangerous at the best of times; even with a full team behind you, you had to secure everyone as quickly and as forcefully as possible. He could already see movement at the back of the house, someone ran from the living room into the kitchen. George stomped down the corridor. 'POLICE!' he roared.

He glanced right. The living room was sparse: a sofa and not much else. No people at least. He found Yarney in the kitchen. He looked the same as in his picture, down to the washed out skin and the scraggly hair, but the pale blue eyes flared wide now. Yarney had backed into a kitchen unit. His right hand was raised high and it gripped a crude-looking kitchen knife. His left arm was pushed firmly into his jacket pocket. George fixed on the blade and reached out with his own hands, showing that they were empty.

'The fuck you doing in my house? The fuck you doing?' Yarney took huge gulps of air as if he was trying to quell his own panic.

'Nicholas, are you alone? Before I start speaking?'

'What? Yes, I'm alone. But I'm the one with the knife, yeah? So don't think that means nothing.'

'I didn't mean it like that. I'm a copper, okay? A police officer. I'm not here to hurt you, but I can't talk to you if there are other people about. I don't want to put you at risk.'

'The fuck you don't! What you doing kicking my door down? You can't be doing that!'

'You're right, Nicholas. You're right. I shouldn't be here. I didn't really think this through. I got a mate back at the nick. He says you might know something that could help me — something I need to know. I got desperate, okay? I didn't think it through and I fucked up. But I do need to talk to you.'

'Talk to me? About what?'

'The shooting. There was a shooting up near Canterbury. Someone died. You might know something about who was there — about who did it.'

'I don't know what you're talking about.'

George's frustration came rushing back, replacing the shock that had come in the wake of his earlier rashness. His voice found force. 'You do. I know you do. I don't have time for games. I don't have time to wait for you to come out of your house so I can make a story about why I'm talking to you. I don't have time to make it look like it was a coincidence that you phoned your handler this morning with some information and I'm at your door a few hours later asking for more.'

'*At* my door? You kicked your way through it, way I see it!' He lowered the knife a little; the body language was changing slowly. He was recovering from the shock maybe. He didn't seem so on edge.

'Yeah, I did.'

'You got no right.'

'I don't.'

'I want your name and number. I ain't having this. I could make a big complaint — maybe get some compensation money.'

'Put the knife down at least. I'm no threat, Nicholas. That's not why I'm here.'

'I'd rather keep it. Your name and number and then you can get out.'

'You can have it, but I'm not giving you anything here. You'll get it back at the police station.'

'Police sta . . . what are you talking about? I ain't going to no police station.'

'You're under arrest for possession of class A — heroin. You do not have to say anything but it m—'

'What you talking about? Heroin?'

'That's what you've been out for this morning, Nicholas. That's what you're holding onto for dear life in your left pocket. Am I right? Do I need to take you down the nick? How much did you get? A couple of wraps? It's hardly worth it for that, is it? Be clever. Talk to me. Tell me what you know and I'll leave you with your score.'

'You forgetting who's got the knife?'

'You might as well put that down now, Nicholas. You're not going to use it. Right now you've got a wrap of heroin in your pocket and a copper in your kitchen. Maybe I shouldn't be here, but you do anything with the knife and all that will be forgotten. You'll go to prison. If you were going to do anything with it you would have done it already. I just want to talk.' George swallowed. He knew he had to stand firm to back up his bluff.

'I don't got nothing to talk about.'

'I know who you are, Nicholas. I know you're connected with people in Dover that are of interest to us. And I know that you might have heard some rumblings about my shooting up near Canterbury. Listen, I went up there. I saw what some piece of shit left behind. If you can help, you should. Trust me on that. This is not someone who deserves your protection.'

'What you saying? That I should be all moral and help you lot out? I don't know how much you think you know about me but the moral angle? That ain't the right one. I lost my morals a long time ago and I got no intention of getting them back to be honest. The world's shit. You gotta be shit to survive. Or at least you gotta be paid.'

George reached slowly for his back pocket. Nicholas tensed his right arm up, but didn't try to stop him. George kept his movements smooth as he pulled out a leather wallet. He flipped it open to reveal his police badge and then pulled out two twenties. He dropped one of them on the kitchen bench.

'Twenty quid? That ain't even going to get my door repaired.'

'I'll sort the door. My mate tells me that twenty quid normally does it.'

'You don't look like you're in a position to barter with me, man.'

'Call it a starter. If you tell me something I don't already know or something I need, you can have the other one.'

'I don't even know much.'

'Then it's easy money, right?'

Yarney's right hand finally dropped to his side. His grip on the knife was looser. He didn't drop it, but George could cope with that. He moved his badge back towards his rear trouser pocket.

'Hands where I can see them, yeah? I been gassed before. That's some horrible shit you lot use.'

George put his hands back out. He pushed his badge into his coat pocket instead.

'I'm not here to gas you. Jesus, Nicholas! Just tell me what you know.'

'I know about this gang. They run the scene in Dover right now. It changes around, you know, but they've been running it for six months. This fella who I was telling your mate about . . . he came down here just a few weeks ago. He was with some crew who go out doing rich people, you know? Out in the country, like. They see a mansion and they go in hard and get what they want. They're not from here. They're into their coke — all of them, probably. I think they move some about too. There are, like, four of them. They've been down here just a couple of weeks but they're big spenders. They got a reputation straight away. That happens when you get a new Billy Big-Bollocks in a small town like this. Then I hear they got the hump with one of the lads on the crew. They all fell out. I don't know what it was about exactly but I think he owed them all money or something. It's always about the money, right?'

George hummed some listening sounds. He didn't want to interrupt Yarney's flow.

'So apparently they're all here because this fella who they've got the hump with, he knows a place with cash stashed up. A lot of cash, yeah? Like a career job or summin' that should at least keep them in lines of charlie for a little while. Whatever. The job goes bent. I guess that's the shooting you're talking about. These boys, they don't do guns. They seemed switched on. They didn't want the attention that comes with it.'

'How did he know though? About there being money at the place? You can't even see it from the road.'

'He knew him — the old fucker there.'

'Knew him? You sure?'

'Stan, right?' Yarney said. George must have reacted and Yarney noticed. 'It is Stan! So you know I ain't giving you no shit. It's amazing what these boys will talk about when they're off their face on coke. "Stan the man," they said. "Stan the man with a hundred grand!"'

'How did they know him?'

'Not all of them did. At least that's the impression I got. Just the lad they had the hump with. Some of them were pissed at being away from home. I think they travel around a bit but they clearly didn't trust this lad.'

'So, the lad they fell out with — did he fire the gun?'

'I don't know that much. I haven't really talked to anyone since the job. I got to hear a few bits late last night, like — that a gun was involved, that it went bent. I knew it would be stuff you lot wanted so I told your man that I was hearing things. I said I would keep my ears out. He told me what he always does — said not to put myself in harm's way and to let him know what I heard. He said he would come back to me later in the week. He never said nothing about no out of control suit coming down here an' kicking my door in.'

'I guess he didn't. To be fair he couldn't have known. The problem we've got with this sort of thing is that we can't be waiting until the end of the week. I need to be doing what I can.'

'I can't help you no more.'

'You don't know where they were staying?'

Yarney looked away and his eyes fell to the floor. There was just a moment of hesitation. 'I don't, man. I don't know that much.'

George stepped in a little closer. 'It doesn't come from you, anything you tell me. We have ways of taking action without anyone ever knowing where the information came from. Think about it . . . if they were off their heads and talking and you know where these people are or where they've been, so do a lot of other people. Is that right? Do a lot of people know where they are?'

'It was just one of the lads, he was the mouthy one. The lad they all fell out with. The guy who picked out the job. He was in Dover. In a hotel. He didn't stay with the rest because he had a missus and a kid. They left him to it and they went off somewhere else.'

'What hotel?'

'Fuck man, I don't know these people. I don't like telling tales about people if I don't know what they're capable of.'

'It doesn't come back to you. You have my word.'

'A man comes to my gaff, kicks my door in, threatens to nick me and then offers me his word. What do you think that means to me?'

'Fine then. The hotel name for the other twenty.'

'Forty quid ain't no good to me six foot under now is it?'

'So make sure you spend it quickly.'

Yarney's face creased into a sort of smile. He threw the knife into an overflowing sink. 'Opposite the train station — the entrance, like. That's all I know. He didn't say no name. I don't reckon he knew it himself. I don't know nothing else. I don't know room numbers or names or anything.'

George dropped the rest of the money hurriedly on the bench. Then turned quickly down the hall and back towards the front door.

'What are you gonna do about my door?' Yarney called after him.

'I'll make some calls!' George called back. It was hanging from a hinge as he stepped through it.

'He won't still be there! At the hotel, I mean! You get yourself involved in something like that and you're long gone, ain't ya?'

George didn't reply. He was already out. He made it back to his car, flushed, hot and bothered. He ditched his jacket on the back seat and ran a quick search on his phone. There was only one real option: the Dovorian

Hotel. It looked to be almost opposite the entrance to the station. It was within a mile. He wanted to jump in his car and go to see Stan. He was the key to all of this, he must know the name of at least one of the gang that were at his house, even if he didn't realise it himself. He would go to the hotel first. He might even get lucky; maybe they were still booked in there. He was damned certain *he* wouldn't be there anymore — more likely he'd left in a hurry when it all went wrong. But people in a hurry made mistakes. They left things behind.

Stan could wait.

Chapter 19

Jenny had gotten dressed as quickly as she could and wasn't properly dry. The clothes stuck to her back and thighs, but at least they were *her* clothes. Whereas she'd felt wrapped up and safe in the warmth of the shower, she'd felt very exposed and vulnerable dressing in front of her captor. He was leaning back on the wooden unit again, the gun still hanging loose in his right hand. She was closer to him now, close enough to take in his features. She hadn't dared before. He had a slim, wiry build and broad shoulders that tapered to a slim waist. His hair was dark and thinning in patches and he'd shaved it close to his scalp. His eyes were deep and dark and played their part in a face that showed no changes in emotion. He had a coldness about him, and though he was no longer pointing the weapon at her, she felt no less fear. He looked her up and down.

'You need to dry that hair. We need to blend in.'

Jenny's frizzy, damp hair fell over her face. She pulled a strand taut over her eyes. 'I didn't think I had the time,' she said.

He checked his watch. 'You have two minutes yet.'

* * *

George took in the façade of the Dovorian Hotel. It was grey, flat and had a layer of what looked like soot that was a darker shade at the bottom. The road that passed close to its front was getting busy with traffic. He crossed over and went through what looked like the main entrance on the south side. It had double wooden doors. Only one of them opened and it was heavy and cumbersome. A slim, blonde woman sat behind the desk. She stood up when he entered.

'Welcome to the Dovorian Hotel, sir.' Her accent was subtle, Polish perhaps.

'Thanks.'

'Do you wish to check in today, sir?'

'No. Thank you.' George felt in his pocket for his badge. He cursed. He'd put it back in his coat pocket after flashing it at Yarney. The coat was lying on the back seat of the car. 'I, er . . .' George patted down his other pockets. He had a pass that hung around his neck when he was at the police station; it had his picture on it and it doubled as access through the doors. He snatched it out and showed it to the receptionist. He hooked the lanyard over his neck. 'Inspector George Elms. I'm a police officer based in Langthorne. I wondered if you could answer a few questions for me? I'm looking for some information about someone who might have stayed here.'

The woman looked a little uneasy. 'Inspector?' She was still looking at the pass that rested against his tie.

'Oh!' He snatched it up. 'Yes, it's a recent thing. This still says *Sergeant*, doesn't it? My replacement's in the post!'

The woman laughed nervously. 'Is there trouble here?'

'Not at all.'

'Is this about the other day? About the car?'

'What happened the other day?'

'There was a car, just outside. Someone shot a gun, I think. The police, they came in here and they asked me. I don't know anything about this car.'

'So you've already spoken to the police?'

'Yes. This car. We do not park here. We do not take car details, you know. They asked if it was from here. I did not know this.'

'I see. This isn't about a car. Do you —or did you — have a couple staying here? They would have had a child with them. They might have been here a couple of weeks.'

'Is this normal? To give information to you?'

'Well, yes. There has been a rather serious incident. Away from here — I mean, there's no suggestion this hotel has any part in it, but I'm trying to piece together what happened.'

'And you are police inspector?'

'I am.' George stood firm. UK data protection laws were stringent if they were adhered to. The guest list in a hotel technically fell under these laws. George should have had the right form endorsed by the right person. He had never needed it before, but then this was the first time he had walked in anywhere without his usual confidence and without his correct ID. He knew that Sarah's call still had him rattled.

'Okay, so here is bookings.' The woman clicked on a mouse and bent to look at something that George couldn't see. She wrote on a piece of paper. 'We have two families that have been here a little while. They come about same time. These are room numbers. I cannot tell you about them.'

'Do you have their details? Their names at least?'

'I cannot tell them to you. This is normal. We do not give information.'

'But you're happy to give me the room numbers and let me go and knock on their doors?'

'If they choose to speak, they can speak. I cannot speak for them.'

'So I need to come back with a form filled out? Is that not a waste of everyone's time?'

'And identification.'

George was starting to get wound up but his anger towards her quickly dissipated. She was probably still doubting whether he was a police officer at all. Her reluctance was his fault.

'I shall have to go and introduce myself then. Have you seen either of them today?'

'Not today. I had day off yesterday. I start, maybe one or two hours. I have number of the girl who worked the night?'

'That's okay. I'll just go and knock on the door.'

The woman looked at him again. She looked less certain — as if she might be changing her mind. She seemed to make a decision and she put the piece of paper on the counter. George swept it up.

'Thanks for your help. I'll just be a couple of minutes.'

George inspected the paper. Both numbers started with a three. With his basic knowledge of hotels, he assumed this would mean they were on the third floor. He pressed to call the lift. His phone rang in his pocket. It was Sarah.

'Sarah, hey.' He stepped into the lift. The three walls that faced him were mirrored. He turned to face the closing doors.

'What do you mean "hey"?' She sounded instantly upset. 'Why are you being like this?'

'Like what?' George suddenly caught up. He hadn't replied to her message earlier. He hadn't had a chance. 'Oh, yeah, I saw your message. I know I didn't reply. I was waiting until I could call you, so we could talk about it. You know I don't like conversations by text message.'

'So you can talk now?'

'Not really, Sarah. I'm just out on some enquiries. When I'm away I'll call you from the car.'

'You know what? Don't bother trying to fit me into your busy schedule. Any of us. I need to get this sorted out with you and Ronnie. For Charley's sake and all—'

'Don't try and pretend this is anything to do with Charley. You're doing this for you. This is *all* about you. If Charley's acting out with this bloke then maybe she just doesn't like him. There's nothing I can do about that. Or maybe she wants her real family back together. Maybe that's what's best for Charley.'

'It's gone too far, George.'

'So you keep telling me. That's all you keep saying. But that's your opinion . . . that's your idea. You might be right, but the mistake you have always made is that you assume something is right just because you think it is. From someone who has made a lot of mistakes, you need to trust me when I tell you that you might be making one right now.'

'I knew you'd be like this.'

'Like what?'

'Obstructive. Stopping me getting on with my life.'

'Sarah, you ran away for a *year*. I have not physically been able to obstruct a damned thing you've done. Do you think that is what was best for Charley? Keeping us apart for a whole year while you worked out what you wanted? And then you get shacked up with some other bloke and you want me to come in and smooth it out so our daughter moves on too. What do you think my answer is going to be to that? I mean, really?'

The doors had long since clunked open. George had moved to stand between them so they didn't shut. The corridor was empty. He was aware that he had raised his voice. He looked around; there was still no movement. He moved into the corridor and the doors moved shut behind him.

'This is a bad idea. All of it. We need to talk to each other. We both need to be clear where we are before you can spend any time with Charley.'

'What do you mean? I'm seeing her this afternoon, Sarah.'

'And where are you now? You told me you had taken the whole day off. I call you on the morning to sort out the arrangements and you're at work.'

'We've got two separate murders over here, Sarah. I'm new in post as the inspector of the area where those jobs sit. I'm just in to tie up a few loose ends this morning. You know what it's like.'

'I do, George — only too well! That's a big part of what I was running away from. I don't know about this afternoon. I wanted you to be a positive influence on Charley, but from the way you're talking you're going to be just the opposite. I'll talk to Ronnie about it. I'll let you know.'

'Talk to Ronnie? About—' George realised suddenly that he was talking to a dead line. He swore — and did nothing to keep his voice low this time. He lifted the phone to smash it back down on the floor — then changed his mind and stuffed it roughly back into his pocket instead. He bunched his fists and concentrated on breathing. He knew where she was: his wife and his child. He would get this done and then he would stand down. Then maybe he could focus on fixing his own life.

* * *

Jenny's hair was dry. She'd pulled it together in a ponytail at the back, two clips in the sides. The man's impatience was growing. She could sense it.

'We need to move.'

'Where are we going?'

'We need to move.'

'Are you not even going to tell me where we are going? Or why?'

'No.'

'Why didn't you kill me?'

'We have another use for you.'

'Are you going to kill me? I've seen films where people get kidnapped. The kidnappers always wear face

176

coverings like you had on when I first came in here. You only have to worry when they don't. Then you know that they don't plan on letting you go. Do you plan on letting me go?'

The man shrugged. He pushed off the wall unit and walked to the door. 'It's not my plan, Jenny. Like I said, I'm here to pick you up. I do what I'm paid to do. And now we are moving.'

The gun still hung from his right hand. He had his back to her and his eye pushed up against the peephole. He was checking that there was nobody about. Jenny's mind was rushing with panic. He didn't want anybody to see her leaving with him — for when they found her body.

'Please don't kill me. Please!'

The man turned back to her. He sighed. 'We'll keep this nice and easy. I don't know what these people want with you, but the one thing I do know is that if you mess me about this will not end well for you. Do you understand?'

Jenny jerked a nod. She tried to concentrate on her breathing; she was in danger of losing control.

There was a tap at the door.

Jenny froze. She stared at the man and he stared right back. He looked questioning — and furious, too. He raised a finger abruptly to his lips. The gun was lifted again, pointing directly at her. She shrugged her shoulders — she had no idea who it was. She put her hand over her mouth to stop any sound from coming out. The door tapped again. The man stepped off to one side and he pushed his finger over the peephole. Jenny was pretty sure it was one-way anyway but it showed his nervousness. He stood side-on to her and held his weapon low, but his finger rested loosely on the trigger as he rested his ear against the door. The handle rattled. Someone was trying it from outside. Whoever it was, they didn't have a key. Jenny's captor stayed still for a long time after the noises stopped. Then he put his eye to the peephole. Another minute passed.

'We're leaving,' he said, suddenly. He pulled the door open — slowly, quietly. He peered through the inch-wide gap, another few seconds passed. He looked back over at Jenny. She hadn't moved; she couldn't. She felt as if her feet were rooted. She knew the man wasn't here to kill her in that room; he'd had every opportunity, and all he'd talked about was leaving. What she couldn't know was what he had planned for her once she left. But it wasn't going to be good.

'I can't,' she said.

'We leave *now*,' he growled, his rage barely concealed.

'You're taking me somewhere to kill me.' Jenny tried to get her legs to move, but backwards, away from the man. She couldn't even manage that. He closed the door again carefully, quietly, and then moved over to her, stepping right in so his face was almost against hers. She felt a tight grip on her right bicep and the barrel of the pistol was pushed up painfully under her chin.

'We are leaving now. You will keep quiet and you will do as you are told all the way until I deliver you. I *do not* fail. Whatever happens to you is someone else's plan, but I will make you a promise now, Jenny . . . if you make this difficult for me, if you cause me a problem then Isobel will be my plan. Do you understand?' His rage was barely controlled, his words were accompanied by phlegm and his grip was tightening with every word.

'You leave my daughter out of this. She's four months old for Christ sake!'

'And she won't know what hit her.'

'You're pure evil!'

'We're leaving now.' He pushed off her arm and the gun jerked out from under her chin. He turned to the door and tucked the weapon in his waistband, against his buttocks. He pulled the door the same way he had before, quietly and carefully. He stepped out, his back towards Jenny. She was moving towards him, but slowly. It was like a dream, as if somebody else was operating her legs. She stepped out and the door fell shut behind her. She followed her captor to the right where the corridor curved around to where the lifts were.

There was another man ahead. He had dark hair and day-old stubble. He was pushing the button for the lift. The man leading Jenny slowed. Jenny thought he might stop altogether, maybe go back to the stairwell that was in the opposite direction. The dark haired man looked up. He seemed to look at them both. Certainly he glanced at her, but it was only a split second before he shifted his attention. The man looked agitated, distracted by something on his phone. They kept walking towards him. The lift arrived, the man who had called it stepped hurriedly in. Jenny's captor lifted his shirt to reveal his weapon for a few moments. He turned to her and made eye contact that lingered. His message was clear. She followed him into the lift.

The man's attention was still on his phone. His head was dipped, his whole focus on the lit screen. It looked to Jenny like he was typing. The ground floor button was ringed in a green light. The lift moved off. The man with the gun digging into his back stood against the back wall and stared over at her. She stood against the left side wall, almost opposite the man still consumed by his phone. She concentrated on trying to get her breathing under control. She became aware that her heart was racing, that her chest was rising and falling quickly. If the man looked up from his phone, he would surely notice. She focussed on him. He was scrolling through something. He was dressed in a shirt and tie but he managed to make it look scruffy. He had a blue lanyard round his neck, a white card attached to its centre. It was an ID card of some sort. She could see it had an image of the man's face on it. Next to it was some writing. She edged closer — as much as she dared. She couldn't quite read the writing. Another tiny movement. She was close enough now.

Detective Sergeant George ELMS along the top line. *THIS IS NOT A WARRANT CARD* on the line below, the crest of a police force in the corner.

A police officer! Her breathing increased again. She could sense the gunman staring at her. She met his eyes. His whole posture carried a warning. His right hand, now hidden behind his back, no doubt clasped the handle of the gun. He must have seen the ID tag too. She stepped back against the wall; she was clumsy and her foot thumped against the metal. She glanced at the policeman, who shifted, his head lifted a little but not enough to look at her. They had called her *Jenny* on the news; they had to be looking for her. Why wasn't he paying attention? She felt like she might combust. He was just a metre away. The lift pinged as it passed the first floor; it would be just another few seconds before it reached ground.

* * *

Stan stood out in the middle of the barn. The sun had burned through the mist entirely now. Its light penetrated the gaps and holes in the ancient walls, and the dust swirled and fell in the rays of sunlight like tiny snowflakes. Stan was tired and needed a minute to rest. He sat on the big wooden lock box he had dragged across the floor into the centre of the barn. It had once held larger items of horse tack. It had been the perfect size. He had used it to reach the exposed wooden beam along which he'd strung the chicken wire. The barn contained no shortage of tools, and the nail gun had proven especially useful — although his shoulders now ached after working with his arms raised above his head.

Once rested, Stan climbed tentatively back up onto the box and tested the wire loop. It felt strong. He tugged on it with both hands then lifted the whole of his frail body from the floor. It took his weight. It didn't budge. The wire finished two thirds of the way along the wooden beam, right at the point where he reckoned Janice had dragged him on that night when they had first met. He'd been sitting on a bale of hay against the left wall. The musicians had been at the back and kegs of lukewarm cider and ale were against the wall where the kitchen now stood. She had walked him out onto the dance floor in the middle of the barn. When he'd hesitated, she'd taken hold of his right hand and placed it on her hip. That moment when they touched was still as fresh in his mind as when it happened. Over sixty years later. The sun was on his face now. He closed his eyes to it, his face creased in a smile.

He turned away from the wire so that he was facing out towards the front where the huge wooden door was ajar and he felt the loop rock against his back. He reached behind him and slipped the loop over his head. The wire felt cold against his neck and shoulders. He knew chicken wire; he'd fenced his whole estate with it more than once and he'd cut plenty of trapped livestock from its clutches. He knew it to be unforgiving. Stanley didn't want forgiveness; he was past caring about that. He just wanted the darkness. He stepped to the edge of the box with just his heels balancing on the rim. He took a last breath in through his nose, inhaling the scent of his farm, of his whole life. He shut his eyes to the memory of everything. Then he stepped forward.

* * *

The lift reached the bottom floor. Jenny felt the sensation of movement as it slowed and finally settled. The doors jerked apart. The police officer, George Elms, was already moving away from her, his head still down. She found herself making a noise from her throat that was entirely unintentional. She also stepped towards him but he gave no reaction, showed no sign he had even registered her existence. Then he stepped out of the lift and turned hard right. She felt an arm across her chest, holding her back as the lift doors slipped shut again.

181

The lift shivered and then there was movement upward. Her last chance was gone.

Chapter 20

George was in a hurry to leave. He stopped to give his number to the woman behind the front counter. She assured him that she would make contact if she noticed either of the families come back. George's phone buzzed in his pocket as he strode away from the hotel. It had been going off almost non-stop. His wife was pulling out of the afternoon's arrangements, it would mean he'd miss out on seeing his daughter for the first time in nearly a year — on her birthday. It buzzed again, longer this time. He ignored the call. He couldn't speak, not while he was in a public space. He needed the privacy of the car. He got back to his vehicle and pulled the door firmly shut. He took a moment; calling her back was the last thing he wanted to do. He just didn't have the energy. He knew it would descend into an argument; there was no way for it to do anything else. He was so angry.

He checked the phone, expecting another angry message or an ultimatum to buzz through. Instead it showed a message from Emily. He had an earlier missed call from her too. He'd ignored her for the same reason he hadn't answered his wife: it would surely end in an argument. The message from Emily didn't appear to be angry at least. It said simply: *I just need to know how it went. Did you get anything you can use? Or, more important, did you manage to protect our handler?*

George typed out the only reply for which he could muster the energy: *It went fine.*

He started the engine. He needed to go and see Stanley. They would need to go through his life in some detail: friends, family, friends of friends, tradesmen. Somebody Stan knew had come back in the dead of night and had killed his wife. Stanley Wingmore was the key to this, even if he didn't know it yet. George stared out over the top of the steering wheel. Exhaustion seemed to have wrapped him like a dark mist. He wondered if he could find the energy to speak to Stan. He considered calling Paul Bearn and tasking him. The buzzing phone interrupted his musing.

'Ryker.' He answered, without thinking.

Emily went straight on the offensive. 'What the hell does that mean?'

'What does what mean?'

'*It went fine?* That tells me nothing.'

'I guess I don't have the time for full updates right now.' George was grouchy.

'What the hell is going on with you, George? Why are you treating me like shit all of a sudden?'

'I'm sorry, okay? I've got a lot going on at the moment. I'm trying to get my head around it all.'

'You think that makes it okay? We're all busy people, George. I take it you mean this shit with your wife? She's still torturing you by dangling your kid out like some carrot in front of a donkey?'

'You don't get to talk about my family, okay? You have no idea what's going on. You have no idea what we've been through. She's not dangling anything. We're just trying to work it out.'

'Like hell! *You* might be trying to work it out but she's toying with you, George, and she has been for years. You need to call her bluff, tell her Charley's your kid, too, and she has to accept that. There are laws, George. She can't stop you seeing your kid.'

'I tell you what, Ryker . . . when you get your own family you can have an opinion, okay? Until then you can keep your fucking nose out, you understand?' George pushed the touch screen on the car's display so hard it bent inwards and made a cracking sound. The call ended. George threw his head backwards into the headrest. Still not satisfied, he did it again but this time harder. He kept throwing his head back in a frenzy of movement, his eyes filled with tears of frustration. As he became still, they ran down his face.

'Fuck!' He said out loud. He stared at the screen. The call information was still on there. He pressed to call back. The call was picked up. There was silence at the other end. George knew there was someone there; he could hear a breath. He peered out of the side window. His eyes had lost their focus.

'I'm sorry, Ryker. I am an arsehole. I've treated you like shit today, yesterday and before. A few times now. I take you for granted and I shouldn't. I'm sorry. I fucked up, Ryker — this morning. I know the rules. I know that people can get hurt if you don't follow them and I just carried on regardless. It's not that I don't care about other people — I just don't care about myself enough to even think about them. About you. I kicked that man's door in — Yarney. I was through it before I even stopped to think because I was angry with my wife. He gave me some information about where a suspect might be staying and I just bowled over there and started knocking on doors, talking to the receptionist, telling her I'm a copper. I know better, Ryker. I know that I should have called it in. We could have considered other options. But I didn't. I didn't because I was angry about my wife. I've missed a call this morning, Ryker, from Stanley. I convinced myself that I was so angry with what happened to him that nothing else mattered, that I could do what I wanted to find these people — and then he calls me up and I didn't even answer his call. Now I don't even have the guts to call him back or to go see him because I'm scared that he'll know. He'll know that I didn't care enough. And I might be all he has at the moment. I've let him down, I've let you down, I let Andy McGuiness down. And I'm not much closer. Not to finding the people that shot that woman and not to seeing my own daughter. I'm sorry, Ryker. You deserve better.' George stared out of the window. Thirty seconds passed. The timer still ticked up on the screen.

'Where are you, George?'

'Dover. I should go and see Stan. One of the gang definitely knew him. That means that Stan knows him. Maybe I should task Paul — everything's just out of control with me right now.'

'Take your day off. Get your head clear. Maybe turn your phone off and start again tomorrow. You're not going to get anything sorted today — with your wife or with your case. You'll be a lot more productive after a day away.'

'Maybe you're right.'

'Tell me what you did, what you know and I'll feed it back to Paul. He can pick up any loose ends. Don't worry about Yarney or McGuiness — I'll smooth that out somehow.'

'What I did? Well, I got to speak to Yarney. He was holding a knife towards me for most of it but he gave me some stuff I can use. Assuming any of it is true. He told me some of the same that he told his handler. Some gang of robbers crossed over the border to do a job out in the rural. He reckons that one of the gang is into the cocaine in a big way. He might have worked himself up a bit of a debt. Anyway, he'd picked out Wingmore Farm as a place for them to score big. He picked it out because he knew

186

there was money there — a hundred grand apparently. And he knew Stan by name.'

'So it had to be someone close.'

'Yarney doesn't know how he knows him? Maybe he's an old farmhand, or it's word of mouth even.'

'Word of mouth wouldn't make sense. They're down from another county.'

'I know.'

'And it has to be someone close. If you have a hundred grand under your mattress you're not likely to be chatting about it over a cup of tea with your sweep-up boy, are you?'

'No. That's true.'

'What's this about a receptionist? A hotel?'

'Yarney got to hear that the crewmember who tipped them off about Wingmore Farm was staying in a hotel. He didn't stay with the rest of the group because he had a wife and family with him.'

'A family? So a gang of robbers set to work in the next county over and one of them brings his missus? Does that sound right to you?'

'Well, no. Not when you say it like that. And a kid apparently.'

'A kid?'

'Yeah. He reckons they were staying in a hotel almost opposite Dover train station. It looked to me like the Dovorian was our best bet. I figured they might still be there or that there might be something known about them we could use. Yarney didn't know the room number, but I went to try one or two where the receptionist said there were couples with kids.'

'The Dovorian? How old did Yarney say the kid was?' Emily suddenly sounded animated.

'I didn't ask to be honest.'

'What about at the hotel? Did they say how old those kids were?'

'Jesus, Ryker, I didn't ask that either. I'm really not functioning today. I'll get someone to go back over what I've done.'

'George, the Dovorian is spitting distance from the shootings in Dover. The shootings where a woman seen running away left her baby on the bonnet of a police car!'

George suddenly sat up. His mind clearing of the fog left by his frustration. 'You think it's the same girl!'

'Well, of course I do! You need to sharpen up down there, George. This crew already has an issue with this lad. Then the job up at the farm doesn't seem to have gone to plan. It's not a giant leap to assume that it's the same crew causing chaos at both locations, is it?'

'No, Ryker, it isn't at all. I'll head back to Wingmore Farm. I'll talk to Stan.'

'What about going back into the hotel? Bottoming that out?'

George looked out of his window at the drab exterior of the Dovorian. 'Nah, she already has issues with me. I'll send uniform.'

'Are you sure you're going to be okay, George? You should still have your day off?'

'We'll soon see, Ryker. And what would I do with a day off now? I am sorry, though, yeah?'

'Just as well. I was just about to call you an arsehole again. I don't even know why I answered.'

'I'm glad you did.'

'Keep in touch.'

Chapter 21

George turned into the drive of Wingmore Farm and saw the marked police car as he rounded the curve. The officer standing next to it reacted immediately, waving his arms as if he was instructing George to pass straight through. He looked agitated and urgent. George pulled up alongside him and whirred his window down.

'You okay?'

'He's in the barn. Left at the house, sir. He's still there — they're working on him.'

'Working on who? What's going on?'

'Are you here about Mr Wingmore?'

'Well, yes, of course. What's going on?'

'He was found in the barn, sir. I had no idea he was going to do that. I'm waiting for an update, I didn't know . . .' The officer dropped his head and his whole body seemed to hang on its frame. George moved quickly away. He followed the curve of the drive round and the house came into view. He took the left fork in the track and passed the house. He could see the unmarked car Paul Bearn had been using and next to it was a first responder's marked car and a full-sized ambulance. There was another marked police car further away. They all looked as if they had been parked hurriedly. George did the same and jogged into the barn.

He saw Stan straight away. He was lying on the floor on his back with two paramedics kneeling over him. A third stood by with a bag of clear fluid from which a tube trailed into Stan's arm. Paul was over to the far right of the barn and a woman was turned into him, sobbing quietly. Paul acknowledged George with a look. George moved over to Stan. His mouth was open at an unnatural angle, a thick plastic tube with an orange top stuck out of it. Stan's eyes were open but George could see they had no focus. A machine beeped and flashed next to his head and two wires trailed to where his shirt had been cut open to reveal his chest. His tie had been cut off and was lying beside him. His suit jacket had been pushed open. George looked up to where a wire noose still hung. It had been fashioned crudely, but it was obvious what it was. George was suddenly aware of Paul at his shoulder.

'Jesus, Paul, what the hell happened?'

'I found him strung up. I picked him up by the legs, his poor daughter had to help me out. I was next to useless with one arm. She cut the wire from around his neck. She must have found something to do it with. There was still some life there then, but I think they've lost him again. It's not looking good.'

'How long?'

'I don't know. It all happened in a blur. We've probably been here nearly half an hour now. I worked on him for a bit, best I could. Louise called 999. They must have been close — it didn't seem long until they arrived.'

'I should have predicted this. I should have read the signs.'

'And done what? I'm here as his FLO. We sorted him out with a friendly face. There was nothing more we could have done. We can't babysit him twenty-four hours a day.

190

He knew his daughter was coming home today. I can't understand why he would do it. Not now.'

George flitted around the interior of the barn. 'We're sure he did? There's no chance—'

'What, that they came back? I considered the same. But when I came in this morning the lad on scene preservation told me Stan had got here an hour ago. Said he'd walked up and said he was going to the barn to make a cup of tea. We've had both entrances covered and an extra officer at the house. There's no way anyone else has been here.'

'But why now? Like you said, his daughter's here this morning. You'd cling on for another day, wouldn't you?'

'Grief, George . . . it's a funny old thing.'

'Poor old bastard. I really thought I could get him onside, get him to focus on helping us out. I thought if he had something to focus on then it would drag him through this. I was so wrong, Paul. I was so wrong.'

'You can't predict people pushed to the extremes of their emotions. This is just what happens. I'm not sure there was anything we could have done that would have had a different outcome.'

'We need him, Paul. There have been some developments. It's quite likely that he knows exactly who killed his wife.'

'How?'

'I have no idea right now. I'll fill you in when I can.'

'What about his daughter? Would she be able to help?'

'I don't know. I don't suppose she's in the right frame of mind to talk right now either. Let's see how Stan gets on. He's a tough old bastard, I reckon.'

'That much is true.'

George looked over to where he could see one of Stan's arms lying on the ground between the busy medics. His hand was palm up and fidgeting as the work on him continued. His skin was light grey and it looked as if it was made out of wax. George had seen that skin colour plenty of times before. Never on the living.

* * *

The man took hold of her and didn't seem to want to let go. They stayed in the lift for just one floor then he pulled her out roughly onto the first-floor landing. He took hold of her hand and pulled it in close to his hip.

'Behave!' he hissed. She didn't reply.

It was clear what he meant and his whole demeanour had changed. He was focussed and urgent. He pushed through the double doors at the end of the corridor and stopped at the landing where the stairs went down to the ground and up to the rest of the hotel. He stayed dead still; it was clear that he was listening intently and Jenny stayed silent too. She didn't want to antagonise him. She didn't know what he might do if the police officer suddenly came after them — not that she considered that might happen, not for one second. He was gone. He hadn't even looked up in that lift. How could that be? *They had used her name!* She could accept they didn't know where she was staying; they hadn't booked into the hotel using their real names. Joseph never did. He always questioned why they needed to know who he was. He always insisted on paying by cash up front and would refuse to leave a card behind the desk. None of the hotels had stood their ground and refused to let them stay.

Jenny's captor seemed happy that the stairwell was empty. He moved suddenly downwards, catching Jenny off balance, and she stumbled after him. He led her out of the same side door through which she had fled just forty-eight hours before with her four-month-old child clutched close to her chest. Her exit this time was much more gradual. The man was being careful; he gestured for her to stay still, then he stepped out onto the pavement. He stood still for almost a minute, took notice of passing cars, checked both directions. Then they were moving again. They turned left.

The way was steep and Jenny had to lean into the gradient. The angle aggravated her sore hip and she had to slow down. The man was pulling her.

'We need to keep going,' he grunted.

'My legs hurt.'

'You can rest soon. Not now.'

A few more paces and they turned left again and started on a road that ran parallel to the back of the hotel. The hotel itself was now concealed behind a row of tight terraced houses that were directly mirrored on the other side. At least this road was level. She started to recover: the pain in her leg had eased and she wasn't so out of breath. She took in her surroundings, this time with a view to spotting any opportunities to run. Hell, she'd done it before. She considered for a second that she might be able to do it again. The man still had a hold of her arm and now he seemed to grip it even tighter, as though he could read her mind. There was an occasional gap in the houses on her right and she could see green trees and fields beyond, where the side of the valley continued. She saw flashes of steep scrubland, thick brambles and exposed chalk. Even if she did manage to get away from him and get into her stride, she didn't think she would get far.

Any opportunity was quickly diminishing. The man stopped at the rear of a small box van. It had double doors on the back that pulled outwards.

'Get in!'

Jenny peered around again. The street was quiet. The van was parked in front of a pub whose windows and door were boarded up and profanities sprayed across them. The rear compartment of the van looked completely empty.

'Where do I sit?'

'Sit on the floor. There's a bag in there. When we stop, put it over your head.'

She had to crawl onto her knees to get in. Then the doors slammed behind her and she was enclosed in darkness. She felt for the side. The engine started and the van moved swiftly off. Jenny stumbled and sprawled onto her side. Her hand fell on something that felt like Hessian and she guessed it was the bag. She managed to pull herself to a sitting position with her back to the van's side. The van lurched, and the back of her head bounced off the firm metal. She immediately leant forward and raised her hand to the back of her head; it stung with pain. Another sudden change of direction and she slid across the floor again. The engine revved hard and she felt them picking up speed. She could hear the roar of the road under the wheels. She curled up on her side in the darkness, made herself into a protective ball and sobbed into her hands.

* * *

They had signs of life. Enough for excited chatter between the medics and a quick transfer into the back of the ambulance. Stan's daughter and Paul followed the stretcher. George could see in; he could see them both trying to stay out of the way as the crew still worked on Stanley. His daughter had appeared to George to be in a constant state of shock. He could understand it, of course, he wouldn't wish her last twenty-four hours on anyone. He moved towards his own car and prayed for the umpteenth time that Stan was going to be okay. He just needed a few minutes with him lucid.

There was a welcome party for the ambulance when they arrived: a white coat and two navy blue uniforms. They swept through automatic doors on a wheeled stretcher, each holding a corner. George followed them until they pushed through to the intensive care unit. Someone was waiting to direct Stan's daughter and Paul into a side room. It was all well-choreographed. George moved to the door and raised his palm to push it open and follow them in so that he could talk to the daughter and find out what she might know. He hesitated. He stopped at the door, his palm flat on the slim panel of frosted glass.

He stepped back, back out into the corridor and turned away. He heard the door open from behind him.

'Are you not coming in, George? The daughter said she wants to talk to you. She might be able to fill in the gaps in case Stan can't.'

'Paul, can you talk to her? We just need a good list of associates, anyone he might have a grievance with, anyone who might know about any money he had at the farm, whether she knows about any money. That sort of thing.'

'You okay, George?' Paul looked immediately unsure. 'I told her who you were. I said you're running the investigation. I think she's expecting you to go in and talk to her. At least introduce yourself.'

'I can't, Paul.'

'You're not okay. Like I said, George, you can't go beating yourself up—'

'It's not that. I just can't, Paul. You've got it covered. You're a good detective.'

'And you're running the investigation. And a better one.'

George took a second. 'Maybe he wasn't telling me everything, Paul. I've played it back in my mind, when he was talking to me back at the house, when I was taking his statement. Maybe he was holding back. Maybe I even knew it at the time but I didn't pull him up on it.'

'He'd just had a terrible thing happen to him. You have to let these people go a bit. He was still shook up, confused—'

George was shaking his head aggressively. 'What if he knew he was going to do this? Do what he did, right from the start? Maybe he was hiding that. I see through people, Paul, I always do. When people have more to tell me, I know, I'm good at it. Jesus, I've made a career out of it. I didn't push him on it because I knew he was struggling and I didn't think I could do anything about it. I ignored it, Paul. I let him down because I didn't have the energy to sit and listen.' George rubbed at his face. He felt he was battling a breakdown. He wanted to give in — to his frustration, to his helplessness, to everything. 'He phoned me. This morning. I ignored it, Paul. What if he wanted to be talked out of it? What if he just needed to know someone was there for him?' George lifted his head and shut his eyes. Suddenly he felt a shove in his chest. He stumbled backwards and opened his eyes as he was pushed through a toilet door. Paul Bearn was forceful in his ear.

'Listen, George, we can't be doing this here. These people have expectations. They don't see past the badge. We don't get to have feelings in front of these people. We don't get to have family troubles. We don't get to be weak or upset and we don't ever let people down. Pull yourself together, *sir*. This is what we're here for.'

George's head shook slowly from side to side. He took a deep breath. He brushed past Paul and tugged the door so hard it smacked off the wall behind him. He took a moment. The door to the family room was almost directly over the corridor. He walked in to be met by a pair of watery eyes. Louise stood ringing her hands. It looked like she had been pacing the room.

'You must be George Elms,' she said. She managed a weak smile.

'I am, yes.'

'And you're going to need to talk to me?'

George exchanged glances with Paul. 'I am, yes. Do you think you're up to it?'

'I don't know if I can help much. I have no idea what's been going on. I speak to my mum a lot. I mean . . . I did. Once a week on the weekend when I could get the time zones right. I feel like I have a lot of questions for you.'

George did his best to look reassuring. He sat down on one of the high backed chairs and Louise took her cue to do the same, perching on the edge of one. George had seen her date of birth; he knew she was fifty-three. She looked a lot younger. She had black hair that was long and straightened. She wore a trouser suit and flat shoes. She pushed slim hands together over an expensive-looking bag. A diamond wedding ring dazzled in the strip lighting. Her expression was expectant. George had met a lot of people under the sort of pressures she was under and in similar circumstances. She was carrying herself well.

'You can start then. What do you need to know?'

'Were my parents targeted? I picked up on something Paul said in the car, that this gang are suspected of making a living out of people like my parents.'

'We have a number of theories, Louise. One of those is that they were targeted by a gang who prey on vulnerable people in isolated locations.'

'Vulnerable? My parents don't strike me as vulnerable—'

'Sorry, that doesn't sound right. It's a police term, we tend to categorise the elderly as vulnerable, not because it is true in every case, but because a criminal would. If they saw your parent's home, the Range Rover on the drive, the nice frontage and they saw your mum or dad coming or going they might assume it to be easy pickings. They were wrong, clearly. Your dad refused to lie down.'

Louise pursed her lips and then said, 'If only he had.'

George shrugged. 'Maybe this wouldn't have happened, but maybe it would. Certainly your dad is beating himself up about it and that isn't helping the situation at all.'

'I understand what you're saying, Inspector. I'm not here to point fingers or to criticise. Who knows what he was going through up there. It must have hit him hard. There's no way my dad does . . . well . . . does that. He would be the last man, I would say—'

'Grief. It does strange things to the best of us. We just need to be sure we are there for him.'

'If we get the chance.'

'When hope is all you have, hope is all you can do. Forgive me, but I get the impression that your dad is a tough old bastard. I told him that myself. He didn't disagree!'

'I'm sure he didn't. And, yes, I think that's a very good summary.'

The door behind was pushed open. George turned.

'Inspector Elms?' A tall, well-spoken man in his mid-fifties approached. He wore a checked shirt tucked into chinos and glasses. George had met enough doctors to spot one immediately.

'Yes, doctor.'

'Do you have a moment?'

'Of course.' George turned back to Louise. 'Forgive me, I'll just be a moment.'

George stepped out of the room and followed the doctor who walked a few feet up the corridor and leant against the wall.

'Is there news?' George said.

'Yes. Good news. Our patient, Mr Wingmore, is awake.'

George couldn't stop the smile — it was relief mainly. 'That is good news. How is he?'

'It's all rather early, Inspector, as you can appreciate. We did very little, to be honest, on his arrival here. The swift actions of whoever found him and worked him initially have given him a fighting chance. We continued with his oxygen treatment and he woke up of his own accord. We have carried out some initial scans on his brain but I will want to do some more detailed tests, especially as he is now back in the land of the living. And, if I'm honest, Inspector, he's very lucky to be here.'

'I guess I should just be thankful for that.'

'We all should. I would normally speak to the next of kin first, but I understand the circumstances around this matter are a little different. If Mr Wingmore is a suspect in a murder case then I know the police get a little upset with relatives speaking to them without the police present. It's up to you how you handle that. I obviously have to go in and talk to his daughter straight away. This was just a little pre-warning.'

'I do appreciate that, doctor, but Mr Wingmore is not a suspect. He was a witness, he's taken it rather hard as you can imagine. I have recently established that he might be a far more important witness than any of us realised. Do you think I might be able to speak with him soon?'

'You might. But I should warn you, Inspector, he is suffering the effects of his ordeal. He is coping with confusion and memory loss — short term at least. He is also sight deficient in at least one of his eyes. That's a preliminary check. It's highly likely that more symptoms will be discovered when he gets up and moving.'

'Permanent?'

'It can be. More likely short term. I have been studying and working on the human brain for over twenty years and I still find much of my time is spent shrugging at relatives, saying the words *we just don't know*. More than once I've considered what my life might have been like if I had specialised in teeth.'

'I guess you know where you are with teeth, doctor.'

'You do. They are rotten, they are broken or they are not. The brain, by contrast, is a baffling and complex ball of utter pig-headedness. The one thing you can be sure of, however, is that if you treat it badly, deny it something it needs, like oxygen — even for a minute — it will have its revenge. Every case will be different.'

'So, the memory loss . . . does he know why he is here?'

'No. Not a clue. I'd better go update the daughter. Oh — and another thing you should be aware of Inspector . . . he is asking for his wife.'

Chapter 22

The van stopped moving and the engine was cut. Jenny sat up and pushed herself against the back of the van. She stared at the double doors in front, at the slit of light that was visible around the handle. There was nothing but silence. She waited for what seemed like an hour but was probably only half that. The doors didn't open and all was quiet. Finally she moved. She felt the back door then pushed her eye up to where the sunlight was leaking through. All she could see was another panel of metal that blocked out her view of anything else. She could hear gulls; they were loud and raucous and she was sure one had landed on the van. She could hear its flat feet slapping against the metal as it walked the length of the roof above her. She tried the door handle. It didn't budge.

More time passed. Jenny couldn't be sure how long, but the harsh white slash of sunlight seemed to have dimmed, suggesting that the sun had moved significantly in the sky. She started calling out. Not loudly at first, just enough for someone close by to be able to hear her. She grew quickly in confidence and her voice got louder until she was shouting at the top of her voice and banging with all her might on the metal sides.

Nobody came.

The slash of light was all but gone completely when she accepted finally that no one was coming to help. She collapsed back onto the floor and waited. Eventually, she drifted into an uncomfortable sleep. Suddenly she heard a voice.

'You need to put the bag on. Like I told you.' The voice was muffled through the door, but Jenny recognised it as the man at the hotel room, the man who had brought her this far. She sat up and rubbed at her arms and legs. They felt cold and numb.

'What for?' she called out, her voice hoarse, her throat raw from shouting.

'You don't need to be asking me any questions. Just do it — or you can stay in there and rot.'

'I'll stay in here then.'

'Put the hood on, Jenny. That's the last time I ask nicely.'

Jenny scrabbled around on the floor. She felt the bundle of cloth and pulled it over her head. 'Done.'

The doors opened almost instantly and she was aware of a bright light shining directly at her, reaching through the weave of the bag. The light seemed directed and artificial — a torch maybe? She felt rough arms grab her and pull her out. She reckoned there was more than one man — at least two. She tried to stand on her own feet but she was unsteady; her legs were riddled with pins and needles. She couldn't walk properly. Something was wrapped around her neck, the bag suddenly pulled tight. Her hands were pulled behind her back and held so that she couldn't move them. There was no time for her legs to recover; she was simply dragged away from the van. She didn't even bother to complain. The bag wasn't quite tight enough and Jenny could see an inch or two if she looked straight down. She could see her feet shuffling over dark stone that was buffed so it reflected the artificial light. She could be sure it was dark. She could no longer hear the call of the gulls but she could hear the movement of a body of water. The breeze that lightly pushed her clothing against her chest also wafted up her nose and it was tinged with salt and the scents of the sea.

'Where are you taking me?' She got no reply, just a shove to quicken her pace. She'd walked a good distance when the terrain underfoot changed. She could see a steel mesh beneath her and, below that, dark waves lapped against thick concrete legs. This was a pier or a harbour breakwater. Instinctively she pulled back against the men who held her arm. They pushed harder in reply.

'Don't be stupid now, love. You don't want to piss me off.' A different voice: harsher and deeper than the man she had been conversing with since the hotel. A few more seconds and she was brought to a stop. She felt pressure on her shoulders, pushing her down. She fell to a sitting position. The bag was still tight round her head. Jenny's body was suddenly so tense that she couldn't move. Her legs were straight out in front of her. Someone reached down and grabbed them roughly. She was spun where she sat. She could just see out of the bottom of her hood still, only just — enough to see she that she was right on the edge of the pier, side-on to the water. She thought for just a second that this was it: they were going to push her in sideways. They didn't. Instead she was held firmly by the ankles. She felt something wrap around them that was pulled sharply tight — too tight. Her ankles were shot through with pain and she screamed out.

'Give over, love. We ain't even started yet!' A new voice. Then laughter. She felt her legs pushed back around so that she was facing back the way she started. The bag was tugged from her head. It hurt her nose and pulled her hair as it lifted.

Jenny blinked. The breeze in her face and the artificial light meant it took a second to focus. She was sitting on the edge of the pier. She recognised it immediately: Langthorne's harbour arm. They had walked it as a family just a few days earlier. It jutted out into the English Channel. The old port on the east side was hidden behind a tall stone wall and there was a sandy beach on the west side — the side she was facing. It had restaurants and bars down its length, but they were open only at the weekends. She'd learnt that the hard way. It was all silent now. She didn't know what time it was but the night was well established. The sea was calm but, at some 600 metres out, the surface still bobbed and frothed. The water seemed to repel the artificial light of the arm from its surface rather than reflect it. It had a black infinity to it. It was terrifying.

Jenny tried to get her breathing under control. She felt surrounded. She had her head and her eyes down; she didn't want to look around, to make eye contact, to antagonise anyone. They were speaking amongst themselves. She wasn't tuned into the words. Someone stood next to her, close enough to be touching her left side.

'Please, I don't know what this is about. I don't know why you want me here. What do you want from me?' she sobbed. The sobs were sudden; she hadn't been expecting them herself.

'We don't need anything from you!' Another voice, this time behind her. She heard footsteps walk round to her right. 'Look at me, Jenny.' Jenny turned her head but she kept her eyes down. She was aware of where the man was standing; she saw his dark trousers. 'I said LOOK AT ME!' The sudden increase in volume caught her out; she jerked her head up and her tears now fell freely.

'What do you want from me?' she said again. It was all she could manage. The man walked away from her. He bent down. Jenny noticed someone else on the edge that she hadn't noticed before. Their figure was lying down, a long back towards her. She narrowed her eyes to try and pick out some detail in the gloom just as the figure was grabbed by the shoulders and pulled into a sit. The man's head hung as if he wasn't conscious. Faint light fell on him as he was turned towards her.

'Joseph!' Jenny put her hand to her mouth; she hadn't meant to say anything but she couldn't stop the words.

'So we were right!' the man replied. Joseph moaned and his eyes flickered open. They were still rolled back. Another man bent down; he leaned over the edge and pulled something up on a rope. Jenny could see it was a bucket. He immediately tipped its contents over Joseph. Joseph reacted: he shouted without making sense; his head snapped up; his eyes opened and he shivered violently; his mouth gaped open and he rushed large gulps of air.

'Yo, Joe! Guess what? Your girlfriend's here!' Joseph's head moved from side to side. Finally he settled on looking over in her direction. His head leaked blood, the water had washed him but already he had a thick stream of red down his left side and over his ear. His eyes were severely swollen and his face was peppered with a red, bloody rash. His lips were swollen and blood trickled from his mouth. It was smeared on his teeth too when he grimaced.

'I don't know her! You boys messed up.' He immediately looked away, out over the sea.

'Oh really? Seems she knows you, Joe. She said your name the second she saw you. And look at her now! She looks like she's seen a ghost!' The man moved towards Jenny, his eyes fixed on her. He crouched down so he was more on her level. 'You really don't know what's going on, do you? I got a good nose for these things, see.'

'No.' Jenny shook her head; her nose dripped with moisture. She tried to look beyond the crouching man to Joseph. He was leaning away from her now and seemed to be vomiting.

'Well, that's not fair, is it? I know who you are, Jenny, so you should know who I am. My name, well what everyone calls me, is Jimmy, and I'm a man who runs a business. I have employees, Jenny, as any business does, and Joseph, here, is one of my employees. He is the cash man, Jenny. He looks after the cash, makes sure it stays safe. My relationship with Joe here is based on trust — much like yours, I would imagine. Does it bother you if I say that Joe here is not someone you can trust?'

Jenny shook her head and sobbed quietly. Joseph still wasn't looking over.

'Joseph here is not an honest man. I guess I knew that. You see we all go out and we take from the rich. Like Robin Hood only with a better business model. 'Ere boys, Jimmy Hood! You havin' that?'

Jenny heard some sniggers. She couldn't tell how many people were around her in total.

'So we don't give any of it away, obviously. Joseph, though, has been taking what he wants from off the top. Skimming, I think you call it. Maybe I shouldn't hire thieves and then be upset when they steal, right? But I'm here to ask for what is mine to be returned — that is all. I have already asked, of course, and so far he has not been willing to help.' The man stood back up. 'I wonder if he will be more willing to help now that you are here? Assuming he knows who you are, of course!' Jimmy chuckled. He turned away to face Joseph. Jenny took in Jimmy's form. He was tall and solidly built. In the dimly lit environment she could still pick out dark hair and dark features overall.

'I don't know anything.' Jenny called out to his back. 'I just want to go and get my daughter. Joseph, whatever this is about, whatever you have, give it back. Just give it back, Joseph, so we can go home.'

Jimmy turned back to face her. 'Well, now, I didn't say *that*, did I? And the child is something else that Joseph had been keeping from me, but then I can understand why. If you are going to steal from a man like me then I suppose you best keep quiet about your family. Or at least not use them to hide what you steal — right, Joseph?' Jimmy grabbed Joseph's hair. He pulled it firmly so that his head faced up. 'Your mother would probably agree, don't you think? If she could, of course.' He let go of Joseph's hair and his head lolled forward. Jimmy moved back towards Jenny and he stepped over her outstretched legs.

'Here we are then, Joe!' Jimmy called out, then made an exaggerated grunt as if he was straining. Jenny looked up to see that he was holding something that took both his hands to lift. It looked to her like an iron dumbbell, but bigger than any she'd seen. Jimmy struggled with the weight before putting it on the ground next to Jenny. She could now see the length of rope that was tied off through its middle. She froze. The rope was short, just enough for it to fold back on itself, but it finished around her ankles. Joseph looked over and he saw it too. His eyes flashed wide. A man appeared on the other side of him; he was holding an identical dumbbell. He put it down on the ground and it made a heavy, metallic sound against the stone pier. It had a rope tied off round its middle too. Joseph's ankles were together. They also trailed a length of rope.

'Jesus, Jimmy!' Joe groaned. 'This is nothing to do with her.'

'I agree, Joe. But this is everything to do with you. You need to make a decision now about what happens next.'

'What decision? There's no decision here.'

'Beating on you did nothing. Threatening to go and get your girlfriend did nothing. So I did it. I've brought her here, to the deep sea with a weight tied around her ankles. I don't think you need me to explain where this ends up next, do you? Unless you *now* feel like talking.'

'There's no choices here, you're going to do this anyway. You were always going to do it!' Joseph's words were rushed suddenly, breathy with panic.

'You might be right. You were always going to die, Joe. You let me down, and I can't have people thinking that is okay. It is not okay, Joe. But the missus here . . . she's your decision.'

Jenny's attention was dragged to her left where there was movement. The weight scraped against the floor and someone picked it up. They stepped right to the edge, where the water rippled below. She braced herself and held her breath. In front of her was a thick chain that ran between two steel posts, a sort of fence, she reached out and wrapped her arms around it.

'How long do you think that will help you, Jenny?' Jimmy leered over at her. 'You do have a bit of fight in you, though. I'll give you that. You gave us the right run around. But we have you now, Jenny, and I won't be giving you an inch.' His attention turned back to Joseph. 'So, decision time, Joe.' Jenny suddenly felt something solid in the back of her head, pushing down. She jerked her head enough to get a view of the man that had been at her hotel holding a pistol to the back of her head. She met his eyes and he stared back. Jenny didn't reckon she could see a flicker of doubt or of humanity there. He was ready to pull that trigger.

'Turn away, Jenny,' he growled. 'Face out to sea. NOW!' He pushed the solid barrel more firmly into her skull. She squealed in pain and turned away. She could just see Joseph in her peripheral vision. Jimmy was stood directly behind him. He had his own pistol and pushed it into the back of Joseph's head.

'Here we are then, Joe. Tell me where my money is and this fate is only yours. Refuse me one more time and you get to see the lovely Jenny there go first. How long can she hang onto that chain for, do you think?' He chuckled. Behind her she could hear more laughter. These bastards would like to see that; she reckoned they were praying for it. Joseph shut his eyes. Jimmy reached down, he had big hands. He gripped the top of Joseph's head and wrenched upwards, forcing his eyelids wide open. 'That won't help you, Joe. My money, Joe. Make your choice.' Jenny's eyes snatched to the left, the solid dumbbell attached to her rolled towards the sea. It stopped right on the edge, resting against a slightly raised lip.

Joseph was breathing hard, but through his nose. Every breath was loud and rushed.

'Fuck it, drop it!' Jimmy called out. There was movement to her left and she took another big breath.

'Wait!' Joseph shouted. He was looking over to her.

'Wait for what, Joe? I am not a patient man.'

'I'll tell you. I'll tell you where it is. All of it.'

Jenny felt the pressure against the back of her head ease off. The weight rolled back a couple of inches away from the edge. Another second passed before she saw Joseph gulp. Then he started talking.

'You let her go. A ten-minute head start. Then I tell you.'

'You bartering with me, Joe? You setting rules now? You lost that chance a long time ago. Fuck this, drop her in!'

'WAIT! Okay! It wasn't at the house. There's a stable block on their land. I've been keeping it there, in a horsebox, parked up. The land is separate from the house. They don't even know about it. It's got nothing to do with them and it's got nothing to do with her. You can let her go. She doesn't even know what I'm talking about.'

'Separate where?'

'You got my phone from the hotel room, right? The notes section has the address for the yard.' Everyone went quiet. Jenny heard the sound of a phone being unlocked. She strained to look sideways. The phone was being lowered to Joseph.

'Yeah — that's it. You've got everything you need. You got issues with me we can talk about it, but she doesn't need to be here.'

'She doesn't need to be here? She doesn't even know what we're talking about, you say? Well, maybe we should educate her. Why don't you tell, Joe? Why don't you tell her what you've been doing — why she's sat on the end of a pier? You brought this on her. The least you can do is explain.'

'She doesn't know nothing, Jimmy. She's got nothing to do with it.'

'So you keep saying!' The man called Jimmy suddenly stepped over Jenny's outstretched legs. He lowered himself down so he was facing her. She could see him up close now. He looked at her intently and she stared right back.

'Quite a pretty little thing, aren't you, Jenny? Wasted on this piece of shit.'

'What do you want from me?'

'Nothing from you. You've done everything I needed.' Jimmy stood up. Suddenly there was a loud *bang*! Jenny shook as Joseph slumped forward. He was leaking blood from the back of his head. In the dim light it was like a thick, dark shadow that quickly consumed his back. Jimmy kicked out at the dumbbell next to Joseph's hip and an instant later she heard a splash. Joseph was moving forward, but slowly. Suddenly he jerked forward. She got a flash of his open eyes as he slid over the edge. She heard a second splash. Some of it flicked into her face. It made her flinch again.

Jenny was flushed with panic. She was alone now. They hadn't tied her hands, the rope already felt looser round her ankles and yet they couldn't let her survive: the man had said his name and then murdered someone right in front of her. She was acting instinctively. There was only one way she might get away from this. She had to run.

Her bound feet kicked out at the weight and an instant later it hit the water. Somebody shouted something — she couldn't make out what. She leaned back so that her body was straight, her right hand lifted to her nose to squeeze it shut and she slammed her eyes tightly shut. She was wrenched forward as if the sea itself had reached out for her.

The chill of the water took her breath away. She let go of her nose; she wanted to flail her arms, to thrash against the freezing water, but she knew she couldn't let panic take over. Somehow, in the pitch black and freezing water with an invisible force dragging her lower she managed a moment of calm.

She reached down to her ankles. They were still tied together, she could feel herself sinking, the pressure building in her ears. She had her eyes open but it made no difference. Her hands were so cold they weren't working properly. She couldn't hear any sounds. The rope felt slippery. She tried to focus on yanking it upwards. It was too heavy — it just kept pulling her down. She concentrated again on staying calm. A few seconds later, she could feel the steel of the dumbbell. It was resting on the bottom. Her hands moved over it, she had seen the locking screw on the side that held the weights on the threaded bar. It ought to unscrew but it didn't budge. She needed a breath. She tried to ignore it, tried to calm her mind. She knew that was the key. She twisted the metal again, focussing all of her strength into her grip. She thought it moved but she couldn't be sure. She kept tugging at it. It was turning. Her panic came back in waves but she twisted faster and the screw came free. The weight was too heavy to pull off the end of the bar, she tried tipping it up but the metal dug into the soft seabed. She planted her feet and tugged it upwards with the last of her strength. Suddenly it was lighter. She was still trying to feel with her hands, then she got hold of the rope and it came free.

Jenny's lungs were bursting. She was a strong swimmer and she could hold her breath, but she was running out of time. She tried to focus on her swim. She pushed off the bottom as hard as she could. Her ankles were still tied together and she tried to kick the rope off but it wouldn't budge. She couldn't afford to panic; she would die if she did. She focussed on trying to kick with her legs together as she pulled upwards with strong strokes. She used her own desperation to power her arms.

Her hand bashed against something firm, she reached out, it felt like stone but it was slimy with weed. It must have been one of the legs of the pier. She pushed off from it, she was desperate for a breath and could do no more to stop her mouth from reaching for the oxygen it craved. She took a huge gulp but she was still under water and it was still pitch black. She took in water — she coughed and swallowed but there was nowhere for it to go, she just took more in. She was drowning.

She could see a flicker of light and she kicked her legs towards it. The light grew bigger — and then she broke the surface. Straight away she tried to take in the air but it still couldn't reach where it needed to go. For a moment, she thought it was too late, that her lungs were filled, but she gagged up some water and managed to keep her mouth above the surface enough to suck in some oxygen. Her arms were flailing, and she tried again to focus on her technique. She calmed her movements, grabbed the bottom of her jumper and scooped a pocket of air like she had been taught in school. She tried to relax and lay back to float. She kicked her shoes off and wriggled her feet together. She felt the rope slipping down and her legs came free. She could hear shouts. Her return to the surface hadn't been quiet. She had recovered enough to tread water but was still coughing as she looked around to take in her surroundings. The pier was in front of her but she had come up on the other side. She could see the tall wall and she knew the men would be behind it. She must have gone right underneath. She didn't have much time. She looked around for an escape route. There was a pebbly beach some five hundred metres away, but they would surely make their way back there and there would be no quick or quiet way of getting out. She had seen a sandy beach further away on the other side. The coast curved away from the pier — maybe another fifty metres — and she wouldn't be able to swim straight for it. She would have to go round the end of the pier, giving it a wide berth, and then head for the beach, as far away as she could manage. She didn't know if she had the strength. She was struggling just to stay afloat and it was freezing cold. She had to focus. She fixed on a point to swim out to. When she got there the plan was to turn and fix on a point to swim back to on the shore. She conjured images of Isobel in her mind, she imagined holding her again. She moved onto her front and kicked her legs.

Chapter 23

Stanley beamed the moment he set eyes on his daughter. To George he looked immediately like a completely different man. He finally showed some colour and some warmth.

'Louise! Did you come all the way back just to see me? You shouldn't have bothered.' Stan's voice was hoarse. To be expected. Hopefully Stan's throat was just swollen and not damaged.

'Don't be silly, Dad. When I heard you were in here I couldn't stay away, could I?' Louise chuckled; it was nervous and awkward but Stan didn't seem to notice.

'What's all this about then, Louise? What am I doing in here and where's your mother? How come you can make it from all the way over in Italy and she can't pop up from home?' Stan was still smiling, waiting for the reasonable explanation. Like maybe she was out getting the teas in. Louise chuckled again. She made eyes at George.

'Well, you know she'd be here if she could, Dad. She'd love to be here.'

Stan's face suddenly creased in confusion. 'Is she not here?'

'No, Dad, but the police are here. They need to talk to you. We all need to know what happened, you see. What went on. This is Inspector George Elms. You've met him, Dad, but you might not remember.'

Stan peered over at George. George stepped forward, he didn't want to, but he had no choice. 'Hey, Stan. I'm glad to see you're awake. You gave us all a bit of a scare there.'

'A scare? What are you talking about? What happened to me, Louise? Why are the police here?'

'They need to talk to you, Dad. I'm going to let them talk to you. I'll be right outside. I'll come back in when they are done. I'll get us a drink, okay?' Louise moved out of the room. She was quick on her feet, her head down, her hand over her mouth. George could tell she was breaking down. He stepped out after her.

'Louise! Are you okay?'

'No, not really, George. I'm sorry. I can't talk to him. I can't tell him about Mum, about what happened. Can you do it, George? Can you tell him — please!'

She turned away. She didn't wait for an answer and then she was gone. George stepped back into the room. 'I'll leave you to it, sir.' Paul Bearn had been stood in the corner. 'I don't want to add to the confusion.'

It was just George and Stan now. Stan shuffled in the bed. He grimaced and struggled to sit up a little straighter. George walked over to him and stretched his arms out to help. Stan shooed him away.

'I can manage. What's going on here? Why isn't anyone talking to me?'

'I'm here to talk to you, Stan. Your daughter is a little upset. I think she's had a long day. Like I said, you had us all worried.'

'Well, I'm fine now. What happened to me anyway? You're police, right? Why the bloody hell are the police here? And where's Janice?'

'Stanley, you called us. To your home address in the early hours of Sunday morning. A couple of days ago, now. You had intruders at your home. They were there to steal from you. You put up a good fight. Do you remember any of what happened, Stan? Does any of this ring any bells with you?'

'Intruders? No! Is Janice okay? Is she injured too?'

'You weren't injured as part of the robbery. Your wife, though, Stan . . . I'm so sorry. She suffered a gunshot wound and there was nothing that could be done for her.'

Stan's head twitched suddenly, like the information was stuck on the way in. 'She's not here? My Janice?'

'Stan, she died on Sunday morning. You were with her. She died in your arms. We're doing all we can to find the people that did this. You can really help us . . .' George trailed off. He had given bad news any number of times; it was never easy. But it had never been this hard. He could see the man in front of him changing again. He was already confused from oxygen starvation and his mind was processing the information slowly. George could see it sinking in; he could see the colour draining.

'My Janice . . . she's . . . gone?'

George was right up close to Stan now. He fidgeted in the bed, his hand rose to his neck where an angry red slit ran through his leathery skin. It was already turning blue with the bruising. His expression was pained as he swallowed too. It was obviously causing him pain.

'I'm so sorry, Stan.'

'My neck is so sore, Inspector. I did this, didn't I?'

George pursed his lips and nodded. 'Are you remembering? What happened?'

'Not really. But I remember this pain. That's why I did it, isn't it?'

'Grief, Stan . . . it can overpower any of us.' George took hold of Stan's hand, as he had done forty-eight hours before. Stan's watery eyes lifted to meet his. 'Stan, the people that did this . . . we think they knew you. Or at least they know who you are. Well, enough to know your name and that you might have something of value at your house. Do you have any idea who might have that information and might be linked to criminality? Or maybe vulnerable to information being extorted? I know it's hard to think right now but I need your help, Stan, if I'm going to catch these bastards.'

Stan stared out beyond George and his eyes appeared unfocussed. George thought he had lost him. He let go of his hand and stepped away. He looked over at the door, considering if now would be a good time to get Louise back in the room. The news would sink in over the next few hours and they'd be back to square one, but at least they still had him. 'I'll go get Louise, okay, Stan? You think over what I said. I'll talk to you again later.' George moved towards the door. He was overwhelmed with tiredness — emotionally drained.

'Joseph,' Stan said.

George stopped at the door. 'Sorry, Stan?'

'Joseph. This will be about Joseph. My son.'

'Your son?'

'Yes. Did you talk to him yet? We don't talk so much, Inspector. We haven't talked since . . . well, since he made clear that he'd chosen his path.'

'No . . . I mean we haven't had a chance yet . . . we can't seem to locate him, Stan. What path is that?'

Stan sniffed. His voice came back weaker. 'He's a bad man, George. Me and his mother fell out about it a lot. She still helps him — I know she does. But some people you shouldn't help, no matter what they are to you.'

George was leaning on the door when it was pulled suddenly open and it made him jump. Louise bustled back in. Her dad was in tears, his hands covering his face. She locked eyes with George and mouthed a *thank you*. George smiled back. She walked over to Stan and they embraced in a deep hug. Paul looked to move back into the room but George stood in his way.

'Louise, we need to get back to work. Are you going to be okay from here?'

'Yes. I've been told I can stay here. They'll be keeping Dad in for the night at least. Tomorrow I'll get something sorted for us both.'

'Very good. You have my number. But I do expect to come and talk to you both again tomorrow.'

Louise nodded. She was leaking her own tears. She went back into an embrace with her dad. George walked away and Paul caught up.

'I take it we're not going to get much out of him tonight, George.'

'He's already said more in the last five minutes than he has over the last two days, Paul. We need to get to the house and do a quick search. I need to find the details of their son.'

'Whose son?'

'The Wingmores'. It would appear they may have a criminal for a son.'

'And you think he's the link.'

'I don't know, Paul. But it took our Stan to be confused and emotional to even admit his existence. There has to be a reason he didn't tell us about him. Then he tried to take his own life. I know he's mourning, but I didn't have him pegged as the type.'

'Did he give you a name? For the son?'

'Joseph. That's all he said. We could assume Wingmore for a surname, but you know me and assumptions.'

'Yeah, I think I do. I think it means another long night.'

George gritted his teeth. 'You don't have to come along, Paul. I can handle this. It's not like I've got a family to get home to.'

Chapter 24

It was just before 9 p.m. when George pulled into the rear yard of the police station. He and Paul Bearn had found a search team at the Wingmore house who had been happy to talk about their finds. It hadn't taken long at all. Even so, they cut tired figures as they crossed the dark expanse to the side door. The lift was waiting for them. George sighed as he leant back on the glass.

'You could have retired, George,' Paul said. 'Walked away.'

'I'd miss it too much,' George said. They both chuckled. The doors parted just two floors up and they walked into the Major Crime office. The main part of the room was in darkness, the meeting room lit brightly in contrast. George could see Whittaker pacing the floor. He looked much the same as when the job had first come in. He could see DS Melanie Richards and DS Jason Carter too, sat at the table with Emily Ryker. Melanie looked like she was making notes. Ryker made a *shh* gesture at George as he walked in and she pointed at the odd-shaped phone that was in the middle of the table. George recognised it immediately as the conference phone. It looked like a squashed star. A voice emitted from it. John Whittaker stopped to hover over it.

'Well, be sure to give me an update after you speak to George. I will be on the phone until late now anyway. I have a number of calls to make before I get to stand down from this incident. If it goes straight to voicemail then please keep trying, John. I want us to talk again.'

'Understood, sir. As soon as George gets here we will see what we know collectively and I'll be able to call you with a summary.'

'Good to hear. Speak soon.' Whittaker pressed the button with gusto to end the call. He expelled air and glanced over at George. 'Superintendent Ian Jackson,' he said, gesturing at the phone. 'He's very interested, as you can imagine.'

George could imagine. Major Crime was his baby. It had been his career to this point at just about every rank. The Chief Constable himself tended to use Jackson to oversee anything that might threaten the reputation of the force. This was clearly something in that category. 'We'd better not mess this up then, sir.' George offered.

'That is precisely what he was just saying. Only I think he used the phrase *coherent response.*'

'Same thing, right?'

'Exactly. And our response *has* been good, people. I think we've made good headway. The coherent bit might have been missing but that's inevitable with such a fast-moving investigation. The idea of this get-together is to talk about what we all know so then we can all know what we all know. Does that make sense?'

'Not really, sir,' Emily offered.

'No, I suppose it doesn't. I think I'm more tired than I thought.'

'We know what you mean!' Emily said.

'Well, good. So I'll start.' Whittaker positioned himself in front of the timeline. It was far busier than the last time George had seen it. 'So, shots fired here, at the beginning of our timeline at around 11 a.m. Sunday morning. Numerous reports. We also have an RTC and patrols are deployed. We now know that a vehicle was being pursued by a dark-coloured van and shots were fired between the two. The crashed vehicle is still with forensics but it has a number of bullet holes and also pellets from what we believe to be a shotgun. So, two different types of gun. The car then comes to a rather sudden stop on London Road, Dover, just outside of the Lucky Inn Chinese restaurant. There is limited CCTV from a premises on the other side of the road that gives a long distance view. The van is then seen to stop on the other side of the road and a person alights from the passenger seat. He is described by witnesses as a male carrying a long-barrelled firearm. Our missing female then gets out of the passenger side of the crashed car and she goes out of view when she walks around to the pavement. Again from witnesses, we know that she got hold of her baby and made off from the scene on foot. The CCTV then shows the armed man approach the vehicle and he appears to fire into the crashed car, through the passenger window. Shortly after this, the van comes back into shot — we can only assume it went around the one-way system — and it stops right by the crashed car. Two people are seen to exit this van and they drag someone from the car and throw them into the back.'

'So it's a kidnapping? I thought he died at the scene?' George said.

'So did we — initially.' Whittaker pointed at a name written on the timeline. 'Oliver Adams is the deceased from this scene. Witness accounts tell that he was walking past, he was on the pavement — going about his daily business. He was carrying shopping bags and lives nearby. The car crash happened close to him and he went to the aid of the occupants. He was seen talking to the female just before she ran away. It is thought that he was in the crossfire when the gunman attempted to stop her from fleeing.'

'Poor bastard.'

'Quite. And of course we know there was to be a poor bastard number two. We'll come onto him. So, our woman and baby run into a supermarket car park a few streets over and she is pursued on foot. More shots are fired and a uniform patrol are drawn into the action. They find a healthy baby girl on the bonnet of their car and no sign of the mother. The woman — and we presume the gunman — have continued on foot down a path that leads alongside the river. And here is poor bastard number two, as promised.'

'Stephen Maddocks?' George said.

'The very same.'

'I still can't believe it. He's a bit simple, he's got a fascination with all things police. A bit of a timewaster, but harmless enough. He probably heard the sirens, he would have come out to see what was going on.'

'That sounds like our man. Whatever his reason for being there, it would appear that Mr Maddocks does his best to help. Certainly he is local to that area and he is seen to walk back towards his house with a female. So we assume he was on the river path and she would have been very distressed. They are followed back to his home address where Stephen is shot dead. The female has again managed to escape on foot. Blood and forensics suggest that she made it out of the back way. And let me tell you, she has done very well. The back yard is entirely enclosed by an eight-foot wall. It seems fear can put a real spring in your step.'

'It would do too. She probably saw Maddocks get blown away right in front of her. You would run, wouldn't you?'

'Yes, you would. And that is the last we see of our girl on that day. We have other possible sightings and they are still being processed and looked into. But the next confirmed sighting is the following day when a female makes contact, stating that she is with our missing girl and wishes to bring her into the police station. This is arranged and the vehicle she is travelling in is ambushed en route. Rather impressively, our girl manages to get away, again on foot. And we've heard nothing since. One can hardly blame her for not wanting to make herself known again.'

'And nothing came from the leak?' Mel Richards directed her question at George.

'No. I mean, there is still work that can be done around that, but nothing immediately. An FCR call-taker received an advance payment and was told to call a number with any information about the missing girl. He did as he was asked. We don't know how he came to be targeted, but I do think it was a case of him being targeted, rather than him being involved. I don't think for a second that he knows who paid him the money.'

'So the trail went a little cold,' Whittaker continued. 'But George, here, has an update that links a job he has been working — and gives us all a lot more work to do. George?'

'Well, yes, you will all know there was a shooting in the early hours of Sunday morning. Stanley and Janice Wingmore, up in Elham, were visited by some unwelcome guests who tricked them into opening their front door. They then demanded money and, when it wasn't forthcoming, they shot Mrs Wingmore dead. Source information tells us that Stanley Wingmore, at least, was known to the gang in some way and they also went there with the belief that there was a large amount of money at the location.'

'Is there?'

'Paul and I are just back from there. The search team are currently doing what they do best. Forensics have been through the house, too. I will arrange for a cash dog to sweep it if necessary. One hundred grand is the figure. That's a lot of paper to hide.'

'Is it a big place?'

'It's a big estate. There are outbuildings that haven't been touched. I can't say it isn't there.'

'A hundred grand though? Where does that come from?'

'I don't know. It's either a lifetime of farming, or a crooked son.'

'Go on?' Whittaker leant in.

'I spent some time with Stan. He's taken it hard — so hard that he tried to hang himself in his barn. Paul saved his life, but his brain was starved of oxygen long enough to cause some damage. He's lost his short-term memory and some of his caution.'

'His caution?'

'Yes, he told me about his son — straight off the bat when he came to. He didn't mention him at all the first time around.'

'So you think he was hiding something?'

'There's no question he was hiding something, it's just whether it is relevant or not.'

'It has to be relevant, doesn't it?'

'I think so. They've found a load of documentation. Some of it relates to a Joseph Wingmore. There's also correspondence with a Joseph Cooper.'

'Same person?'

'We shall see. We'll be giving the house back to Mr Wingmore tomorrow when he and his daughter come back from the hospital. They will have some questions to answer too. I also happen to know a very good intelligence officer who has made a career of getting to the bottom of this sort of thing.'

Emily sat back in her chair, her arms folded. 'Sure. But in the morning, George.'

'Oh yes, Emily,' Whittaker cut in. 'We are most definitely done for the day. I will be back in around seven. Is there anything more to share, George?'

'No, sir. I think that's about it. I want to revisit Stan. Like I said, he'll be discharged tomorrow. Hopefully the timing will work out and we will clear the scene in time for him to go home.'

'What's the deal with the short-term memory, George? Is that still going to be a factor?' Whittaker asked.

'Yes, sir. The neurologist couldn't tell me how long it would last for. He doesn't think it will be permanent but he couldn't promise that it wouldn't be either.'

'But our Stan . . . he knows what happened?'

'He didn't, not any of it. I had to give him the death message, sir. I had to break his heart all over again.'

'Jesus, man, that's not ideal. What about the house? Is there the need for a clean-up? I can't have the poor old bastard turning up to that.'

'I've sorted it, sir.'

'George paid for it out of his own money, sir,' Emily cut in. She eyed George as she did. 'This was before he had any memory issues. George didn't want him cleaning up what was left of his wife.'

'Quite right, too. Why didn't you use my budget, George? I won't have you paying for something like that.'

Emily was quick again, 'I think sometimes George forgets that other people care about our victims, sir. It's a fault. A good one, but a fault all the same.' Emily's gaze was still locked on George. Her discourse was impossible to miss.

'Well, we've had a long day and we're all very tired.' Whittaker announced. 'I think budget is definitely something that can wait for the morning. The way I see it, this investigation splits two ways . . . George, Paul and Emily . . . I want you to continue your work on Stan and the son. Mel and Jason will stick with me and the rest of the incident room and we will carry on trying to find our missing runaway. Somewhere between those two are all the answers we need. Does anyone have anything to add that we might need to know right now?'

There were mumbled negatives around the table and then they all got up. Emily was out of the door before

George could even call out her name. He watched her through the glass as she made for the exit. Whittaker was right: they were all tired. They would achieve nothing more that night.

Chapter 25

Jenny saw bright lights, unsettled and moving quickly. They were coming towards her. She was exhausted. All of a sudden the lights were gone. The sea washed over her; she felt the weight of it on her back, she could taste it strongly in her mouth and it stung her throat. She scraped against the beach. The pebbles moved underneath her; they bumped and smacked against her as the waves slid back out. Her breath came in short gasps.

The lights were closer and shone directly in her eyes. She reached out her hand to try and grip the beach and stop herself being sucked back into the wash, but her strength was spent and there was little she could do. The water rolled back over the top of her and she felt the pebbles on top of her this time. She was being buried and drowned at the same time. She was resigned to it. She stopped trying.

She felt rough hands under her shoulders. The grip was firm and strong and her face emerged from the sea. She was above the water now, looking down at it. Her bare feet scraped on the pebbles. She heard excited shouts.

'That's it! Get her out!'

She tried to take in a deep breath but still choked on salty water.

'Alright, love, stay calm. You've taken on some water.' She was lowered down, still fighting for breath. The beach was solid and unforgiving on her back. She was tugged on to her side and was promptly as sick as a dog. It just kept coming: water and bile that frothed like the sea from which she had just been pulled. The lights were still bright, she couldn't make out any details of the people around her. They were still talking, they still sounded excited. She finally got her breath.

'You're going to be okay,' someone said. The same voice then shouted, 'SHE'S OVER HERE!' He must have moved his feet; she felt pebbles push against her head. She still gulped the air. She was facing the sky. She could make out the stars. Her whole body shook violently in a shiver. She no longer felt cold, though — just numb.

She was aware of more people around her. More lights. The first voice she heard was back talking to her, telling her she was going to be okay. She could see a bit of him now. He had a boyish face and was wearing a head torch.

Someone put a blanket over her. She was rolled back onto her side, and when she was rolled back again it was softer on her skin. Then she was lifted into the air. She was on a stretcher of sorts and was moving up the beach. She could hear heavy footfalls on the pebbles, as if they were struggling with her. It seemed like an age before the scrunch of pebbles stopped. By then, vivid white light was all around her and she narrowed her eyes to it. Someone bent over her, a woman wearing a lurid green with yellow epaulettes.

'How are you feeling?'

Jenny tried to talk. She opened her mouth and could only grunt. Her body was shivering so hard now; she couldn't stop.

'We're going to strip you down and then bring you back up to a good temperature, okay? It's not really the night to be out for a swim, you know!' She chuckled but Jenny could see the concern in her face. 'What's your name?'

'J-J-J-J-Jenny.'

The woman smiled. 'Jenny, right?'

Jenny jerked a nod, her whole body still contorted in shivers.

'Well, Jenny, it's lovely to meet you. Another few minutes in that water and I don't reckon we would have. But you're going to be just fine now, okay?'

Jenny managed another nod. She felt the warmth of a tear on her cheek. She was aware she was being pulled around, the woman gave her another reassuring smile as she hovered above her with scissors. She cut off her top and it was replaced quickly by a blanket that rustled like foil. A softer blanket was laid on top of that. The woman spoke to someone, her voice raised a little. Jenny was again aware of being moved. She didn't know where. She didn't care anymore.

Chapter 26

George was lying on his sofa at 5 a.m. again when his phone went off. He had been asleep this time though. A shopping channel played softly on the television. George instantly felt terrible.

'Hello?'

'George! Sorry for the rude awakening, old boy.' John Whittaker sounded wide awake.

'Don't worry about it, Major. Seems like it's the week for it. What can I do for you?'

'Nothing really, George. I just wanted a chat, you know. I couldn't sleep.' George's eyes flicked to the clock hanging on his wall. He was about to make a point when Whittaker started laughing.

'Very good, Major.'

'Too early for banter, old boy? I've had a call. There's been a development.'

'That sounds more like it. Where do you need me?'

'William Harvey Hospital.'

'I'm on my way.'

George was there in twenty-five minutes. He made for the accident and emergency entrance since he knew it was open twenty-four hours and it was the only place with any movement. Sure enough, Whittaker was in the waiting area, sat on the edge of a plastic chair. George took in the waiting room and did nothing to hide his surprise at how many people were having medical emergencies at five thirty in the morning. Whittaker stood up and then George noticed that Ryker was there too. Whittaker nodded and immediately walked into the corridor, away from the waiting masses. Emily followed but stayed silent and didn't acknowledge George.

'Has there been some sort of natural disaster I wasn't aware of?' George said. 'I thought this was the quiet time for A and E.'

'State of the NHS these days, George. Some of these poor bastards have probably been here for hours.'

'Where are we going then, Major?'

'Well, I was going to wait for Mel Richards, but we appear to have an opportunity, George. I received a call from the night duty DS. Seems a female was pulled out of the sea last night. A group of night fishermen found her. She was in a bad way, suffering the effects of exposure, exhaustion and a few other bits and pieces. Half-drowned by all accounts. It took a little while for them to work out who she is, but it's our girl, George. It's the runaway.'

'You're sure?'

'Certain. I mean, I haven't met her yet, but she's spoken briefly to a couple of uniform officers and told them as much. She's shaken up, I hear, but I wanted to talk to her before we lose her to medical procedures and sleep.'

'I agree with that.'

'Well, good. I figured this is your thing. I mean, I was determined to find a use for you somewhere!'

'Very good, Major.'

'Of course we just need to find her first.' George could see Whittaker was peering up at the hanging signs. He stopped and looked in opposite directions. He set off again. George tried to catch Emily's eye and rolled his eyes playfully at the old man struggling with his directions. She was still ignoring him.

A passing nurse helped with directions. It was obvious when they were getting close to their witness. George could see two bored-looking firearms officers in chairs that had been placed untidily out in the corridor. They snapped to attention as Whittaker approached.

'Morning, men. Thanks for coming out. We have a VIP it seems?' He grinned and they both relaxed.

'As we understand, sir. We have both corridors covered with patrols. I can hear from the radio chatter that there are other patrols coming down to sit out the front.'

'Good stuff. Sounds like you have it covered. Do we have someone in with our young lady?'

'Yes, sir. A local patrol.'

'Very good. Is she just through there?'

'The door on the right there, sir.'

'Excellent. And have you been well looked after? Did anyone get you a tea yet?'

'No, sir. They all seem rushed off their feet to be honest. I certainly didn't like to ask.'

'No. Quite. I will though.' Whittaker chuckled and stepped to the door. George followed him. He stopped. 'We think she's *Jenny*, right?'

'So you said, Major,' George replied.

'I was just checking that was what I said. Don't get old, George. Not if you can help it.'

Jenny lay on her side. The standard white sheets of the NHS were mostly covered with a thick-looking blue blanket that was plugged into a box that whirred. The cover on the box flexed slightly as if it was breathing. George had seen such a device once before; it was designed to keep the body temperature constant. Jenny looked to be asleep. The sheet was tucked in tight around her.

'Good morning.' Whittaker was cheery for the female officer who stopped writing in her book. 'How has she been?'

'She's not talkative, sir. At least she hasn't been with me. The nurses have been in and out and they seem to be very happy with her. I think it's all observations now. The big challenge we've got is that she's shattered. She talked to me earlier but every word was a fight.'

'What did she say?'

'She was terrified, sir. She said they killed her boyfriend, she said she saw it and she escaped by jumping off a pier. They'd tied a weight around her legs. It sounds like quite an ordeal.'

'Blimey! It does at that, the poor thing. And this is just today's episode. This young lady has had quite a time. When did she last speak to you?'

'Oh, at least an hour ago. She's not been sleeping soundly, sir. She's very restless. The nurse said she would be while her body sorts itself out after the hypothermia. Her stress levels won't be helping either.'

Right on cue, Jenny murmured. She fidgeted under the thick blanket and moved onto her back. Her head rocked from side to side and it sounded like she was trying to form words. Whittaker and George leaned closer as her eyes fluttered open. Her eyes rolled in their sockets as if she wasn't quite awake.

'Hey, Jenny,' George said, softly.

Her eyelids flickered and then opened. He was close enough to see them focus.

'You're okay. You're in hospital and you're safe. I'm Detective Inspector George Elms and I'm—'

'George Elms . . .' Jenny murmured. Her eyes moved around and she grimaced as if confused.

'George Elms. I'm a police officer. Take your time, okay? You're safe here . . . we're going to help—'

'George Elms!' she screamed. Her eyes opened wide. Her arms and legs thrashed under the cover. George took a step back and looked over at Whittaker and Emily. Jenny screamed again, it was long and more powerful. George stepped further back.

'Not him! Not him!' She fixed on him, then over at Whittaker. Emily pushed past George and placed her hand gently on Jenny's forehead.

'Hey, hey, Jenny! Shh . . . it's okay, honey. It's okay.'

Jenny settled down a little though her breathing was still rushed and loud and her eyes searched the room.

George moved further away.

A nurse appeared at the door. 'What the hell is going on here?' she demanded.

'It's okay. I think Jenny woke up a little confused and surrounded is all,' Emily said.

'Not him! George Elms! He was there. He was there!'

'Could you please leave?' The nurse held the door open and she looked over at the two men. Whittaker led the way back out into the corridor.

'What the hell was all that about?' Whittaker said.

'I have no idea? She can't know what she's saying.'

'Does she know you?'

'No, Major, of course not. She's just woke up from hypothermia. She's all over the place.'

Whittaker sighed. 'I suppose you're right. I was kind of hoping she would come to and immediately regale us with her last three days. I suppose that was a little ambitious, thinking about it.'

'We'll get there. It'll just take time. Ryker's still in there. If anyone is capable of getting information out of someone, it's Emily Ryker.'

A few more minutes and both men glanced at the door. Emily Ryker appeared looking agitated. 'Seems you've made quite the impression, George.'

'What was that about?'

'I'll tell you what it was about, George. She saw you. At the hotel. While she was being kidnapped. I can't get too much detail out of her — she's repeating herself over and over. She's very traumatised but says she was stood right opposite you. She just keeps saying that you wouldn't even look at her.'

'Jesus, Ryker. I swear I've never seen that woman before in my life.'

'Which is what she is saying!'

'At the hotel?'

'The lift. She said you were in the lift with her. You were on your phone? I think that's what she means.'

'Jesus!' George brought his hands to his face. He couldn't look at Whittaker or Emily either. He turned away — and heard Whittaker's voice.

'Is that all she said? Can she not tell us more?'

'She won't engage. I struggled to get that much. She said she won't talk to me.'

'To *us* — because of me,' George said. 'She's lost all faith. You can't blame her.'

'We had no idea who she was, George,' Whittaker said. 'Even if you were looking right at her it wouldn't have made a blind bit of difference. You can talk to her when she's a bit more compos mentis and explain. She's had a traumatic time. Lord knows how she ended up in that sea.'

'She must have known who I was, that I was a copper. She must have been looking right at me, knowing that I should be helping her. She would have been leaking fear from every pore. I've been letting people down, Major. I didn't even realise this one.' George was still facing away, down a long, straight corridor. He started walking. He didn't know where he was going, but he needed to get away, to clear his mind.

'You okay, George?' Emily called out.

'Yeah, Ryker. I'll find us all a coffee or something, yeah?'

George kept walking. He hadn't gotten far when he saw a courtyard through the window. A bare square of concrete surrounded on all sides by corridors leading to different parts of the hospital. He stepped out through a door that clanked shut. Two wooden benches faced each other and a man stood leaning on the back of one of them. He had a drip on a wheeled holder and he was wearing pyjamas. He smiled at George. George ignored him, his back found the glass window and he slunk down to sit on the ground. The man was smoking and took a deep drag. George was aware he was still looking over in his direction.

'Shit day?' the man said. 'Or shit news, more likely, in this place.'

George knew he was going to have to engage. 'Shit day,' he said. He quickly looked back down at the floor.

'Shit news,' the man said.

George looked up at him.

'For me, I mean.' He sucked on his cigarette for a last time. It dropped to the floor and he stood on it with his slipper. 'You any good at telling families shit news? 'Cause I've been out here for three of these now and I still can't think of how to do it.' The man expelled some smoke in a sort of laugh. George thought he might break down. That was the last thing he needed. But he couldn't help but feel for him. The man's head dropped, he turned away as if he had accepted that George didn't want to talk.

'How shit?' George said. He forced himself back to his feet and moved over to the bench that faced the man. He sat down.

'There's nothing they can do. That shit.'

'That's right up there with the shittiest, friend. I'm really sorry.'

'Ah, don't be. If you don't look after your lungs they can come right back at ya! Who knew?'

'The problem isn't not knowing though, right? It's not caring. We've all been young and invincible.'

The man smiled ruefully. 'Yeah we have. And now I get to be middle-aged and dying. I got a year, max. My kids . . .' The man broke off.

'They'll be fine. Trust me, they will. How old?'

'Adult.' It was all he could manage.

'And now you know you've got twelve months to make the most of them. To make sure their memories of you are what every kid should have of their dad. Most people don't get that. I'm not saying anyone would swap with you, friend, but, actually, you get something most of us don't. You get a timetable. You get a motivation to make the next twelve months the best time you have ever spent with them. And it will be.'

The man's eyes were heavy and red as he peered over at George. 'You do this professionally? Did they send you after me?'

'Do what?'

'Talk to people when they walk away from a prognosis like I got? Making people feel better?'

'Goodness, no!' George couldn't help but laugh. 'I don't think I have the right qualifications for that job.'

'Not a job anyone would want either. Talking to the walking dead.'

'We're all walking dead, right? At least you have that timescale. When you tell your family, tell them that you have good news. That the next twelve months are gonna be the most amazing of your life — of *their* lives. It's still going to hit them hard but at least then you start off on the right foot.'

'I might just try that. I just want to see if I can go with no regrets, you know? That's the dream, right?'

'I think it is.'

'Not going to be easy, though. Me and my ex . . . we were great together. We had the kids but it went wrong. She had her head turned by her personal trainer. I'm a walking cliché, right? I was working all day and tired all night, so I guess it was inevitable, but I took it bad. I was so angry, it put a chip on my shoulder I never managed to get rid of. She hates me now. I mean, I know what she did, but I made her life hell.'

'Is that your regret?'

236

'No. I mean, it's *part* of it. It's the kids, see? She used to get upset and the kids would see her upset and they would know I caused it and . . . well, we all fell out for a while. We didn't talk for a few days, then a few weeks, then it was months and in the end it took years to sort it out. I never should have done that. I should never have let my pride stand between me and my kids.'

'Well, you've got twelve months to make it right.'

The man smiled, and this time it looked more genuine. 'You're right. Thanks for talking to me. I'm sorry I vented. I guess you were just the first person I saw.'

'No one sent you?' George quipped. 'To talk to me, I mean? Seeing as you accused me of the same?'

'What do you mean?' The man stopped in the doorway on his way back into the hospital.

'Doesn't matter. Good luck with it all, yeah?' The man left. It wasn't long before George turned to another voice.

Emily Ryker stepped out. 'Well, this place is fucking grim, isn't it?'

'The hospital?'

'Well, yeah, but I mean this little area. I would picture outside areas at hospitals as being like gardens, with flowers and stuff. This is like John Major's screensaver.'

'I suppose it suits it.'

'Not a fan of hospitals?'

'Who is?'

'You okay?'

'Fine. I was just thinking it out. The next step.'

'And there was me thinking you were out here beating yourself up. The boss was right, George. We didn't even know who she was then. It didn't matter whether you were looking at her or not.'

'Maybe you're right. It just puts us back a few paces. Do you think she'll talk to you? We need what she knows.'

'I don't think so. Not any time soon.'

'Dammit! Between her and Stan I feel like we've got all the keys now but we can't find the door.'

'We'll get there. Do you want me to find the coffee then?' Emily moved back to the door.

'Oh yeah, I'd forgotten about that. I'll have a tea if you're going.'

'Are you staying here?'

'Just a few more minutes. I need to make a couple of calls and then I'm going to go back in there and have a chat with our Jenny.'

'I think you're the last person she'll talk to, George. Are you sure that's a good idea? We don't want to piss her off and push her further away.'

'I think she'll talk to me. I just got an idea.'

'Why does that always fill me with a sort of dread?'

'I'll be five minutes behind you — in time for the tea at least. Just let me make this call.'

Emily lingered on him for a few seconds. She looked like she had more to say, but she moved back into the hospital. George watched her disappear from sight. He pulled his phone from his pocket and scrolled through to his wife's number. He pressed to dial and held the phone to his ear.

Chapter 27

George was very uncertain when he stepped back into Jenny's room. Jenny had fallen back to sleep; the monitoring equipment beeped a gentle rhythm around her; the blanket still breathed in and out as he approached. He had forgotten how tiny a baby could be. Isobel lay across his arm, tucked in tight to his chest. She was sleeping. She had squirmed a little when she was handed to him but her eyes stayed shut. Her breathing was rhythmic again and she looked peaceful.

'Jenny!' George said. Jenny stirred a little. 'Jenny, I've got Isobel here to see you.' Jenny's eyes fluttered open. She took a few moments, her eyes half-open. Suddenly they opened wide.

'Issy!' She pushed herself back in the bed and held out her arms. George laid Isobel gently in her grasp. He stayed close, the nurse had told him she was weak and she might not even realise it. She pulled her child to her chest and held on tight. There was no way she was going anywhere. George backed off a little.

'I'm sorry it took us so long to bring her down but we had to be sure you were okay first. How do you feel?'

'Great now!' Jenny beamed. She didn't take her eyes off her sleeping child. Isobel took a firm grip on her outstretched finger. 'Oh, my little Issy! I knew I would see you again!'

'I've arranged for a cot to be brought in here. She shouldn't have to leave your side again, Jenny. I thought you'd appreciate that.'

'Thank you.' Jenny now looked at George. 'Are you the man I shouted at earlier?'

'Yeah. I let you down, Jenny. But I wanted to exp—'

'They already did. The girl. She said that you didn't know what I looked like. You got my name from someone who heard Joseph shouting at me. It's okay.'

'It's not okay. I can't imagine how you felt in that lift. I must have been so close.'

'Closer than you are now. I read your tag. I saw you were police.'

'I am sorry.'

'It's okay. I know'

'I wanted to get off to a better start, Jenny — with you, I mean. We need you, we need your help desperately.'

'I thought you might. I'm not sure what I can do though. I'll be honest with you, Inspector, I just want all of this to go away.'

'Please, call me George. Unfortunately that isn't an option right now. The man in the car with you when this all started, is that your other half? We know he was taken from that car. We need to find him and—'

'He's dead.'

'He's dead?'

'I saw it. Joseph. He was with me on the pier. They shot him in the head. I was right there. Jesus!' She broke down. George cursed himself, immediately he knew he had underestimated what this girl had gone through. He looked around the room. There were two padded armchairs against the wall on the other side of the room. He pulled one over so it was next to her. She took a hold of herself a

240

little and nuzzled into Isobel. 'I'm sorry, George. I've had a hell of a few days. I thought Joseph was dead all along. I saw them shoot into the car, that's why I ran. I didn't even look back. Then I saw him on that pier and I was so confused. Not just because I thought he was dead, but because I knew that he was the reason I was involved in all this. I couldn't hate him though. I saw him there — he was all tied up and helpless. He tried to act like he didn't know me, but when they made him — when they said they knew all about me, he did what he could to save me. They shot him. It was like they were putting down an animal, George! How could someone do that?'

George still hadn't sat down; he simply leaned on the back of the chair. 'I really don't know, Jenny. No matter how long I do this job, no matter what I see or hear, I can never understand how people can be so evil. There's something fundamentally wrong with these people, Jenny. They need to be off the streets. The only way the rest of the world is safe from them is if they're in prison. You need to understand your situation, Jenny. You've witnessed a terrible crime. These people cannot let you live. They've proven just how far they will go to hurt you. Right now you're safe. You're being protected by six armed police officers at different points around this hospital — with more on standby. I can help you, Jenny. I can keep you safe. But we have to help each other. The only way to guarantee your safety is to put these people behind bars. They can't hurt you there, Jenny. I'll make it as easy as possible. I've got a video camera. We'll set it up and forget about it. Then we just talk about what happened. No writing. No checking it back over. We just talk.'

'I don't want to talk! You can make me disappear. I've heard about it. I've seen it on TV — witness protection, right?'

'That's right, I can do exactly that. But to get witness protection, you have to be a witness. That means someone who is giving us evidence that will put these people away.'

'And if I don't, I'm on my own? Is that what you're saying?'

'Honestly? No. I'm not about to turf you back out and wish you luck, Jenny. But we can only do so much to protect you and we can only do it for so long. And you have to know that Social Services have arranged foster care for Isobel here—'

'Well, they don't have to now. I'm back, aren't I?' Jenny flashed angry, her cheeks burned red.

'You are. But think about it . . . will the police and Social Services let you have care of young Isobel, here, if you're considered to be a target for serious harm?'

'So you're going to take my baby away? Because I saw a murder and someone shot at me?'

'That's not what I'm saying, Jenny. I want to keep you both safe and I want to keep you both together. That's my favourite outcome. But if you take a decision that makes that impossible, then I will do what I can to keep Isobel out of harm's way. Because she isn't old enough to make a decision that is in her own best interest.'

'So you just came in here to threaten me with taking my baby away if I don't help you? You're no different to those men, they just used guns to threaten me.'

'I'm very different. If you don't help me I will still do all I can to keep you safe. I will still do all I can to find those men and to put them in front of a judge who can send them down for a very long time. And if I manage to do that without your help then I will help you get Isobel back in your care. I don't want you dead. That makes me your best option, Jenny. I haven't got off on the right foot with you. That was my fault. I still feel like I let you down, and because of that I will work harder and faster. But you need to help me. You need to tell me what you know and you need to let me put that into evidence. Together we will get these bastards. They've already given me the hump by shooting a defenceless pensioner dead in her own home. Help me, Jenny, please.'

Jenny snuggled back into Isobel. She kissed her lightly on the cheek. Isobel still slept soundly. 'And then you'll move me away? The new identity. A place to live? So I can't be found by them or their mates?'

'I will.'

'You promise?'

'I have a daughter too, Jenny. She's nine though. She does this thing — it's called a pinky promise. You have to link your little finger on one hand. There's nothing that can break a pinky promise.'

Jenny stared at him. She looked more than a little unsure. George held out his right hand, his little finger extended. Jenny shook her head, the slightest curl of her lips. Then she locked her finger with his.

When George emerged from her room Whittaker and Emily Ryker were stood outside waiting for him.

'You were ages in there, old boy. I take it you got her talking?'

'I did, yeah. It's a hell of a tale.' George lifted up the DVD that now contained her account.

'Where are we then, George? We all need to get back together at the nick. I'll need the team to sit and watch it so we all know what there is. Are there any fast-track actions, though — anything to do straight away?'

'There are, sir. I need a surveillance team and an armed tactical team that can be available round the clock.'

'Okay, I agree we need some safeguarding in place. I'm not sure I can get you a whole tactical team—'

'It has to be a tactical team, Major.'

'Okay? Are you aware of something that you are not divulging, George? You understand my position as the SIO. I can't have anything kept from me — especially if you want me to start writing blank cheques for tactical teams.'

'It's nothing like that, Major. There's more to this. We're not being told the whole picture here. I think there's still more to play out and we need to be ready. That will be our chance to nab these bastards.'

'I'll see what I can do. Teams of seven specialist officers don't come cheap. It can be done, but you need a damned good reason for not being content with sticking up a camera and putting a marked car outside the address. That would do the same job for a tenth of the budget.'

'They're preventative, sir. You can still do that by all means.'

'So you don't want the tactical team at the Wingmores'?'

'No, sir. And I would rather they didn't know.'

'Do you think this gang intend on coming back? That maybe they have unfinished business and this is a ploy to flush them out?'

'I don't think they will return there, sir.'

'You have me confused, George.'

'We still don't know the real story. We're getting snippets. I'm getting half-truths, half-stories and downright lies. Right now I can't pick out which is which. I figure if I'm not being told the truth I might try sitting back and seeing if it gets played out in front of me. You don't have to like the idea, Major, you just have to not dislike it enough to order me not to.'

'Oh, I definitely dislike it enough for that.'

'Are you ordering me not to?'

'Well, no, George. But we need to go over what you want to do. Then at least I know what I'm not ordering you not to do.'

Chapter 28

George was in the foyer of the hospital when his phone rang. It was Ali.

'What's up, Ali?'

'George, I'm done up at the house, but I've just had a rather strange call. The source of that call kept apologising and said that his orders had come from some bloke called DI Elms and that he didn't know any more. He seemed new, like he might be frightened to ask any questions. Maybe even new enough to respect you.'

'Blimey. Must be fresh out the box.'

'I know. And seeing as I don't particularly care about rank an' all that, I thought I would call you direct and find out what the hell is going on.'

'And I'm glad you did,' George chuckled. 'You know I always like to help. What do you need to know?'

'So I'm finished up at the house. But I'm being told to wait for a couple of other marked vehicles to get here. Then I'll be told when the scene can be stepped down and we all have to leave together in some sort of choreographed convoy?'

'That's right—'

'Then I need to make my way directly to Langthorne beach and — this is my favourite bit — this DI Elms joker needs me to create a crime scene using my body tent and some police tape. So . . . my question is probably obvious, George, don't you think?'

'Yeah. You're going to ask me what colour tent you should use. I know you have the yellow hi-vis one or the plain white. Personally I think you should go for the plain white. I think that's a bit of a classic.'

'You're not funny.'

'I am, Ali. You get told something enough and you do start believing it.' George ducked into a disabled toilet cubicle that had become free.

'Strange you should say that. You hear something enough about someone and you can start believing it too, George.'

George chuckled again. 'And I bet you haven't been hearing about how funny I am, have you?'

'Not even once.'

'So you want to know why on earth you would be leaving in a big convoy and then setting up a body tent over a mound of pebbles?'

'Well, yes.'

'It's a very long story, Ali, one that you are very welcome to hear right now or you can trust me and let me buy you a coffee in a day or so when this is all over. Your choice.'

'*How* long?'

'I-haven't-really-got-the-time long. The shortest version is that we had a girl go into the water off the pier out there. I need the people that were with her to think that she washed up dead. You're perfect for the job. This might be the only way I can get hold of these bastards. I can't tell you how important you are. That's not just me buttering you up either, Ali. I'll explain it all and you'll know I'm right.'

'I don't trust people, George — I've never been good at that. And doesn't that mean that we have another scene? On the pier, where this girl was pushed?'

'I didn't say she was pushed.' George was deflecting. He didn't want to tell her about his expectation of finding a body at the bottom of the sea, tied off on a dumbbell. CSI got twitchy around bodies in water, especially seawater. If forensics was your thing it was possibly the worst environment on earth.

'You've not said much!'

'Like I said, you can have the long story now or the coffee and full explanation later. You know you can trust me. You remember my face, right? How trustworthy it is? Hold that image in your mind. I think it'll help.'

'You're something, George. That's an image I really don't want. You'd better find these people and then you need to do better than a coffee and a cake.'

'I never said cake.'

'I haven't said yes.'

'Help me out, Ali, and you get whatever you need.'

'Done. Your cleaners have turned up, by the way.'

'Cleaners?'

'Yeah, I've kept in touch with the woman you spoke to who runs the cleaning company. They're at the address now. They should be done in the next hour or so. She doesn't like you either.'

'I don't need to be liked, Ali. That's good news, though. I'm waiting for Stanley now. I'm taking him back home. He should be with me any minute, and as soon as we get him home that's when the scene can be stood down.'

'Can't wait.'

With the call finished, George stepped back out of the toilet to see Louise in the distance. She was obviously looking for him. He had asked her to meet him here alone before he took her and Stan home. He got her attention with a wave and led her into the first vacant room he found. There were seats and he offered her one, then took one himself.

'This has the feeling of bad news, George,' Louise said.

'There's no way of hiding it, I'm afraid, Louise. It would appear that I am about to make your day darker.'

'What is it?'

'Your brother. Joseph.' George waited for a reaction. She bit down on her lip and waited for him to continue. Certainly there was no denial of his existence. 'I'm very sorry to have to tell you this, Louise, but we've received some intelligence that suggests he was shot dead earlier today.'

Louise brought her hand up to her mouth. Her eyes flashed wide in shock. 'Shot? Dead?'

'It appears to be almost an execution in style. I'm sorry, there's no easy way to say this and I can't spare you the details. I think it might all be linked to what happened to your mum and dad. I need to ask you again if you can think of any reason that someone might be targeting your family?'

Jenny flopped back, her body suddenly limp. Her eyes stared up at the ceiling and filled with moisture. 'No. I have no idea what is going on. Oh God, Joseph! I should have stayed in Italy.'

'When did you last see your brother?'

'Years, Inspector. Many years. We don't talk. The only time he ever used to call me or turn up at my door was to ask for money. The same with Mum and Dad. When he was much younger, he got himself involved in drugs. He had a problem. They put him through rehab — spent tens of thousands of pounds on trying to get him right and all he did was throw it back in their faces. My dad lost all faith, practically banished him. I don't think they've spoken since then either.'

'What about your mum?'

'What about her?'

'Did she still speak to Joseph?'

'Not that I know of. I mean, I very much doubt it. He's not even an easy person to find if you wanted to. His life is chaos. He moved away. Portsmouth, I last heard.'

'I've been able to find out a little bit about him, Louise. There are signs that he might have been looking to settle down. He's got a partner. They've been together a while and . . . well, he's a dad.'

Louise snapped up straight. 'Joseph!'

'Yes. A little girl. She's four months old. She's a lovely little thing.'

'You've met her?'

'She's here, strangely. Her mother was taken ill but she's going to be just fine. You're an aunty, Louise, and your dad out there—'

'A granddad! He always wanted grandchildren. I mean they both did — my mum was even worse. I remember telling them I couldn't. It was worse than telling my husband. They were absolutely devastated. They tried not to show it, of course.' Louise was back to sobbing silently behind her hand.

'This is why I wanted to speak to you alone. I wanted to talk to you about the best way to tell your dad.'

Louise leant forward. She composed herself; she took her time. 'It's hard to tell, really. They never got on, but he's still his son. The baby thing as well . . . it's all going to be a lot to take in. He's still struggling. He gets confused. Oh! This is all such a mess!'

'I think we have options, Louise. I can tell him now and we can manage the fallout between us and take him home. Or we can let him get some sleep in his own bed and I'll come and see him tomorrow. We can talk to him then.'

Louise was shaking her head. 'I don't think I can be with him all night and not tell him about Joseph. It's massive. It would be like a weight and it isn't fair. He would want to know.'

'I'll talk to him, then. We can bring him in here and—'

'No. Drop us home. I'll sit him down at home and I'll talk to him.'

'Are you sure that's the best way?'

'I think so. Maybe. What about the baby? What is the situation there?'

'What do you mean?'

'He's had his heart broken. I'm about to give him more bad news. Can we see the child? Maybe meet the mother? Maybe my dad will react to his grandchild. I think he might.'

'I can ask the question. I don't see any reason why she wouldn't want you to meet her daughter. You are family, after all.'

Louise managed a smile. 'I can barely believe it.'

'Your dad will struggle too. I'll have a word. I think she will be able to go home soon. Maybe I can set something up for tomorrow. That way your dad gets the news tonight from you, but has something to look forward to tomorrow.'

Louise nodded. She pulled a pocket mirror from her bag and checked her makeup. She stood at the door. 'That just might work. I'll go and get him.'

Ten minutes later, George was back in the foyer and Stan appeared. He was walking, supported on one side by his daughter with Paul Bearn hovering close to his other arm — just in case. Paul looked genuinely concerned. George loved that about him. He hadn't been a career cop; he'd been late joining and he was all the better for it. He was as sharp as they came and yet had none of the cynicism that had most cops already making their minds up, believing they didn't need to consider the evidence.

'Hey, Stan. How are you feeling?' George said.

'Fighting fit.'

'There'll be no fighting today, please, Dad.' Louise said. She looked at George. 'Let's go home then shall we?'

'Of course. I've arranged for a marked police car to be stationed at the end of your drive. It'll be around for a few days at least but I can't promise how long I'll be able to spare it.'

'There's no need. I think my dad here just wants to get back to normal.'

'I can understand that. But your dad, here, is a witness to a murder. He's a target. I'd feel better with a copper on your drive for as long as possible. We've also installed a panic button. It's exactly as it sounds — a big red button that's linked to our control centre. One push and we'll all be on our way. I've also had the farm added to the standard patrol route for our firearms teams who are working nights. Paul here is going off right now to make sure you're added to the briefing for every copper coming on duty. You'll be well looked after.'

'I'll see you soon, though, Stan.' Paul shook Stan's hand and nodded at George before he left. They would get back together at the police station.

'We appreciate all you're doing,' Louise said. 'I don't think anyone will be coming back, though, George. If they have any sense they'll be getting as far away as possible, right?'

'Well, I would if I was them.'

'I'll be staying with Dad for a little while — until he gets back into the swing of things. This has all been such a shock.' Louise lingered on George.

'Louise, I already told you that I don't need to be getting into the swing of anything,' Stan protested. 'Stop talking about me like I'm not here. I'm not the useless old fool you seem to think I am.'

'Please, Dad, I don't think you're a useless old fool. You need time to recover. You don't have your strength back yet. No one would have.'

'My strength! You mean until I'm strong enough to tie off a noose again? It was a mistake. A stupid thing, and I know that now. I'll be fine.'

George looked to step in. 'I understand Louise doesn't get over too much. If nothing else, you can spend a few days with your daughter, Stan. Don't think of it as anything else. That's a big old house to be rattling around in on your own.'

'The sooner I get used to that the better — right, George? You'll all go back to your normal lives when you're happy you've done all you can. I can never get back to that. Don't you people worry about me. I'll survive. Now take me home.'

* * *

The start of Stan's drive was clear. The car that had been on the outer cordon was now on the gravel just outside his front door. Ali's CSI van was there too, as were another two marked cars and a marked 4x4. All the cars were occupied and the officers manning them looked expectant as George pulled up. A small, plain white van was also parked off to the left, close to the side entrance. A woman in a white paper suit leant against its side. She pushed off as George approached. George guessed it was the lady he had spoken to from the cleaning company. He would address her first. He asked Stan and Louise to wait in the car for just a moment.

'Hey! It's Kerry, right? My saviour who owns the cleaning company.' George held out his hand in greeting.

'Well remembered.' She peeled off a glove to take up the handshake.

'I never forget the names of the people I'm in debt to.'

'You paid your debt. Over the phone as I recall.'

'I still feel indebted.'

'Well, now I have your invoice. So you can wave this at your finance people. Good luck with getting your money without a battle. I never did.'

252

'That's a real shame. You don't know the difference you make. I couldn't imagine Stan there coming back to this house if you hadn't done your bit.'

George looked over at the car. Kerry did too. Stan was in the front passenger seat. He was looking forwards but beyond them at his big, empty home.

'Well, you know where I am if you reckon you can get a better system in place. It was a good contract. In theory.'

'I told you I would do something about it. I'm a man of my word.'

'We shall see.' She smiled. George knew it was genuine. He waved at her van as she drove away down the drive. He spoke to the officers. Most had stood up out of their cars. Some had moved closer. A female officer with PC EDEN on a Velcro badge on her chest moved to give him the house keys.

'Thank you.'

'It's been checked through, sir — just to make sure there was no police equipment left. It's all good. We've been out a little while. We were told that we all need to leave together?' She looked at him as if she was confused by the request.

'That's right. Are you all ready to go?' He got a round of nods. 'Perfect. Can you make sure the scene log is dropped into Major Crime — whoever has it?' Someone waved the book at him. 'Ideal. Thanks all for your help. I know Stan in there appreciates what you've all done for him.'

George moved the car forward so they were closer to the front door. He stepped out in time to see the convoy of marked police vehicles meandering down the drive. There was no way anyone could fail to notice that.

Chapter 29

George walked into the kitchen behind Stan. He had some paperwork to complete following the search of his house. Two signatures and he could leave. Louise immediately excused herself to use the toilet.

'I'll make some tea, George,' Stan said. 'Can I interest you in one?'

'No, thank you. I had better get straight off. Are you sure you don't want me to make it? Why don't you have a sit down?'

'No, I'm fine, thank you.' His tone carried a little annoyance. Maybe he'd heard enough concern over the last few days. The kitchen was spotless. Ali had been right: they had done a great job. You would never know it had been the scene of a horrific murder just a few days before. Stan must have been thinking the exact same thing.

'It's like they were never in here, George. It's like it never happened.'

'I know what you mean. They've done a good job tidying it up.'

'So, now what? It's all straightened up and scrubbed down in here, so life just goes on? It seems disrespectful almost. I don't know what I mean, it just . . . doesn't feel right. Me, stood here making a cup of tea, my Janice . . .'

'I know what you mean, Stan. It's human nature. We feel guilty when we lose someone close and it will happen a lot. I lost someone close to me once and I remember the same. The first time I laughed, the first time I felt like I was enjoying myself or if I went a few hours without thinking about her, I felt ashamed. Like I had no right to just move on.'

'That's it. That's it exactly.' Stan had the kettle in his hand. It hovered over the Aga, the liquid sloshing inside. For a moment he looked unsteady, the kettle thumped down on the hob as he regained his balance.

'You okay?'

'Yeah. My balance is still a bit shot.'

'They said it might be for a while. You're supposed to be resting. What would your daughter say if she knew I was letting you make the tea? She could walk through here any minute!'

'Ah, she don't scare me, George.'

'I'm not talking about you, Stan! She scares me. I reckon she's got a lot of your strength.'

'She's a good girl. I wish we'd seen more of her in the last few years. I suppose if we had known . . . well, they get their own lives, don't they?'

'They do. I meant what I said. Try and make the most of having her here for a few days. Try not to put up any walls for her — she only wants to help.'

'I know that. Sometimes you can have too much of a good thing though, right, George?'

'Makes sense to me, and I can take a hint. I'll get going, okay? You're sure you're happy for us to leave?'

'Yes.'

'The emergency button, you know—'

'Press it. I mean, that's it, right?'

George chuckled. 'Yeah, I suppose it isn't rocket science. It's on a toggle, Stan, so you can wear it. That way it's always on you.'

'Noted.'

'We won't let it out of our sight, don't you worry about that!' Louise had entered and must have heard the last of the conversation.

'Well, good. You both have my number. Don't hesitate to call me if you need me. I did say to Louise I would come over and see you both tomorrow. Just to see how you're settling in.'

'Thanks, George, but don't you start fussing, too.'

George tugged his coat closer as he stepped back out onto the gravel. The temperature was dropping with the sun and he instantly missed the constant heat from that Aga. He stuffed his signed paperwork in the glove box and drove slowly back down the drive. He turned left and accelerated away. It was always a strange feeling leaving a scene when you knew it was under surveillance. George had instructed the Covert Rural Operations Team — CROPS — to cover Stan's property. They were the experts in surveillance outside of the towns and cities. They would be dug into a woodland hide or unmoving in a treetop or in thick bushes. George couldn't see any sign of them — that was the whole idea. If they did as they were instructed, no one would notice them, not any would-be robbers returning to get rid of the only witness to a terrible murder. And not Stan or Louise.

George called Emily as soon as he was clear.

'George.'

'Hey, Ryker. I need your help.'

'Well, of course you do. I don't think you know any other type of call.'

'I know you like to feel wanted.'

'I'm still pissed off with you, George. This had better be good.'

'Our friend at the hospital . . . she talked about some land separate from the Wingmore estate. It might still be owned by them — or at least rented. What can you find out quick-time?'

'I can run land registry checks. That usually takes a few days but I have ways of speeding it up in emergencies.'

'Sounds ideal. That won't cover if they are renting though, right?'

'No. It only shows up anything they own. What's the land being used for?'

'There's a stable block on it. That's all I know.'

'As a business?'

'I couldn't tell you, Ryker.'

'You don't like to make things easy, do you? I'll do some digging, see what I can find out.'

'Thanks, Ryker.'

'Whatever.'

George's next call was to his chief inspector.

'George.'

'Major, do you have any news on my tactical team yet?'

'You mean the team you want on permanent standby, but we can't tell them what for? Do you have anything more to tell them yet?'

'No, sir. That is still the briefing.'

'You don't like to make things easy, do you, George?'

'Apparently not, Major.'

'I have a team of four. That's the best I can do tonight. They're sucking me dry for overtime too. I haven't managed to resource tomorrow yet.'

'That'll have to do for now. Thanks, boss. I know it's not ideal.'

'Nothing's ideal until we get a result, George. Get that and nothing matters.'

'I'll see what I can do, Major.'

'Don't you always.'

Chapter 30

'How did I know you would still be here?' Emily must have been silent on entering the Major Crime floor. Certainly George didn't hear her coming. It was late. The day had flashed past and George didn't feel like he had got much done.

'Because you know just how dedicated I am, I suppose.'

'Yeah, that must be it. It definitely won't be that I know you have no life outside of this place.'

'Well, I'm working on that. You're hardly the socialite yourself, Ryker!'

'True. I don't really like people.'

'I know the feeling. Please tell me you have something for me? Right now there are a number of people who don't like me and I have to add a bored tactical team to the list. I've just got off the phone. They don't seem to understand that sometimes they might need to wait for nothing to happen.'

'I thought that would be something they were well used to.'

'They're on overtime, too. I can honestly say that this is the first time I have heard a team complain about being offered overtime to effectively sit on their arses.'

'I have something.'

'Go on.'

'Land registry shows the Wingmores have owned a lot of land, but it's largely what you've seen — the farm estate. It stretches over roads and parks. It has a lot of complicated paths, bridleways and right-of-ways attached to it. But, when you get down to the detail, it's relatively simple.'

'Have owned?'

'Yeah. They sold off a lot of it around a decade ago. Now it's just eight acres of land with the house sat in the middle.'

'Just eight acres!'

'I know! But compared to what they had before — three times that or more — it's not much.'

'So they would have come into a lot of money.'

'I'm sure they would have been comfortable after the sale, yes. But it's commercial land. Specifically it can only be used for farming. So it wouldn't be as valuable as, say, housing land.'

'Okay. And you said *largely* what I've seen? I'm always interested in what I haven't seen.'

'What you haven't seen is a much smaller plot that is separate from the main house. It's still registered in the name of Janice Wingmore and it was purchased just over five years ago. Since then they have built outhouses on it, which are registered as stables.'

'Excellent! That ties in.'

'I thought that. There's a little more to it. The plot is jointly owned. A Miss A. Jeffries is listed on the agreement as part owning. I did a little open source research — basically seeing what was available online. There's the trace of a Miss Andrea Jeffries at Companies House. She registered a business around five years ago, with her company address as being this stable block. It's Whitsun Avenue, the address shows as Canterbury but it's the outskirts of Elham really.'

'So not far from Wingmore Farm.'

'Not far at all.'

'I also found an old social media profile for her and some online advertising. It's pretty clear that she was running stables there. She was advertising for people to house and exercise their horses. There was also a manège facility — that's walking your horse about, according to Google.'

'"I like walking the horse about!" Shame she didn't ask you to help her with her advertising.'

Emily pushed the folder onto his desk. 'It's all in there. She has an old phone number listed. That's in there too, for when you want to call her with your questions.'

'How did you know?'

'When have you ever not had follow-up questions?'

'Fair point. Do you have an address for her? I prefer the turn-up-and-knock method.'

'I knew you'd ask that too. I found a listing on the electoral register. She's a bit closer to Canterbury, but not too far out.'

George stood up. He scooped up the paperwork as he did. 'Do you fancy a trip out?'

'You're going now?'

'Right now. I mean, I know you probably have a date with all your mates . . .'

'What do you need me for?'

'Maybe I don't need you for anything. Maybe I just thought you might like a trip out, you know? Get you out the office.'

'You know I'm off-duty, right? That I'm already three hours past finishing?'

'I was aware of that, yes.'

'So again, what do you need me for?'

'Fine. I need you to make a call. Get an out-of-hours technical request done.'

'An out of hours? What for?'

'I need a lump — a tracker stuck on the bottom of a horsebox. And I need it geo-fenced. The tactical team will have the monitoring equipment. Then I need an intelligence officer to brief them to stop it if it moves.'

'You need . . . that makes no sense. What horsebox? I just told you . . . even if this plot exists, how would you know there's a horsebox there.'

George smiled. 'I tell you what . . . if there isn't, then we all get to go home.'

Emily rolled her eyes. 'I won't hold my breath.'

* * *

Andrea Jeffries pulled the door open roughly. Her face wore an expression that suggested that a knock on her door at eight in the evening was not something she desired. Over jeans, she wore a tight-fitting Aran jumper that finished high on the neck. Her house smacked of country cottage to George. It was small, whitewashed and pretty. Perfectly formed. George stood at the front door that was dead centre.

'I'm sorry to bother you, Miss Jeffries.' George paused for a reaction. He got none and knew he was talking to the right person. 'I'm Detective Inspector George Elms. I'm working out of Langthorne Police Station. There's nothing to worry about, but I was hoping to have a few minutes of your time.' George held up his badge.

The woman's expression changed all at once. Where she had looked ready for an argument, she now looked unsure. She stepped back into her property. 'Did you want to come in?'

The inside of the property was immaculate, everything in its place. George was led through to the kitchen where a slab of expensive-looking work surface jutted out towards the centre with high stools around it. She gestured for George to sit.

'Can I get you a drink, Inspector?'

'No, thank you. I don't expect to be here long and, please, call me George.'

'Thank you, but I prefer to keep these sorts of things formal. What did you say your surname was again, please?'

'Elms.'

'Like the tree?'

'Well, like a couple of them, I suppose.' He smiled, trying to lighten the mood. She made a show of writing down his details. 'Did you need my force number too?'

'No, thank you. That won't be necessary. My partner plays golf at Etchinghill with a few of your bosses. Sometimes I tag along with the other wives. I just wanted to be sure I know who I'm talking about.'

'Oh, well, I'm sure they'll all know who I am.'

'Quite. So how can I help you, Inspector? Can I assume this is about this awful business up at the farm?'

'Which farm is that, Miss Jeffries?'

She pursed her lips. '*Is* this a formal conversation? I can't say I've ever had a formal conversation with a police officer.'

'I can imagine. Good people rarely do, until something terrible happens.'

'So you are here about Wingmore Farm? This is a small village, Inspector. I'm sure you understand how word gets around.'

'I do. So tell me, what have you heard?'

'Poor Mrs Wingmore, I heard she was murdered up there. A robbery gone wrong. I mean, my partner could probably find out all the details but I told him not to. We need to let the police do their thing. We need to trust them to keep us safe.'

George bit his tongue. The next time she implied or mentioned links to senior officers he might not be able to. He came across it all the time, people thinking they needed to put you in your place from the start. Playing golf with a senior police officer might have meant something once. It certainly didn't anymore.

'You're right, of course. But sometimes we need help to keep you safe. I understand you were close — to the Wingmores, I mean.'

'Then you are misinformed, Inspector.'

'Close enough to be business partners? To buy land together?'

'An investment, a business proposition that they reneged upon is a more accurate description. I spoke with my solicitor just today in fact to establish whether the events at the farm impact on our situation.'

'What situation is that?'

'Once again, is this a formal conversation?'

'Depends what you mean by a formal conversation, Miss Jeffries. I am trying to find out a little more about the use of the plot you co-own with my victim. If you tell me there is a dispute over that land, then of course I am interested in that too.'

'A legal dispute you understand, nothing more. I am extremely frustrated, Inspector, but I don't hold any personal grudges. I happened to be very fond of Janice. I think we all were.'

'We?'

'The Women's Society. Janice and I were both active members. She hasn't been coming quite so often recently. I think she became aware of the tension over some of her husband's recent decisions.'

'What decisions were they?'

Andrea Jeffries sighed. 'I met Janice through the Women's Society. We had a mutual love of horses and we built a friendship around it. It escalated to the point where we agreed to acquire a plot of land where we would rent stables and I would be able to offer a few other services. We built an exercise yard — one of those all-weather affairs — and we had some agility equipment and a few other bits and pieces. I was even getting involved in the selling of some tack up there. I had a supplier who offered me a reasonable cut. It was worth my while.'

'So what happened?'

'To this day I still don't know, Inspector. We were making money. I was and Janice certainly was. Janice was very much a silent partner — it suited us both. This was my business and my passion and I have youth and ability on my side. Janice was happy for her cut on the stable rent and a smaller cut on the other elements and for my rent on the land. It was regular and it was on the up. Then she suddenly announced that the land couldn't be used anymore for the business. She held all the cards you see. I was more than a little naïve in the creation of the contract between us. She purchased the land and I paid for the facilities. So of course she had the ability to determine its use. Or at least to determine what it was not to be used for. Out of the blue, I received a letter from a solicitor informing me that the land could no longer be used for any equestrian activity. I was effectively out of business overnight.'

'Why would she do that?'

Andrea shrugged. 'A fair question, Inspector, and one I still haven't had a reasonable answer to. Around eighteen months ago they suddenly didn't want any equestrian activity on that land. Reading between the lines, I don't think they wanted *anyone* on the land at all. Initially they tried to chuck me off but they realised that we had registered a business together and thankfully that gave me some protection. Then I received an offer to buy me out, which was worth more than the money I had put into the plot, but my argument remained that they should buy me out of the *business* I had built up, not the land. I suspected they were trying to force me out so they could start up the same thing again and claim the profits for themselves. All the hard work was done after all. Had they bought the business, the figure would have been much higher.'

'So you turned them down.'

'Of course I did. I worked bloody hard to get that business up and running. The stables were full with a two-year waiting list no less and the sales and services I was offering were increasing month by month. I had a staff of four. We were all suddenly out of a job. All my money was sunk into that plot so it wasn't like I could just go somewhere else and set up again. I'm afraid they put me in a terrible situation and for the last eighteen months I have hardly moved away from it.'

'I imagine that made you very angry.'

'Frustrated, Inspector. Like I said, I want answers, really. But if they would have just let me start back up again I would have done it. My partner has a job in the city. He works long hours and stays up there most of the week. That business was our key to an easier life and a retirement plan. And I should be well on the way to it by now.'

'Have you been there since?'

'For the first few months I went up there a lot. I was trying to get something going and I just kept ending up there. I think I was in shock. I just couldn't understand why they would just suddenly stop something so good. They wouldn't even talk to me, save a few letters of correspondence from their solicitor. I had another silly offer for the land, then I had warning of a compulsory clearance order — they can't do anything with the land while the business is in dispute, you see. I knew that was a bluff, as any court process would find that I had done nothing wrong. Eventually I stopped going up there and I stopped trying to talk to them. I have a solicitor — who fortunately is a friend of ours — otherwise I wouldn't be able to afford her. She is trying to get some movement. I'm not sure what this all means for us now.'

'Were you here Sunday evening?'

'Yes. You're not suggesting I would drive up there and shoot the woman, are you? I'm very upset with it all

— damned frustrated — but I do draw the line at murder, Inspector! My partner and I were both here. We were alone. I think we ordered takeout, though, so there might be some sort of record of someone else having seen me here.'

'I have to ask!'

'I'm sure you do.'

'Was the land still being used? After you closed down and while the dispute was going on? Any suggestion of the Wingmores using it for something else?'

'Well, at first I was trying to make a point. There were vehicle tracks so I knew it was being used. Some things were moving about. I saw one of the horse transporters being towed there one day and I ran over with my phone and started taking pictures. They had made a fuss about how the land couldn't be used for anything equestrian and of course I was hoping to trip them up. But the box was empty. The driver was some rough-looking lad. My solicitor said it wasn't proof enough. I went up there a few times after that, and then I had this single moment of realisation. It came on a beautiful summer's evening when the sun was just setting — so it would have been around 9 p.m. and I was sat in my car, tucked behind a bush close to the entrance to the site. The transporter wasn't there and I was waiting for it to come back with a horse in it. I suddenly thought *what am I doing*? I had wasted a beautiful summer's evening. It wouldn't have solved anything either. I realised at that very moment that I'd become obsessed and it wasn't helping. I don't think I've been back since.'

'Are you aware of anyone else who has a dispute or a grievance with any of the family up there?'

'I'm afraid not. I don't really know who else would have anything to do with them, Inspector. I hope that doesn't make me suspect number one!'

'I don't think so, Miss Jeffries. Just don't leave the country! Thank you so much for taking the time this evening. I know where you are if I need to come and ask any more questions.'

'So it seems. Do you think that land has anything to do with what happened? Is there anything I need to be aware of?'

'We can't rule anything out right now, Miss Jeffries. I'm sure you'll hear all about it over a game of golf.'

George waited until he got back into his car to make a phone call to Emily. She sounded even grumpier than she'd been before. She did confirm that the technical team had been able to install the tracker as he had requested. They had found a horsebox on the plot. The tracker was concealed under a wheel arch. The tracker linked with a computer programme via a mapping application. The map had defined points that formed a virtual ring around the horsebox — a 'geo-fence.' If the tracker was moved outside of that fence it would immediately send a text message to three defined phones and could then be tracked via a laptop. The tactical team sergeant had the laptop and one of the phones, Emily had the second and George pulled out the third from the armrest pocket in his car and switched it on. He sent Emily home. The tactical team were to remain at a police office within reasonable distance of the stables. George himself was heading home too. There was nothing more he could do now. And he had no idea how long things might take.

Chapter 31

3 a.m. One phone ringing, the other making a shrill alarm sound. The geo-fence had been breached. The ringing was Emily Ryker.

'I got it, the box is moving.' George shifted across his living room. 'How long for?' He was still groggy; he had drifted off on his sofa. He was still fully clothed, including his shoes. His car keys were still in his pocket. He was out of the flat in less than thirty seconds. The cool air of the early hours of morning hit him all at once.

'It's stopped just outside the perimeter from what we can see,' Ryker said. 'I'm on the air with the tactical team. Are you monitoring the radio? We're running on a talk-through.'

'I will. Standby.' George turned the handset on. It took a few seconds to connect to the network. He had left it monitoring the right channel. It was dedicated to his operation and no one else should be monitoring so they could talk to one another easily. The screen lit up immediately, and he heard the distinctive tones of the tactical team's sergeant, Harry Robson.

'Did you get my last, Emily?'

'Sorry, I was updating the guvnor. He should be monitoring. Can you repeat, please?'

'Yes, yes, the asset is on the move. We are making ground. Inspector Elms, confirm you are monitoring?'

'It's George. Let's keep this informal. I am monitoring.'

'What do you want from us, sir? Sorry, George.'

George was in his car. His headlights raked across the beach as he turned round and accelerated.

'What I want is to put a stop on the asset. I'll leave the tactics up to you, Harry. If you're not happy to stop it then I just need to know where it ends up and we will get a perimeter on it until I can get you more resources. Assume they are armed and assume they will use extreme violence.'

'Received that. We are in two unmarked vehicles. I will make ground and try and get a visual. Yankee Two, stay close, but out of sight. We'll have to play this one by ear.'

George heard a confirmation from the other call sign. He could hear the excitement in their voices — this was what they lived for. He had concerns though: four officers and two cars was a lot less than would usually be sent to do an armed stop on a moving vehicle. He didn't think Harry and his men would attempt it. He couldn't blame them really.

'Ryker, you still there?' George had abandoned the phone in the passenger seat. It had connected to the car and the timer ticked up on the screen.

'Yeah, George. You sure you want to leave Harry in charge of the tactics? They're not the most subtle.'

'I'm not looking for subtle, to be honest. If they choose to stop that car with just four officers they will need to be anything *but* subtle. Are you turning out?'

'I can if you want me to. Or I can head back into the nick and run the intel cell. Once you get them nicked I can make a start on a report for the morning.'

'Yeah, okay. Makes sense.'

'Are you coming into the nick? There's nothing you can do now the armed team are on their arse. Apart from get in the way and get yourself shot. I'll put the kettle on.'

'Don't be silly, Ryker, I can drink tea any time. It's not every day you can go and get shot at.'

'There's me thinking you might have had enough of that?'

George chuckled as he pressed for the call to end. He could feel his own excitement growing. He was in the one-way system that took him to the top of the town. He needed an update. He picked his radio back up.

'George to the team . . . do we have a last location? I am in Langthorne heading out towards Canterbury.'

'Yes, yes. The asset is in North Elham. They are on the Elham Valley Road, headed in the general direction of the A2.'

The A2. It was a major road that provided a link from the port of Dover to London and eventually became the M2. It would make sense for a gang based out of the county to make for it. It was the closest main road — the best option if they were looking to flee the county. George could only assume that was their intention. He didn't like knowing so little about them. 'Understood. I'll take the A260 and join the A2. Have you caught up with it yet?'

'No, no. We're five minutes out. It's not travelling fast, but we might not get to it before we get to the A2.'

'Dammit!' George spoke out loud but not into his radio. The team's start point must have been too far away. Somewhere that did good coffee, he guessed. This time he did speak into the radio: 'Received. Consideration for calling up on the main channel and getting a rolling road on the A2? You could get a sterile area to work in.'

'Yes, sir. Doing it now. The A2 isn't ideal though, George. You can't cover the slips.'

A 'rolling road' was a police term for a marked unit blocking all lanes of a major road or a motorway and bringing it down to a crawling pace or even a stop. It worked better on motorways where the options for cars to join it were limited. Harry had a point: cars could join the A2 from too many points to make it truly sterile. George focussed on his driving. He was making good progress, the flashing blue lights in the grille were vivid in the darkness, so he didn't even need the sirens. He passed through the village of Hawkinge and powered towards the A2. He wasn't too far behind.

The next update seemed to take an age to come through. *'All patrols, the asset is approaching the slip for the A2. Local patrols and traffic are a long way out. They are making their way, but we are unlikely to get a sterile area. We are still making ground . . . we should have a visual in under a minute.'*

They must have picked up speed. George was close to the slip to the A2 himself; they were all converging together.

'We have a visual. A dark-coloured Land Rover Freelander with a horsebox. The vehicle is stop. Stop. Standby.'

George was just a minute behind. The radio went quiet, it was a sure sign of police activity — everyone caught up in the moment and forgetting to relay what was going on. He got to the slip, the last location he knew them to be in. Immediately he could see the darkness shimmering in blue in the distance. He couldn't see the source. He slowed up. To his left was H's Café, a solid building just off the slip that was popular with bikers. George reckoned the blue lights were coming from the other side of that, further up the A2 maybe. They didn't look to be moving.

George edged forward. The road split in to two forks: left led around the back of the café; right took him onto the A2 where he would be committed. He took the left fork. A yard opened up in front of him. To his right was the shadow of a large, square building. George knew it had been a hotel once. It had been closed down for almost as long as he could remember. The blue lights were still further away. The road turned into a track as he passed along the front of the building. He could just see part of a static caravan in the distance, tucked around the side of the old hotel.

George rounded the building and the blue lights were immediately blinding. Two cars, both flickering their lights, blocked in a Land Rover with a horsebox attached to the rear. Both the doors to the Land Rover were open. George could hear shouted instructions but he couldn't make out the words. He knew he should hang back; the armed team would be moving in with their guns and body armour. He was dressed in a shirt and trousers with a small torch — hardly ready for anything. He moved a little closer then stopped. He hesitated, unsure as to whether he should continue, not wanting to go back. Suddenly he heard a loud *pop* — a gunshot — then another two in quick succession. There were more shouted instructions. George couldn't stand still any longer. He moved forwards.

Sergeant Harry Robson was immediately recognisable, despite his ballistic helmet and partial face covering. George expected to be shouted at; to be sent away while they neutralised any threat. Instead, Harry met him with wide eyes, his gun still levelled.

'They wouldn't listen, George,' he said, the shock clear in his voice.

George strode past him. Two more officers were kneeling on the ground. They were fussing and barking at each other. George could see a pair of legs sticking out from under them. He moved closer. A man was lying on the floor, his front soaked in blood, his eyes wide open and unmoving, his skin already draining of colour. George knew a dead man when he saw one. One of the officers was pushing a clump of gauze into the dead man's chest; the other was doing his best to carry out CPR. George looked around; he counted three officers. There were four on the team.

'Harry, who's missing?'

The sergeant still had his gun covering the scene on the floor. His eyes were fixed on the activity. He seemed rooted to the ground.

'Harry? HARRY!'

His eyes flicked to George. 'They wouldn't listen, George.'

'You had no choice, Harry, okay? It happens. You did your job. Where's the fourth man? There were four of you, right?'

Harry seemed to come to his senses. He looked panicked. 'Goddes. He ran after the other one. They went into the woods.' He pointed to a path behind George. It ran off parallel to the A2. George shone his torch in the general direction. The path twisted away and it was impossible to see far down it. He could hear shouting from further along the path. George broke into a run.

PC Goddes was just twenty metres into the woods. George lit him up from the back. He could tell from Goddes's stance that he had his weapon levelled. It was pointed at the ground and had a torch strapped to the top.

'Don't move!' he was shouting. 'Hands where I can see them.'

George got to him. A man was on the ground in front of Goddes. He leaked blood from a wound under his right eye — it looked superficial. He was in just a T-shirt and jeans. Both were filthy. The mud under him was damp and reflected George's torchlight.

'Don't shoot! I've got nothing, yeah?' George could see this was just a boy — late teens maybe. He lifted his hands, his palms towards George and PC Goddes.

'Get on your knees!' Goddes said. 'Place your hands on the back of your head. Any sudden movement will be seen as aggression and you will be shot dead, do you understand?' Goddes stepped closer, the barrel of his gun just a few feet from the boy who moved to his knees. His head jerked in a nod. 'Do you have any weapons?' The boy shook his head. 'Sir, can you pat him down. Stay out of the line of fire. Do his top half first. When you're happy, step away and I'll stand him up, okay?'

'No problem,' George said. The instructions were clear. PC Goddes's training had well and truly kicked in. George was careful to walk behind the boy. 'Keep your hands still and on your head or he will shoot you. Do you understand?' The boy nodded again. George could see his waistband was clear, his T-shirt had ridden up when he had lifted his arms and George could see a few inches of his back and stomach. George patted the centre of his back and his armpits.

'Top half done!' He called out.

Goddes took over the instructions. 'When I tell you to, you will stand up slowly. Keep your hands on your head at all times. Any movement will be seen as aggression and you will be shot dead. Do you understand?'

The boy nodded once more. George could see that he was physically shaking.

'Stand up now, slowly.'

The boy did as he was told. George waited for a nod from Goddes. He went through his pockets and down his legs. He patted his ankles and untied his laces.

'Kick your shoes off,' George said.

The boy didn't hesitate. He was wearing loose-fitting trainers and no socks. He put his bare feet back down in the damp mud.

George searched the shoes. 'Nothing,' he said.

Goddes's body language relaxed a little. He kept his weapon levelled. The torch on the top was bright and the boy narrowed his eyes to it. He relaxed a little too. His head dipped and he sniffed. George didn't want him to relax. He needed information.

'What's your name?'

'Cole. People call me Cole. Colin.'

'Where's your mate, Cole?' George said.

'What mate?'

'Don't fuck about. You're part of a gang, right? So where's the rest of your gang?'

'There was two. Only two of us. I wasn't even driving. I just came out to help. I got nothing to do with this.'

'Nothing to do with what?'

'Any of this. Jimmy . . . he just said to come out and help him pick up a trailer. That was it. I did what I was told.' The boy sniffed again and his eyes flicked away, back to the muddy ground. George knew he was lying. He'd had enough of being lied to.

George lunged at him and grabbed him by the scruff of the neck. He pulled Cole's face in close to his own. 'You were there, right? When the old lady was shot . . . when she was murdered? Did *you* pull the trigger, you piece of shit?'

'What? What are you talking about?' The boy stammered over his words. George wrenched him to his feet, grabbed his arm and twisted it up his back. The boy cried out in pain. George shoved him back down the path, forcing him to walk on his tiptoes, his bare feet scraping over the woodland floor. He pushed him back into the clearing. The car lights and torches lit up the scene. George pushed the boy onto his knees — just a few metres from where his accomplice was lying dead on the ground, on his back, his head lolling towards them, his eyes bolt open and reflecting the pulsing blue lights. The two police officers who had been working on him had the same shocked look as their sergeant.

'Jesus, Jimmy!' Cole said.

'He's dead, Cole. Shot dead. Who else was here?'

'No one else! No one else was here. Me and Jimmy were sent out. It was a simple job — get the trailer. There's a lock box in the back. Two man job.'

'What happened at the farmhouse, Cole? You shoot that lady?'

'Sir?' Goddes stepped towards him. George raised his hand; his attention was still fixed on Cole.

'I don't know what you're talking about.'

'He's dead, Cole. Look at him. LOOK AT HIM!' George grabbed Cole again and dragged him another metre. Cole was now so close to Jimmy that they were nearly touching. Jimmy's wide eyes stared into nothing, his lips already a dark blue in the torchlight. Cole recoiled, but George grabbed him by the hair and forced him to look.

'What the fuck are you doing, man? You can't do this!' Cole screamed.

'He's dead. Jimmy's dead, Cole. All I've got left is you. I'm gonna make sure you go to prison for the rest of your life for shooting that woman. I promise you that.' Cole tried to move his head.

'I didn't shoot her, alright? We were just supposed to be there to pick up the cash. I didn't know what it was all about. Next thing I knew it all got out of hand and I was running for my life.'

'What happened?'

Cole was starting to break. He clenched his eyes shut to the torchlight and the vision of his dead mate.

'Joe and Jimmy never got on. Everyone knew it. Joe didn't think we were getting enough of the cut, so he started skimming some. Joe said we could stash a bit up at a farm down here. We were going to share it out and fuck Jimmy off. We'd drop a bit down here and there. It was far enough that Jimmy wouldn't find out.'

'So what happened?'

'We get up there and the old lady comes out to meet us. Joseph knew her, I didn't know, but it's like his mum or something. That's why we went to see her. She moved the cash about the place apparently, so her old man don't find it. Then he comes down — the old man. He's proper angry. Joe argues with the lady about his sleeping pills. I think she was supposed to load him up. The old man's got a gun. Fuck knows what for — we all knew he was just shitting with us. Even when he shot one off over our heads, I never thought nothing. Joseph called him out —

said he didn't have the balls. He was winding him up. He come stomping out. The old lady shouted at him and he just shot her, man! I didn't see it coming. It was like it was from nowhere.'

'Who shot her?'

'The old man. She begged him. She begged him to leave Joe alone and then she was on her back. The second she hit the deck we were gone. I mean, I never ran so fast. We got in our truck and we were gone. That night, though, it was such a mess that Jimmy got to find out about what we did. One of the crew called him up. I think we figured that he was going to find out and he would know what to do. We were all shitting it. We all played Joe. We got our stories straight blaming him. It was his fault after all. We said that we thought we were there to get the money for Jimmy. We said that Joe had told us that's what we were doing. Joe tried to run. Jimmy was pissed. I mean, I've never seen anything like it. He was on some rampage. He had like a shotgun and something else tucked in his waist. It was the middle of the day! We got hold of Joe and he went after his girl. He wanted her dead real bad. He wanted to be the one to tell Joe when he did it too. There's summin' wrong with him in the head.'

George pushed Cole back to the floor. He stepped away. He was suddenly aware that all the officers were staring at him. He could hear sirens too, more patrols arriving. Harry must have called up on the main channel. Harry still looked in shock.

'We need to get him away, George. We need to clean this up.'

George nodded. 'Yeah, we certainly need to do that.'

Chapter 32

7:30 a.m. George pulled down the drive of the farmhouse with Paul Bearn in the seat next to him. Their car disturbed a layer of light mist that hung under a blue sky. The farmhouse appeared as a dark outline at first. George could see cars parked on the drive outside. One he recognised: an unmarked police car that was the same make and model as his. He knocked the door and was answered almost immediately by a smiling Louise.

'George! Good to see you. I didn't think you would be coming up so early.'

George stepped in. Paul followed him in behind. They had come in through the main entrance. The kitchen was straight ahead, the large living room off to the right. George hadn't been expecting anyone to be there, least of all Jenny. Hers was the next face he saw. She stood just inside the living room. She turned to smile at him too. A suited man stood next to her; George had worked with him some time before on a witness protection case.

George moved into the lounge. At the far end, in front of the fireplace, was Stanley Wingmore. Baby Isobel was in his arms. Stanley hadn't noticed George yet. He didn't look like he would notice anything; his attention was fixed on the tiny bundle that slept soundly in his arms. He was spinning gently on his scuffed floorboards, slowly and with a rhythm no one else could hear. George was close enough to hear his soft humming by the time he was back round to face him. Stanley raised his head, his face flushed with colour. George recognised it as pride.

'Did you know? About little Isobel here?'

'I did, Stan. We didn't work it out straight away. When I knew, I spoke to Louise about the best way to tell you.'

'It's the circle of life, George, that's what it is. A tiny miracle. The family goes on. The next generation. I had no idea.'

'I need to talk to you, Stan. Alone.'

Stan pushed his little finger into Isobel's fist and she gripped it, her eyes still shut. Stan looked up at George. His expression didn't change. The pride and the colour remained.

'I thought you might. Jenny, love!' Jenny moved over and Isobel was gently transferred. 'Jenny here is going into protection for a little while. You probably know that already though, right?' Stan said.

'I do. I promised her we would look after her. I didn't know she was coming up here to see you, though, Stan. It was something we were looking to arrange.'

'I know. Louise said you were going to sort something out, but we just couldn't wait. Louise tracked her down. She knows someone who works the reception at the hospital. An old friend from before she moved. They were able to get a message to Jenny here and she was happy to come up and see us. I'm so happy she did.'

'You're welcome, Stan,' Jenny said. 'She's your granddaughter after all.'

'She's beautiful, Jenny. Absolutely perfect.'

'I think so too.'

'Do you mind if I just have a couple of minutes with the Inspector here? I think he has something important to talk to me about.'

'Of course.' Jenny moved out of the room. Louise stood at her shoulder.

'Can I stick around?'

'No, love,' Stan said. 'Don't worry. I'll make sure you're kept up to speed. We need a few minutes is all.'

Louise made eye contact with George. She hesitated for a few seconds but she did move away. She pulled the door to behind her. George walked over and pushed it all the way shut.

'There were some developments last night, Stan. I got hold of one of the lads who was here that night.'

'I knew you would, George. I told Louise it was just a matter of time.'

'We had to bed him down. It was quite late by the time we got him inside a custody cell. But he told me a few things, Stan, and I'm pretty certain he's going to repeat them again in his interview in a few hours.'

'Did he now?'

'How's that short-term memory problem of yours?'

Stan's smile fell away a little. He took a deep breath. 'Genuine to start with. A blessing it was. Of course I was cursing it at the time. I desperately wanted to know what was going on, what had happened. I wanted to be able to help you. Then it started to come back. It was like being shown drawings at first. I couldn't see the details but I got outlines. I knew what happened though. I remember that much.'

'You remember how Janice died?'

'I do, George. More and more of it every day. Joseph never came to this house without causing trouble of some sort. If he hadn't turned up that night we would have both slept soundly in our beds and woken up to breakfast. I got disturbed. I heard someone talking. I got out of bed and I could hear Joseph's voice. I heard him checking with

Janice that she had given me my medication — my sleeping pills. He was checking she had drugged me! I got my gun George, I was just going to make a statement. I wanted him to know once and for all that he couldn't come back. Not ever again. I just had it broken over my arm. I didn't even put any cartridges in it at first. I walked away from the gun cabinet. But, for some reason, I went back and put two shots in. I kept it broken. It was a present from my wife, that gun. Beautiful thing — a Browning over-under.' Stan stopped to compose himself a little. 'She knew I had been courting it for a little while. She wouldn't let me buy it. I got angry with her for that. I didn't know she had already bought it for me — I ruined that night too.'

'How did it happen, Stan?'

'I was furious, George! I can't tell you how angry I was — as angry as I've ever been. I don't remember the details still. Joseph was stood in my kitchen. He was making fun of me. He said I would never use the thing so I might as well put it down. Janice convinced him to leave. I followed him out and we argued some more. He had a few of his cronies with him. Druggy scum, the lot of them. They stayed out the back. They said something about wanting their money. I fired a shot over their heads. They all backed off but Joseph didn't. He went back into the house. I shouted at him, I told him to come out. I said I wasn't messing about. He shouted back at me. He said that his mother had made her choice, that she had been helping him for a long time. She had been hiding money in the house, in the barns — on my land, George! Drug money! I told him again to come outside. I closed the gun. I pointed it at the door. I could hear Janice, she was pleading with me, George. She said to just let him go. She begged me. I heard Joseph — he said that she was choosing him again over me. He was goading me. I heard him at the doorway. I could see his outline. There's a bright floodlight over the door and I couldn't make him out. I pulled that trigger,

George. I wanted to kill our son. Just in that moment, but I did. I meant it. My Janice . . .' Stan became unsteady. Paul stepped in to guide him to the seat. George didn't move. 'My Janice — it was her in the doorway, not Joseph. I think Joseph took one look at her and he ran! What sort of a son does that? He did what he always does when life gets tough. Now I hear he finally found something he couldn't run away from.'

'You know what this means, Stan?'

'I do. I've known it from the second that gun went off, George. I tried to run away from it, too, in my own way. The barn, that's what I was doing. I was running away from my responsibilities. You have to stand up and be a man when you're wrong.' Stan pushed himself to his feet. He was still unsteady. He stepped closer to George.

'Thank you, George.'

'For what?'

'You kept your promise. You said you would find the bastard that killed my wife. Now you need to make sure he gets what he deserves.' Stan reached out with his arms locked together.

'You're under arrest, Stan. For murder. You do not have to say anything, but it may harm your defence if you do not mention, when questioned, something which you later rely on in court. Anything you do say may be used in evidence. My advice is to say nothing more, Stan, because now I'll have to start writing it down.' George met eyes with Paul, who nodded and felt his pockets for his car keys. They had spoken on the approach up here. They needed to get Stan out of the house as soon as possible. George immediately led Stan towards the door, taking hold of his right arm. Louise was on the other side of the door.

'All done?' she said, then her expression swiftly changed. 'What's wrong?'

'I need to go the police station. I'm sorry, Louise. I'm so sorry.'

'What do you mean? Why do you need to go to the police station? What's going on, Dad?'

George led him straight out of the front door. Louise's questioning continued; she was getting more and more upset. Stan got in to the back of the car. George had to put his arm out to stop Louise getting hold of him. He forced the door shut. She turned on him.

'What are you doing? He's an old man! He's a witness to a terrible murder — of his wife! Why are you treating him like this?'

George moved around to the other side of the car. He opened the driver's door. Paul was already in place in the seat beside Stan.

'I'm sorry, Louise.' George looked at her over the top of the car. 'He's not a witness. Not anymore.'

Chapter 33

George was running a few minutes late, he needed to hurry into the building. The heavy wooden door crashed shut behind him and he grimaced as faces turned towards the noise. The girls were already dancing. The parents were seated on long, wooden benches as they faced the performance. George looked beyond the tutting and the shaking heads. He could see his daughter; she was out the front. She saw him too. She squealed and broke from the formation. She sprinted through the gap in the seating and to the back of the village hall where George was already on his knees, his arms out to meet her. He swooped her up, tears in his eyes, and he buried his face in her hair. Her torso shook, she was crying too.

'Hello, monster,' he spluttered.

'Daddy!'

George rocked from side to side. It took a few moments for him to realise the whole room had stopped and turned its attention to him. He opened his eyes and scanned the faces. The dance teacher was in the background with her hands on her hips. Sarah was sat down, off to the right. She wore a beaming smile. Her eyes were puffy with emotion.

'Charley, I think you need to go finish your dance.'

'I don't want to leave you, Daddy. I don't want to.'

'I'll be right here. I'm going to watch you dance, honey, I'm not leaving. Not ever again.' He put Charley down. She took a step back and wiped her face. She reached out towards him with her little finger outstretched.

'Pinky promise?' she said.

George wrapped his little finger gently around hers.

'Pinky promise,' he said. Then he swept her up again and carried her back towards the dance floor.

THE END

Thank you for reading this book. If you enjoyed it please leave feedback on Amazon, and if there is anything we missed or you have a question about then please get in touch. The author and publishing team appreciate your feedback and time reading this book.

Our email is office@joffebooks.com

www.joffebooks.com

ALSO BY CHARLIE GALLAGHER
BODILY HARM
PANIC BUTTON
BLOOD MONEY
END GAME

MISSING
RUTHLESS
THEN SHE RAN

Made in the USA
Lexington, KY
20 July 2018